LEARNING TO WALK

LEARNING TO WALK

A Soldier's Story

By Clifford Beck

Clifford Beck
Cover design – Clifford Beck
Copyright©2019 Clifford Beck

For my brother, Randy

For my Brother, Randy

"The hottest place in Hell is reserved for those who remain neutral in times of great moral conflict."

> Martin Luther King, Jr

Chapter 1

Everyone thinks the desert is always hot and dry. That's not necessarily true. Afghanistan has both mountains and deserts. It sees both blazing hot days in the desert sand and frigid temperatures in the mountains. Their main export is heroin, grown on the fertile slopes of the Afghan mountains. Recently, it was discovered that the Afghanis had begun producing heroin that's ten times more potent than they had previously produced and of course, the largest consumer of Afghani heroin is - you got it, us. The addicts here who get their hands on this stuff are dying before they get the needle out of their veins.

You might be asking yourself right now, 'Why should I care?' The world is going to hell and there seems to be little, if anything, any of us can do about it. I don't know, maybe it would be better if good old planet Earth took a hit from a mountain-sized asteroid. After all, as big as the universe is, who would miss us? People don't seem to understand how insignificant we truly are, but that doesn't mean we can't make a difference. Maybe not to the whole of humanity, but sometimes it only takes one person to step up and do the right thing. I'm not talking about God or anything.

Personally, I'm not so sure there's anything out there that could provide anyone with a sense of purpose, whether you want to call it fate, determinism, the will of God, or whatever it is that people call it. The truth of the matter is we're all alone, at least in this neck of the woods anyway, and all we really have is each other. But, I try not to see humanity as the random collection of sexually driven animals that others see us as. You know the people I'm talking about - the politicians, the corporations, the wealthy, and all the other power-hungry, self-delusional idiots who seem to have talked themselves into believing that they're somehow better than everyone else.

The line between right and wrong often becomes blurred when money and power are involved. Many times, the rich walk while the poor get locked up and forgotten, treated as if they're nothing more than the eyesores of society. Unfortunately, there's nothing that one person can do to better the world, but one person does what one person can. My name is Clarence. But in the eyes of the government, I have another name - Private Taylor. So, I suppose for the sake of accuracy, I should refer to myself with my proper government-assigned name. So, let's start again. My name is Private Clarence Taylor. My current address is a charming neighborhood in hell called Afghanistan. And this is my story.

I was born in Bangor, Maine in 1986. I went to school, did my homework, and studied hard enough to graduate in the top ten percent of my high school class. My parents tried hard to instill in me a strong set of ethics and to make something of myself. They taught me not only the meaning of compromise but that there would always be times when compromising could not be achieved. They also taught me the importance of doing the right thing, no matter what the cost.

I wasn't raised with any kind of religion. It's not that my parents thought it was a waste of time, they simply believed that if there was anything that could control our fate, it would have started by cleaning up the mess left over from a species 'it' created in the first place. I never saw the universe as possessing some grand scheme or divine plan, and if you asked that age-old question - 'What is the meaning of life?' - you would have been disappointed by the answer. And what is the answer? Life has no meaning. Life is simply an event that happens wherever the conditions are right for its development. To be honest, I came to see that question as something of a cop-out, one that's asked by people who are unable or unwilling to take a good hard look in the mirror and deal with their own emptiness, insecurities, and misery.

The question that people don't seem to want to ask is, 'What is the meaning of 'my' life?' It's a hard question to ask because it demands not only reflection but accountability. And let's face it, we are all too willing to blame everyone else for the problems that we create for ourselves. And without accountability, indifference often raises its head. We've all heard the words 'Why should I care?' spoken far too often. Don't get me wrong. I'm certainly not perfect, and I don't expect the whole of humankind to suddenly achieve enlightenment. It would just be nice to watch the news someday and see more people doing some good for the world. I know that's asking a lot, but I guess it's just a little wishful thinking.

Chapter 2

Well, like I said before, I went to school in Bangor. After high school, I did what was expected and went on to college. My parents wanted me to major in something 'marketable' but as something of an idealist, I chose to study philosophy. Besides, there was still grad school and I could still earn a 'marketable' degree. But at the time, I just wanted to explore, and it seemed like philosophy would be an interesting way to find some direction. Classes were both interesting and deep - logic, existentialism, and philosophical psychology. I couldn't get enough.

In the shelter of academia, there weren't a lot of other things the average student needed to think about, but I didn't keep myself locked up like some cloistered monk. I went to a few parties and tried to fit in. However, the last thing any girl wanted to talk about was Plato's Republic or how Aristotle's ethics had become lost in a not-so-blind justice system. I took a class in Buddhism and found it refreshing that someone could follow a spiritual path without being compelled to answer to a divine authority. The concept of karmic law seemed more than reasonable to me. This idea states that we, as individuals, are responsible for the consequences of our actions and that our lives are guided purely by the decisions we make. But, there's a downside. As creatures possessed by humanness, we are incapable of seeing all possible outcomes for any one decision. So, although we can try to do our best, in the end, we're still, more or less, flying by the seat of our pants. Then again, if we could see all the possibilities we would no doubt become consumed by them, and without uncertainty, the search for meaning becomes pointless.

Now, for some reason, subjects like this weren't generally well-received at social events where liberal amounts of alcohol were consumed. Either people weren't interested or they were too incoherent to understand, and I quickly became thought of as something of a nerd and found myself largely excluded from the campus social scene. I didn't really mind. In fact, I found it rather difficult to relate to most people. I guess I was just in a different place than most. Not that I ever considered myself to be 'special', perhaps I just wandered onto a different path. I found it troubling when people began referring to me as being 'different'. I didn't really understand what that word was supposed to mean and eventually, I reached two conclusions. The first was that the word 'different', in this context anyway, was and will likely always be used by small-minded people. We all know people like this. They will never understand what makes you tick and because they seem to be so caught up in themselves, they will never give themselves the opportunity to find out who you really are. They have already judged you based on the perception that, for some reason, you just don't fit in. The second conclusion I reached was that there's nothing wrong with standing away from the crowd, refusing to follow the herd.

You don't have to fit in, and never bow down to the egos of those who stand at the tops of their ivory towers, judging everyone but themselves. Eventually, I learned to not only accept the fact that I was somehow 'different', but to embrace it. I came to enjoy being as different as people saw me, and felt as though a heavy weight had been lifted from my shoulders. I had spent a good portion of my life being resentful of the opinions most people had of me. Now, I just didn't care anymore. Their opinions mean nothing to me. I can only live my own life, and they're just going to have to figure things out on their own. So, what I guess this all comes down to are two simple words. Fuck them. Not that I'm angry, and please don't mistake these words for hostility. It's just that I've come to a place where I find it pointless to make a personal investment in people who will probably always see themselves as being better than everyone else.

I always seemed to have my head in a book, usually philosophy, history, or literature. Not that there's anything wrong with reading novels, it's just that I see life as a learning process, a chance to grow. Besides, what's the point of living if you're burying yourself in other people's fantasies? And I'm sure that my penchant for learning has cost me more than a few social opportunities. But, my college life wasn't entirely devoid of socialization, either. There were one or two girlfriends. I'm still not sure what they saw in me, but they must have seen something. Relating to girls was never something I was good at. Maybe it's because my head always seemed to be somewhere else. In fact, I found it difficult to relate to people in general, and I still do sometimes. I suppose that socialization is a constant learning process too. Some people would tell me that I think too much, and they're probably right. My mind always seemed to focus on loftier things, but at some point, I started reading the news. A lot. I'm still not sure why. I always believed that the world sucks anyway. Maybe I began to feel a need to get connected, to raise my own awareness of why the world is the way it is.

I discovered, or perhaps rediscovered, that civilization is in the midst of moral decline and no matter where you look money always seems to be at the center of it and I reached the conclusion that humanity is burying itself. We're simply on our way out. It'll be a very long process and who knows how the final stroke will arrive. Maybe we'll go out fighting, or, maybe we won't see the end coming at all. I know this seems very pessimistic - even grim, and some people might think that things can't get any worse, but I disagree. I think that things can and will get worse - much worse. And I'm sure that anyone who takes the time to see the world as it is likely would agree as well. The question is: is it too late? I honestly don't know.

Chapter 3

The spring of 2000 came without so much as a warning, and I wasn't ready at all when graduation arrived. It's amazing how quickly four years can pass, but I did see graduation as the beginning of a time when I could use my new education to do some good. At the time, I was absolutely terrified and found myself confronted by the question: 'What the fuck do I do now?' I had lived the last four years of my life sheltered by the relatively quiet atmosphere of college. Now, I was expected to go out and get a job, make a living, and face the world with a noble smile. The problem is that the world is not a noble place and jobs are very hard to come by. Even graduates with marketable degrees were finding it hard to get work, and many of them were forced to settle for work outside their chosen fields. So, where does someone with a degree in philosophy go to find work? The answer? Anywhere they can, and after a few weeks, I took a job in the human service field with an agency here in Bangor. The pay wasn't very good, but I thought that this might be an opportunity to make a difference. I worked as a teacher for the developmentally disabled, but after about three months it dawned on me how naive I could be. I found myself both stunned and disappointed to discover that many of the people who get hired into these jobs are hired out of desperation, as long as they pass a background check. To my shock, I also found that in many instances, the staff tends to have more issues than the people they were there to serve. I still don't know quite what to expect from people, but I do know that the idea of 'normal' is nothing more than a pipe dream. Once I fell into the routine of the job, I started to notice that the staff had divided themselves into cliques. I had experienced this mentality to some degree in college and came to deeply resent it. The idea that someone could have the audacity to think of themselves, or their group, as being better than everyone else sickened me. Sure, it's all fine and good for high school students to adopt an attitude. After all, people of that age group seem to be rather idiotic, simply by virtue of their youth. However, at some point, one should develop the realization that they are not at the center of the universe. So, if you're not going to do anything meaningful with your life, you should pick up your attitude and step aside. Then a question came to me. If the staff walked around thinking they were so much better than everyone else, what must they think of the people they are paid to serve? I didn't even want to think about what the answer might be and quickly began to feel that I was not taking the proper direction.

The job was both routine and boring. Sure, once in a while I got the chance to counsel someone who might be on the edge of losing their self-control, but I wasn't feeling challenged by what I was doing. I also found out that anyone could do this job and the employment opportunities for someone with a degree in philosophy were non-existent. So, while I decided to stick with a job I didn't like, I also decided that it was time to regroup. I spent weeks looking at colleges online. The thought of going out of state did occur to me, and although my parents would understand they still wouldn't like me being so far away. I decided to spend the next few months looking at my options. After all, going to grad school is a major investment of both time and money and I wanted to be certain about the field of study I was going to apply for. But one thing was certain, I had to move on. Working with the disabled seemed to be a good idea at the time, but there was no real future in it and most people who worked in this industry eventually went back to school anyway.

As fall arrived, that feeling of being out of place became magnified by the desire to go back to school. I thrived on knowledge and missed the academic atmosphere. Reading literature or philosophy gave me a great deal more pleasure than the idea of burying myself in a novel. I never saw that there was anything to learn by immersing myself in someone else's fantasy world. What I wanted was to grow, not to withdraw. Life will never come to you. You have to pursue it. So, I started ordering a few books online. I suppose I was also looking for things that could take me away from my job. It seemed to work, most of the time. In November, I took the GRE at the University at Bangor. Unless I did well, I would never be considered. So basically, grad school was my only hope of not only getting a good job but also finding some direction, a way to make a real contribution. There will always be people to care for the disabled. Don't get me wrong. It's not that I don't care, I'm just looking for something that I can uniquely fit into and still be able to do my part.

I arrived at the campus early. There were a few familiar faces, mostly professors. It was an all-day event. But, as exhausted as I was by the end of the day, I walked away with the distinct feeling that I had scored high enough to ensure my acceptance. Two agonizing weeks later, I received a letter from the university. As I suspected, my GRE scores were more than sufficient and were made part of my graduate application. By this time, I had decided on a program of study and the university accepted me to their Master's program in social work. I'd be able to work in any part of the country, even become a licensed social worker, and open a practice somewhere. I felt like I was on top of the world, finally finding my path - my calling if you will. I'd get to help people who had real problems without having the headache of state-funded sheltered workshops or day treatment facilities. These would be people whose situations threw them to the wolves - people with psych issues, marital problems, and addictions. The state was obligated to care for the disabled, but the people I'd deal with would be lost without someone to help them make sense of their lives.

Winter came with a vengeance, and Bangor lies far enough from the coast that we manage to avoid storms coming in from the ocean. But, nor'easters always came up from the Midwest and by the time they got here, they were monsters. Places like Portland seemed to dodge the bullet most of the time. Even though it was on the coast, most of the bad weather just seemed to go around it. A few years ago, a Nor'easter blew its way up the coast, slamming into the entire state. The power was out for days, and many people in northern Maine were in the dark for up to three weeks. Without power, Bangor had become a ghost town overnight. The storm was so ferocious that the wind began to sound like wolves howling at the winter moon.

Most people hated winter, but I found something in its icy solitude -- the blizzards, the long nights, the feeling that, under the right conditions, the entire city could go black at any time. For me, winter brought an intensity and anticipation that nothing else could even come close to. One night, the frozen, snowy earth would be blanketed in silence under a clear moonless sky. On another, the earth would tremble in fear as the persistent roar of a fierce winter onslaught approached. Winter in Bangor offered no mercy and would not be tamed even by God himself.

But as much as I enjoyed winter, spring was always a welcomed reprieve, and this spring was certainly no exception. As winter held the earth in its dark, icy grasp, spring would force open its frozen grip and breathe new life back into the landscape. In Maine, it is well-known that there are, in fact, five seasons - summer, autumn, winter, spring, and mud. With all the snow that came with winter, rain, and flooding would soon follow, and we were now right in the middle of mud season.

Aside from the mud and rain, a noticeable chill remained in the air until almost the beginning of June. For me, summer didn't really get underway until the first thunderstorm, and, a summer without at least two was a huge disappointment. A good thunderstorm brought the same intensity as a blizzard - the way the sky opened up; the sight of lightning as it seemed to split the air, and nothing's better than a thunderstorm at night. If there was a good chance that a storm was on its way, I'd stay up late listening to the thunder and watching flashes of lightning fill the night sky. The heat, however, was a different matter. For as long as I can remember, I never had much of a tolerance for the heat, and sleeping in the summer was all but impossible. This summer brought a different feeling, dragging by as I anticipated going back to school. As with most things, waiting was the hardest part.

Chapter 4

I gave notice at my job on the first of August and quite honestly, I was very glad to be leaving. It was routine and boring and, like most companies, the management never seemed to get around to praising the staff. They seemed to think it wasn't necessary simply because we were just doing our job, but in two weeks, I'd be done with it - the politics, the attitudes, and all the other bullshit that went into a largely thankless job. Don't misunderstand me, the people being served should always receive care, but it's a dead-end job. Even a nearly toothless thirty-year-old stripper can be trained to do it. I'm certain of that because that's what one of my co-workers was, at least before she started doing this job. But I am no one's judge. I just wish that places like this would be a bit more selective in who they hire. After all, these people are not only disabled but defenseless and I don't think that a background check is enough to weed out those who could be potentially abusive.

I left two weeks later. There were no goodbyes -- no 'it's been nice working with you'. Even on my last day, most of the staff continued to avoid me, just as they had during the past year. I walked out the front door of the building and never looked back. But, I can say that I did learn something from this experience. I learned that it's hard, if not impossible, to care about people who only seem to care about themselves. This would reshape my perspective on people, but I would not allow it to make me cynical or jaded. We all have our issues. However, these people seem to think they're above having any issues at all, and I don't think they would agree, but I think that the word 'perfect' loses its meaning when applied in human terms. But, that's just me, and one person's opinion usually amounts to nothing in the face of insurmountable self-absorption. I don't hold anything against them personally. It's the quality of arrogance I despise, and all it seems to do is hold us back from making any real progress as a people. A friend of mine would have said that someone had come along and 'pissed in their gene pool.' But enough about that.

Classes started a couple of days later. I was back in my element and the previous years' memories quickly became replaced by textbooks, discussions, and assignments. I realized just how much I really missed the world of academia. It allowed me to not only grow but to hide from the world, even if temporarily. With all the studying I was doing, there was no longer time to watch the news or read the paper, and I actually felt a bit relieved about that. There were too many bad things going on in the world, from violence in the Middle East to incompetent leadership here at home. Then, about three weeks after classes began, something unthinkable happened. This was an event that would not only change my life but the lives of millions of others, not just in this country but everywhere. I arrived on campus at seven thirty in the morning for an eight o'clock class in clinical psychology. It was Tuesday and class began as usual with the professor checking attendance. At the graduate level, if you missed even one class, it was almost impossible to catch up. If you have a serious health issue, you might as well start over next semester.

The class was two hours long and held on Tuesday and Thursday mornings, but as exhausting as it was, I still felt riveted by its content. At about ten minutes of nine, a teaching assistant entered the room unannounced.
"Um, excuse me," she said.
The professor looked at her with obvious irritation.
"I'm in the middle of teaching a class," he said. "Whatever it is, it'll have to wait."
She looked at the professor as though she'd seen a ghost, and a tear began to roll down her face.
"New York's just been attacked," she said.

Everyone in the class was now looking at the teaching assistant with utter disbelief. She was not able to repeat herself and suddenly bursting into tears, ran out of the room. The next few moments were agonizingly quiet as the professor excused himself and left the room. Returned minutes later, he dismissed the class, saying that for reasons of security, the entire campus would be closed. I left the building with a strong sense of denial.
"We can't possibly be under attack," I thought. "Probably some kind of accident".
I stepped outside to see countless other students entering the campus center. Many of them seemed just as confused. In the cafeteria were two televisions, both set to the same channel.

As the images portrayed a large, burning tower, it had been announced that at eight forty-six Eastern Standard Time, a commercial jet had collided with the north tower of the World Trade Center in New York. It was believed to have been an intentional act carried out by a terrorist group. What was not known was which one. Time stood still for everyone as shortly thereafter, at the reported time of three minutes after nine in the morning, a second jet slammed into the south tower. Some students began crying, as people could be seen jumping from windows to avoid the fire of burning jet fuel. The television cameras intermittently focused on fire and rescue crews running into the towers to evacuate as many survivors as possible. Later, it would be reported that many of them would die in service to their fellow human beings, and the only thing that anyone could do was watch.

All told the number of dead came to two thousand nine hundred and seventy-six. But, that would not be the 'official' tally. In truth, the actual number would never be known. We all watched in horror as both towers collapsed under the increasing stress of melting steel. The smoke, dust, and debris now acted as a shroud for the dead. Those who had not been crushed by falling concrete and steel wandered the streets in a state of catatonic shock. They had been forced to stand on the line that lay between life and death and some of them would later realize that there were, indeed, things that were far worse than dying.

I left the campus an hour later, as did many other students. The media would continue to report the attacks and, as with anything else, pound it into the nation's traumatized psyche for weeks. By the time I got back to my apartment, the area had been buzzed by a small squadron of military jets. Airborne patrols had been scrambled up and down the entire east coast as the country was put on high alert. I had not been in the habit of watching the news for quite some time, but when I got home, my attention became glued to the television. It's not that I needed to witness the grotesque nature of this event. I just wanted to know why it happened. Who could we have been pissed off so much that someone would organize something no less than mass murder? I was certainly not alone in the asking of this question.

As newscasters and intelligence analysts struggled for an answer, the names of certain organizations came up. It was hypothesized by the media that one of three groups was responsible, the Taliban, Al-Qaeda, and the Mujahideen. All three were notorious terrorist groups that were well-funded by a few wealthy members of the Middle Eastern aristocracy. It would later be discovered that money was being funneled to them by one or two governments, including Pakistan, who would later be referred to as our 'frienemy'. The true meaning of that word still escapes me.

At some point, the grief that had swallowed up the country became something else, something that was entirely unexpected. People came out to celebrate, and what was being called an 'attack on America' had generated an expression of public loyalty that caught even the media off guard. It was incredible. People came out of their homes waving flags. They lined the streets chanting 'USA, USA…' They came together as one, in every corner of the country. Not out of political loyalty, but out of love for their country. That day not only changed the course of history but left a painful wound on the collective psyche of the country, one that would never completely heal. But, I had to see it for myself, and I was close enough to downtown that I could easily walk there within only a few minutes. What I saw beyond belief. People stood shoulder to shoulder, waving small flags, while passers-by honked their horns in support. Those who were not holding flags held lit candles as an expression of remembrance for the victims of that day. The words 'nine eleven' would be permanently etched into the collective consciousness of the entire country and everyone would remember where they were on the day when the world, as we knew it, came to an end.

Chapter 5

The campus reopened the next morning, but everyone was preoccupied with yesterday's events. Upon investigation, it had been discovered that one of the attackers had flown into New York from Portland. The fact that he was under our very noses terrified people. During the Cold War, things were different. We knew who, the enemy was and the only thing we had to worry about was nuclear war. Now, we faced an enemy that seemed to be hiding in plain sight. They were nearly invisible, yet seemed to be everywhere. What was worse was the fact that they - whoever 'they' were - also attempted to attack the Pentagon, as a small plane was flown into the side of the building. Coincidentally, another jet had crashed in western Pennsylvania and although there were no survivors, it had been determined that it had been hijacked and into turning back towards D.C. leading some to believe that the White House was the next target. I wondered how someone could get that close to us. How long had they been here? How long had they been watching and planning? And if they were under government surveillance, why weren't they stopped? Everyone seemed to be affected for days. Different people expressed different emotions about it. Some were tearful and depressed, while others became angry and vengeful. Personally, I didn't quite know how to feel. Maybe I was trying to make some sense out of something that was clearly senseless. I guess I just wanted to know why.

The media, of course, did what they do best - take a story and drive it into the ground. Not that the events of yesterday didn't deserve our fullest attention, but the rapid onset of media overkill was enough that some people just tuned out. They just wanted to forget, and that was okay for them, but many people would not let it go. They wanted to do something. But, what can you do in the wake of so much death and destruction? It seemed that the only thing people could do was to be there for each other. Naturally, the media had to report and over-report the cleanup as well. Bodies could be seen being taken inside for identification. Occasionally, a cell phone would ring as someone tried to reach out in an attempt to locate a family member. Rescuers were ordered never to answer them, that families would be notified in an orderly, respectful manner, and as the names of the dead were listed over the next few days, it was found that a graduate of this university had been killed in the attack. This brought the events of nine eleven much closer to home, and some students organized a small memorial service for them.

Everyone wanted to do something. Donations were made to a nine-eleven fund that would go toward the victim's families. Bake sales were held. Raffles and charity auctions also became common. But, people wanted to do more, and putting up a memorial website didn't even come close. Of course, this marked the beginning of other problems. Once it was uncovered that an Arab terrorist group took responsibility for the attack on the World Trade Center, people began giving the Arabic community a second look. Obviously, we have better things to do than focus on the color of people's skin when there are so many problems in the world. However, another side of this prejudice developed and people became vigilant, even if out of paranoia. In time, those with ties to terrorist groups would be apprehended. The existence of 'sleeper cells' would also be discovered. These were loose groups of people who had already been living here. Some had been here for years. They had jobs, families and were educated in American colleges. As it would turn out, they would be found as highly trained killers taught to blend seamlessly into our population and culture. On the fourth of July, they could be seen waving the American flag, but in secret, they were tinkering with electronics and mercury switches. They were drafting up plans for dirty bombs, studying maps of the country's largest cities, and acquiring architectural drawings of buildings they considered to be potential targets. The only thing they were waiting for were orders. Apparently, they had been planning this for quite some time.

Now, I found myself in a position where I wanted to do something. But in grad school, there wasn't time to do anything outside of studying. Many lined up at recruiting offices and joined the military. It looked like the same kind of reaction that swept the country during World War Two. People suddenly became patriotic, and it needed to seem to matter if they were fighting terrorists or Nazis. As far as everyone was concerned, they both fell into the same category - cowards. I found arrogance nauseating, but cowardice enraged me. I try to accept people for who they are, despite their flaws and imperfections, but there's nothing worse than a coward, the asshole with a gun who would use a woman or a child as a human shield. Now, there seems to be another kind of coward, and this one goes by the word 'terrorist'. And yes, it did cross my mind to enlist in the military.

Several weeks went by, and it was getting close to midterms and no matter how much time I spent studying, it seemed like it just wasn't enough. I was confident that I'd get through it, but secretly I was terrified. I suppose it was a bit comforting to know that more than a few of my fellow students felt the same way. I stopped watching the news and read the newspaper but only for the comics section. After September eleventh, it seemed like a little humor was in order. The media was still broadcasting footage of the attacks. I felt bad for the families of the victims, but the constant news coverage put me into media overload. We get it already. It happened and nothing would make it go away, but enough is enough! As if that wasn't bad enough, there was a marketing frenzy of products designed to play on people's grief. There were coins, collector's plates, wall posters, T-shirts, and a myriad of other items that were being pitched as 'memorial products', or 'in remembrance of'. I found it incredible that companies run by human beings would stoop so low as to try to make a few bucks at the expense of so much pain and grief. One night, I became so angered by one of these commercials that I picked up a coffee mug and threw it at my television, shattering the screen. I'd had enough. It was time for me to get off my ass and do something, and I was fairly certain what that would be.

Chapter 6

Some people might think I'd become too invested in my reaction to the nine eleven attacks. I don't see how anyone could just let it go. If you were someone who didn't care, then you were part of a larger issue, but that's an entry for another time. Now, I began to feel that in order to do anything at this point, was to take a direct approach, so I started thinking about military service. Up to this point, I had spent so much time in school that I knew nothing about the military outside the media. Beyond that, I knew that the military promoted order, structure, and discipline and if you were in the wrong place at the wrong time, you could be killed. Yet, I suppose that one's chances of being killed went up dramatically simply by crossing the street. I also came to admire what the military had been doing over the past few years. A good example might be 'Operation Restore Hope'. The Marines had been deployed to Somalia to hand-deliver food and water, feeding thousands of starving men, women, and children. Since then, I came to think of them as 'humanitarian warriors'. I know that sounds a bit grandiose, but I am at a lack for any other description. Now, in the aftermath of nine eleven, I wanted to be a part of that. The idea of making a difference on such a personal level was too compelling to ignore. So, on a day off from classes, I went down to the local recruiting office.

I spoke to the recruiter of each branch, spending about two hours there. They all had pamphlets to hand out and videos that glamorized their particular branch of service. It all came down to two questions: Which branch would I join, and did I want to become an officer? With a four-year degree, it was possible that I could become an officer, but a degree in philosophy wasn't exactly in high demand, although, the Marines would accept at least a two-year degree in any area. So, that was a possibility. After giving it some thought, I decided that I probably would not be of much use behind a desk and wanted something more 'hands-on'. Now, it was just a matter of which branch to join. I didn't want to make a career out of the military and I did want to continue with my education, so I began to take a good look at the army. It would be a four-year enlistment. But, the decision maker was when I was told about the G.I. Bill and that the army would pay for college when I got out. I considered the other branches, but I wanted to go where help was needed, and I thought the Marines might be a bit much for a philosophy student and four years would earn a lot of tuition.

There didn't seem to be too much of a downside to my decision, or so I thought.

I thought it would be best to finish out the semester. At least I'd have one semester done and wouldn't have to start over four years down the road. When classes ended in December, I went back to the recruiter's office and made an appointment to take the ASVAB test. This was the aptitude test given by the military that would tell them what field I would be best suited for, and it had been determined that I would be most useful as a cavalry scout. They said my reasoning ability and spatial perception made me an ideal candidate for training in that field.

Now came the hard part. How do I tell my parents that I had essentially volunteered to kill terrorists? With that thought, I realized exactly what I'd be doing. Could I actually kill another human being? I suppose it depends on how you define 'human'. Some people believe that we are born human, that we are born with something that animals are not - a soul - whatever that is. Even Plato, in his theory of emanation, suggested that we, as human beings, are an expression of God but not nearly as pure. Yet, B.F. Skinner tells us that we are born with the potential for humanness and that the qualities of being human are learned. I'm not sure how complicated this issue is. Maybe issues like this are only as complicated as we make them. But, I don't think it's right for one person, or even a few people, to decide what's human on behalf of all humanity. I guess if I'm going to end up shooting people, I need to find an answer for myself. What does it mean to be human, and can the answer justify killing a complete stranger without so much as a thought? I wouldn't have an answer to those questions until much later when the act of killing was staring me in the face.

Christmas found me at home with my family. For days, I'd been thinking about how to tell my parents what I had decided to do. I still hadn't come up with the right words, but my parents knew there was something on my mind. I guess I seemed pretty preoccupied. Both my parents were Harvard graduates. My father was a graduate professor of bioethics and had written several important papers on medical ethics. His latest writing was specifically on the subject of 'terminal sedation', where one of the questions he asks is: Do people have the right to face death without medical intervention? He also brought up the argument between the rights of the individual versus the intent and decisions of the family. Certainly, there are more questions than answers, but his work has been reviewed by politicians, hospitals, and ethics committees across the country. My mother, on the other hand, is head of the research and development arm of a large pharmaceutical company and has the final word on how new drugs get tested. She also holds the chair of the company's ethics oversight committee, deciding how far to go with both human and animal trials. If it's one thing she'd learned during her career, it's that not everything works out as intended. They met at Harvard. I'm not even sure how they managed to get along all these years. They always seem to be arguing. Not over marital issues or anything like that. It was always over ethical and philosophical points, especially where world events were concerned. I think they found the arguments intellectually stimulating and would be bored to tears without them.

After dinner, we sat in the living room and opened gifts. The wind howled outside as a Nor'easter was making its way up the coast. The living room had become warmed by the crackling of the fireplace, brought to life by the glow of dancing flames. My father was sitting in his favorite chair holding a brandy snifter and glancing at me from the corner of his eye.
"So, Clarence," he said. "What's on your mind?"
I could no longer avoid the conversation, and I still didn't know how to tell them.

"I've decided to put grad school on hold for a bit," I answered.
His expression went unchanged, preferring to know all the facts before reacting in any way. My mother, however, looked up in complete shock.
"On hold?!" she said. "Are you out of your mind?!"
"Now hang on a second," my father began. "Let's not react too quickly."
My parents seemed to be polar opposites of each other. My mother was the excitable one, while my father was usually the calm voice of reason. He looked back at me with an expression of concern.

"Alright," he began. "What led to this decision?"
I took a breath and glanced down at the floor.
"Well," I started. "Ever since nine-eleven, I've felt… lost. I need to do something. I know that I can't fix the world, but I feel driven to do something. I need to get involved - to fight back. So, I'm going to join the Army."
I thought my mother was going to faint. The last thing she ever imagined her son doing was marching around carrying a gun. My father, however, was putting a great deal of thought into my response.
"So," he began. "You want to go over to the Middle East and fight?"
"Yes," I answered.

"Okay," he said. "Why you?"

Now he was testing me. He wanted to be sure that I knew why I wanted to do this. He wanted me to think.

"I just need to do this," I replied. "I'm sick of the way things are. I know that I can't change anything but these people should be stopped and if this country is going over there to stop them, then I want to be part of that. You always told me how important it is to do the right thing. Now, it's time for me to step up to the plate."

My father nodded his head.

"What about grad school?" he asked.

"Well," I began. "It's just four years and when I get out the G.I. Bill will help pay for grad school. It might even be able to help pay for a Ph.D. program."

"You know, Clarence," my father responded. "We can continue to help you pay for grad school, just like we did for your bachelor's degree."

"I know, and I've always appreciated that," I said. "I just don't see how anyone can appreciate getting an education if someone else is picking up the tab."

He looked down at the floor and slowly nodded his head.

"So, you've figured this all out?" he asked.

"Yeah," I answered. "I've given this a lot of thought. I need to do this."

He calmly looked over at my mother, who was looking at him like a deer caught in a car's headlights.

"You can't possibly condone this!" she said.

"This isn't up to us," he said. "Not this time."

My mother became panicked. I suppose it's a mother's prerogative to want to keep her children out of harm's way, but the real world is full of hazards, and any idea of a relatively safe world came crumbling down with the Twin Towers.

"I suppose there's nothing I can say to change your mind," she said.

She was slowly beginning to understand that the reasons for my decision were both important and personal. She also understood that I was no longer insulated from the pain that the world could inflict. However, she would never resign herself to what I was about to do.

"When are you leaving?" my father asked.

"I don't know yet," I answered. "More than likely after the first of the year."

I thought it would be a good idea to leave after New Year's Day. I could spend a bit more time with my parents over the holidays - maybe do some reading. I found out through the news that some of our troops were engaged at the caves of Tore Bora, somewhere in the Hindu Kush Mountains of Afghanistan. The caves had been there for thousands of years, but they were now being occupied by members of the Taliban and al-Qaeda. The military had been sent in to clear the caves with whatever force was needed. Some of these terrorists simply surrendered themselves, while most tried to put up a fight, only for their bodies to be dragged out by U.S. troops.

We were all on the same page now, even though my parents were far from comfortable with my decision, but at least they understood why I was doing it. My father and I continued to talk about it. My mother, on the other hand, wanted nothing more to do with it. It wasn't that she didn't care. She just didn't want to think about it and over the next couple of weeks, she managed to find a lot of things to busy herself with, so she wouldn't have time to stop and think. New Year's arrived and naturally, we were invited to the yearly holiday party. This year, it was being hosted by a family whose daughter had just returned from Stanford University with a Master's degree in law. Her parents, like mine, had also attended Harvard and like many people of that level of income, they saw me as something of an oddity. While most of the people my parents associated with were unable or unwilling to see beyond their wealthy, well-insulated lives, I chose to see the world without the dollar signs. There's much more to the world than gated communities and well-manicured lawns or who possessed more net worth. To be honest, the idea of status symbols and old money made me sick. Perhaps, deep down, there might be a bit of a socialist hidden inside me. I know it's more than a bit of a contradiction - an idealist, growing up in a wealthy family of Ivy League graduates. But, I wasn't rebelling against my parents. They didn't seem to have that 'rich bitch' attitude I saw in other people associated with my parents. Conversations always seemed to come back to them and how many lawyers they had or how many businesses they had invested in. Some of them even tried to speak what I would call 'sanitized English', speaking with such perfectionistic accuracy that they often dropped their contractions - 'I've' became 'I have'; 'didn't' became 'did not'. They tried very hard to seem important in a world that likely didn't give a shit about them, never realizing that they were just people who had fallen into a very fortunate set of circumstances.

Given the direction my life was about to take, my mother did what almost any mother would do. She tried to hook me up and, walking over, took me by the arm.
"Clarence," she said. "There's someone I want you to meet."

Her tone of voice made it obvious that she had an ulterior motive and began dragging me into a large, crowded room, where I immediately felt overwhelmed by the clamoring sound of conversation. The hosts of the party called it the 'great room' because of its size and opulence. To me, it was just a space surrounded by walls.

"Mom," I replied. "You know how I feel about crowds."

The truth of the matter was I couldn't stand these parties. It wasn't just having to deal with all the people, it was the attitude. They seemed to spend a lot of time patting each other on the back. That is when they weren't patting themselves on the back.

"Oh, come now, Clarence," she said. "Mingle a little."

She pulled me over to a slim young black-haired woman.

"Clarence, this is Gloria," she began. "Her parents are hosting the party tonight. Gloria, this is my son, Clarence."

It was one of the most awkward moments of my life. We shook hands and uncomfortably exchanged hellos as my mother disappeared into the crowd. Gloria was stunningly beautiful, wearing a royal blue cocktail dress that came down to just above the knee. Her hair was jet black and her eyes a deep brown. For a brief moment, I found myself getting lost in them, only to be torn away by a sudden flash of self-consciousness.

"So," I began. "I understand you just got back from Stanford."

"Yes," Gloria replied.

She spoke with an elocution that one could only learn at an Ivy League college like Stanford.

"I've been back for about a month or so."

"So your degree is in law," I said. "What do you plan on doing?"

She hesitated as a shy grin came to her face.

"I'm not entirely certain," she began. "My parents want me to go into bankruptcy law, given the direction of the economy."

"Oh, yes," I replied. "But, what do 'you' want to do? I mean, you can make all the money in the world and still be unhappy."

She looked at me with a slightly puzzled expression.

"I don't think I ever considered that."

A tense moment quickly grew between us. Gloria took a breath and quickly changed the subject.

"So, your mother tells me you're going into the Army, why is that?"

She was completely bewildered as to why someone from a wealthy family would enlist in the military. I couldn't really blame her. She had become so well insulated by her family's wealth that she seemed unable to see beyond the walls of privilege, and I had a feeling that Gloria would not understand the direction I had committed myself to.

"Just trying to do my part," I answered casually.

"I see," she said. "Will you be enlisting as an officer?"

I actually held out a bit of hope that she might be anything but superficial, but now she was trying to tag a status symbol on me.

"Actually, no," I answered. "I think I'll get a higher quality of life experience by skipping the whole officer thing."

She hesitated again. But this time, it was with a slight expression of disappointment.

"Oh," she said.

She became somewhat uncomfortable as she glanced off to one side.

"Would you excuse me?"

"Oh, of course," I answered.

She left before I could even finish speaking and as the moments ticked by, I suddenly felt as though everyone in the room was watching me.

After that brief moment of embarrassment, I walked out of the room with the impression that Gloria was just another spoiled rich bitch and that she wasn't worth getting upset over. Not that I was upset, but I was angry about what I believed to be a 'holier than thou' attitude. Now, I just needed to get some air and I thought that the January chill might help to take the edge off the resentment I was feeling. It wasn't just Gloria's attitude. It was about all of them, with the exception of my parents who seemed to always have their feet on the ground. However, none of these people would ever understand anything about the world beyond their offshore accounts and private planes.

After about ten minutes, my mother walked up behind me and touched my shoulder.
"Clarence," she began. "What are you doing out here in the cold?"
"I just needed some air," I answered. "It's a bit too crowded in there."
She again took me by the arm and gently pulled me back inside.
"So," she began. "What do you think of Gloria?"
I didn't have the heart to tell her what had happened, nor my opinion of Gloria. She was obviously trying to give me a reason to stay.
"I don't think she's my type," I replied.
"Oh, nonsense," my mother said, "She's gorgeous! You just need to give her another chance."
There was no arguing that Gloria was very beautiful, and any man would be lucky to have her on his arm. I just didn't see myself as that man.
My mother walked me to the dining room, where everyone was now gathering. There were nine

large mahogany tables set up in such a perfect arrangement that it could only have been done by someone with OCD. Several well-dressed servants were waiting for everyone to be seated, while ushers showed each guest to their place. Naturally, my mother had arranged for me to sit next to Gloria.

By this time, dinner was being served. The main course was Quail served with a white wine sauce. Personally, I would have been happy with chicken fingers and a cold beer. At this point, I just wanted to leave. The idea of spending money on that kind of food just to satisfy the appetites of the wealthy made me sick and, of course, they had to be fashionable about how they ate, meaning that no one ever finished what they were served and rarely accepted seconds. The thought of all that food simply going to waste infuriated me, and it was a pretty good bet that no one in the room ever gave to a charity unless their accountant told them it would be tax advantageous to do so. As I approached the table where an empty chair sat next to Gloria, I turned back to my mother with a hand on my stomach.
"Mom," I began. "Suddenly, I don't feel all that well."
"Well, have some dinner," she replied.

I looked back at the table while dinner was being served and noticed that Gloria was doing a poor job of ignoring me.

"Mom," I said. "I really don't handle rich food all that well. I think I'd rather go home and get something small to eat."

My mother gave me the look of concern that only a mother can as she nodded her head in resignation.

"Alright," she said. "I'll have someone bring the car around."

I told her that I preferred to walk, but she quickly pointed out that it was the middle of winter and insisted that I be driven home. It was true that my stomach couldn't cope with the food that was served at these parties. But truth be told, I just didn't want to be there. I couldn't stand the atmosphere; the people were arrogant and judgmental and there were way too many of them.

The valet was kind enough to drop me off at home, but before I got out of the car I handed him a one-hundred-dollar bill.

"Oh, I can't accept this!" he said.

"Do you have a family?" I asked.

"Yeah," he answered.

"Then you take this," I continued. "And tell them happy New Year for me, alright?"

"Yes, sir," he replied. "Thank you, sir."

I hesitated as I opened the door.

"And my name isn't sir, it's Clarence, okay?"

"Gotcha'," he answered. "Happy New Year!"
"You too," I replied.
He drove off before I could get his name. I always thought that if you do something for someone you should at least get their name. I also felt that was especially true if they were doing something for you.

Chapter 7

A couple of days later, I went back to the recruiter's office and scheduled my entry date. In five days, I would have to be in Augusta. I'd have to go through a physical exam and sign a contract, giving the Army the next four years of my life. One part of me was looking forward to the challenge of military service. The other part of me was terrified. Then, there was the question that occasionally rose up from a small fear of the unknown - 'What the hell was I doing?' But, I knew that what I was about to do was right. It was right for me, and no one could convince me otherwise. Over the next four days, I talked with my parents -- a lot. I called a few friends and visited the university. That was probably something I shouldn't have done. The university was my second home, and the idea of leaving school felt worse than the idea of leaving home. But, I comforted myself with the knowledge that I would come back in four years with what was sure to be a new perspective and that would only add to my continued educational experience.

I spent some time reading as well -- partly to take my mind off the idea of leaving home and partly to mentally prepare myself for military life. I read

Sun Tzu's 'The Art of War' and found a lot of interesting ideas in it, but it seemed more like a guidebook for management, and I wasn't planning on becoming an officer. I did, however, read up on the Roman philosophy of warfare. The ancient Romans, it seems, took a strong position for conquest based on the complete and utter devastation of the enemy. Orders were strictly followed without question and the warrior was seen as more than just a soldier, brutally molded into a highly disciplined killer, able to shut off his conscience for the sake of bringing the glory of battle to their emperor -- whom they considered a god. For the Roman soldier, there were no rules of engagement - no code of conduct - only orders. The idea of ignoring the need to survive in order to bring one's enemy to its knees made sense to me. Wars cannot be fought with survival instincts. To cast off one's need to survive for the fray of battle, it seems, requires something that most people do not possess, and I'm still not able to put a word to it.

While most ancient cultures had little need for battlefield ethics, the armies of today's developed world fight by a code of conduct, largely guided by the Geneva Convention with the assumption that a moral war could be fought. History shows us that this assumption is misguided for the simple reason that not everyone plays by the rules and as far as I'm concerned, there's a big difference between being a warrior and being a murderer. However, it also occurred to me that sometimes the line that divides the warrior from the murderer can become blurred, leading somewhat civilized human beings to regress to their animal nature.

It's amazing how time flows so quickly when you're about to throw yourself into a life-changing event, and before I knew it, the day of my departure had arrived. My parents drove me to Augusta. Naturally, my mother cried for most of the way, still believing that I was making a huge mistake and had spent the last five days trying to change my mind. When we arrived in Augusta, we followed a set of directions to the federal building, where the enlistment center was located on the third floor. There was a large group of people, both men and women, who were also there to be processed for enlistment. Women, of course, were shown to a separate processing section. My parents waited in the hallway as I lined up with the rest of the group. I was not aware of it at the time, but there were about a dozen or so people in the group that I would spend the next ten weeks with, and almost all of them, including myself, would be sent to the Middle East.

With the exception of underwear, we were told to remove our clothes. We stood single file through every step of the physical exam, inching forward like a slowly moving conveyor, and they examined everything. They also drew blood, testing for recreational drugs, HIV, hepatitis, and a battery of other health issues. They didn't want anyone to ask questions. Unless you were asked to speak, you kept your mouth shut. This was made very clear to us on several occasions - not that I had anything to say anyway.

After the physical exam, they took small groups of us to be seated in a separate room where a rather intimidating looking uniformed man stood in front of us and as we sat down, he seemed to be looking us over very carefully. With his first question, it became obvious that this was the psychiatric portion of the exam.
"Has anyone here ever been in a psychiatric hospital?" he asked.
Surprisingly, or maybe not so surprisingly, one person raised his hand and announced that he'd been recently discharged from the Spring Harbor Psychiatric Hospital in Portland.
"Get your stuff," the uniformed man said.
He was promptly escorted from the building.

None of the questions surprised me - had anyone experienced depression, heard voices, hallucinated, thought about, or attempted suicide? I tried hard to believe that the military was doing a good job of keeping weapons out of the hands of unstable people, but with a psych exam that consisted of nothing more than questions and answers, I just couldn't bring myself to be convinced. We were probably sitting there for an entire ten minutes while he continued his questions, trying very hard to read everyone's reactions. It wasn't exactly a clinical assessment, but it seemed to be good enough for the military. Now, we were again shuffled to another room, where another uniformed man stood behind a podium. In the back corner stood an American flag on a wooden pole. We were lined up in rows and told that we were required to take the oath of enlistment.

"Raise your right hand," the man ordered. "Now repeat after me."

I've found that not many people can be taken at their word. So, I'm not sure about how much value an oath really has. After all, people lie to Congress under oath on a fairly regular basis. Maybe the oath of enlistment is nothing more than the first step in a lengthy indoctrination process designed to instill a strong sense of loyalty. At any rate, this is the oath I took:

"I, Clarence Taylor, do solemnly swear that I will support and defend the Constitution of the United States against all enemies, foreign and domestic; that I will bear true faith and allegiance to the same; and that I will obey the orders of the President of the United States and the orders of the officers appointed over me, according to regulations and the Uniform Code of Military Justice. So help me, God."

Obviously, these are very dramatic words, and I couldn't help wondering why God would be mentioned. 'So help me, God'. I don't think I'll ever understand what that phrase means. I do understand the importance of faith in the military, especially at times of war when one's life is immediately threatened by battle. I imagine that many people use the idea of God to find the strength to do what needs to be done – to kill the enemy. I guess my question is, 'What kind of God would advocate war?' If the Christian idea of God is true, then why doesn't God wage His own wars? I suppose a divine war is fought by divine beings.

Historically, we have always waged war with the belief that we do so as part of God's will - whatever that is. But, we also go to war believing that God supports us in our slaughter of each other and everyone seems to have God on their side, regardless of the name given to that god. I wonder what conversation would arise from two people meeting on the battlefield - each the enemy of the other, both are out of ammunition and each claims to fight for God. Would they sit and talk about their respective Gods? Would they ask each other why they are there at all? Or, would they draw knives and kill each other for their respective Gods? I think that the idea of God is certainly well-meaning until you introduce people into the equation. Apparently, God is the weapon of choice for warfare as faith becomes the substitute of reason. If there is a God, I don't believe that He would act on our behalf. I think there is a very clear difference between religion and spirituality. In religion, we do what we're told - we go to war for the same reason we go to church. In spirituality, we are guided by compassion and a sense for doing the right thing without the restraints of church politics or religious laws. I am certain that the idea of loyalty is blind by virtue of the idea of God. Perhaps this is the idea behind the phrase 'God bless America'.

Chapter 8

My picture and fingerprints were taken after I signed several copies of the enlistment contract. Now, I was officially government property. Of course, my parents would have preferred that the family attorney review it first. I guess that when you're born into wealth, the family lawyer becomes as much a member of the family as the family dog, but in a good way. Finally, by mid-afternoon, I met up with my parents.
"Well, this is it," I said.
My father shook my hand.
"If you really believe that this is the right thing to do, then you have my full support," he said. "Just keep your head down, alright?"
My mother was not one for public displays of emotion, but as I turned towards her, she threw her arms around me with tears in her eyes. I knew that she wanted me to finish grad school, but it wasn't about that anymore. She no longer saw me as a Ph.D. candidate but as her son - her only child - who was now about to put himself in harm's way. To my mother, it didn't matter why I was doing it. She simply saw her son going off to war. After the longest five minutes of my life, we were again lined up alphabetically and in single file. Airline tickets were passed out as each recruit was called

by last name. This was when I found out where I was going. There are four Army bases in the country dedicated to basic training - Fort Jackson, South Carolina; Fort Benning, Georgia; Fort Sill, Oklahoma; and Fort Knox, Kentucky. I was on my way to Fort Jackson. I was in the middle of a Maine winter, so the change in temperature would prove to be interesting, to say the least. Shortly after, we were loaded onto buses and taken to the airport. We were divided into groups based on our destinations. Those going into the Air Force were being flown to Texas. Recruits going into the Navy were flying to Chicago, while new Marines were going to Parris Island. By this time, I had a pretty clear understanding of the phrase 'hurry up and wait'. Those words easily summed up the entire day.

We waited at the gate for about an hour as a man in uniform stood nearby. There were seven of us going to Fort Jackson, and it was obvious that we were all nervous. Finally, we boarded our flight. Naturally, there was a delay. The plane sat at the end of the runway while another plane was allowed to land. After that, we began moving as the plane's engines roared to life. More than halfway down the runway, I felt the nose of the plane rise up from the tarmac. My ears popped as we rose higher, leaving the earth farther and farther below us.

After several hours, we landed in Columbia, South Carolina under a full moon. The change in temperature was dramatic and upon walking out of the plane a warm breeze wrapped itself around my body. I found it strange that near the beginning of January, there could be a place where nor'easters didn't occur. I knew that not every place on the planet gets snow, but I had never traveled outside of Maine before. Knowing there are places that never see snow is one thing. Setting foot on them is quite another and after picking up what little luggage I brought, I was escorted to what was now a much larger group and onto one of two waiting buses. There were two very stern-looking uniformed men standing off to the side. Their uniforms had been pressed to a fault, and they wore what could only be described as 'Smokey the Bear' hats. I didn't know what else to call them. They ordered - yelled, actually - that we line up and get on the buses as quickly as possible. I took an aisle seat, somewhere near the middle of the bus. While each of the uniformed men boarded a bus, the man on our bus stood at the front with a clipboard in his hand and an angry look on his face. His intimidating appearance worked because

no one made a sound, and any whisper of conversation was met with an immediate response.
"Hey!" he yelled. "Shut the fuck up!"
The effect of his reaction was instantaneous and from that moment on the bus was deafening quiet.

After a very long thirty minutes, the buses turned onto the entrance of Fort Jackson. The main gate was very well-lit and staffed by more uniformed men. These men, however, carried guns. They stepped out onto the road and motioned for the drivers to stop. I.D. cards were checked, and authorization papers were examined, after which we were allowed to proceed. I'd never seen anyone carry a gun outside a police officer. This site drove home the reality that I was about to embark on a military life. It wasn't long before we pulled up in front of a large cinder block building. We were very sternly told to get out and form a line shoulder to shoulder. I quickly realized that there were several uniformed men, all wearing the same 'Smokey the Bear' hats. They called themselves 'drill instructors'.
"Jesus fuckin' Christ!" one of them yelled. "What kind of goddamn freak show is this?!"
The thought crossed my mind that knowing what to do is largely based on knowing what to expect, and I had no idea what to expect. I stood absolutely still, only to leap out of my skin when

one of the drill instructors suddenly approached me, our faces only inches from each other.
"Are you one of these freaks?!" he screamed.
The tension was immediate and I answered without thinking.
"No, sir," I replied.
"No, sir?!" he yelled. "Is that all you have to say?!"
I felt a huge sense of relief as he began pacing up and down the row of recruits.
"From this day forward!" he yelled. "Everything you say will begin with the word 'sir' and will end with the word 'sir'! Do I make myself clear?!"
We all answered with the same words.
"Sir, yes sir!"
Some were louder than others, but any sense of time was completely absent.
"I didn't hear a fuckin' word of that!" the drill instructor yelled.
He turned to another drill instructor.
"Did you get any of that?!"

The other drill instructor shook his head in disgust.
"They sent us a bunch of fuckin' retards this time," he said.
I noticed that they spoke with a slight southern accent. It wasn't something I thought to expect, but I wasn't surprised. I momentarily recalled a conversation with my recruiter, who told me that

the drill instructors would do a lot of screaming and yelling. He told me not to take it personally and that it was part of their job not only to create stress but also teach us how to cope with it. So far, it was working.

"Let's try this again, assholes!" he yelled. "From this day forward, everything you lowlifes say will begin and end with begin and end with the word 'sir'! Am I understood?!"
This time, everyone responded with one voice.
"Sir, yes sir!"
"I didn't hear you!" the drill instructor yelled.
"Sir, yes sir!"
This was repeated several times. We were then taught how to stand at attention - back straight, shoulders back, head up, heels together, knees slightly bent, palms in, fingers curled, thumbs pointing down, and touching the outside seam of the pants. It was nine o'clock at night, but training had already begun. We were ordered to turn to our left and escorted into the building. There, we were taken into a large bay lined with freshly made-up cots and footlockers. Each of us was assigned a cot. This, of course, was done alphabetically. The drill instructor told us that we were guaranteed a full eight hours of sleep - no more, no less.

By morning, I realized, to some degree, the level of comfort I had been living. Sleeping with a roomful of complete strangers on a four-inch-thick mattress was an adventure in itself. But, I was confident that things would get much worse. The drill instructor stormed into the room while a recording of Reveille played over a speaker. Five o'clock in the morning had never arrived with such cruelty.

"Get up, morons!" the drill instructor yelled. Looking back, I think my senses had been partially on during the night because I woke immediately. Those who didn't wake so readily faced the drill instructor's wrath as he screamed in their faces, taunting them into a state of wakefulness
"Get your shit out!" he screamed. "Get into the goddamn lavatory! Shit, shave and shower! C'mon, move your asses!"
I had the good sense to go quickly to the lavatory - or, the head, as it would be called. Every once in a while, the drill instructor would stand at the entrance of the shower and loudly prompt us to hurry.
"Hurry the fuck-up, girls! Get your asses in gear!"
Within twenty minutes, most of us were done and dressed. Those still in the head were chastised repeatedly. We were, once again, lined up and escorted to the dining area. I have to admit, the

food was not as bad as I expected. In fact, it was actually pretty good. The drill instructor repeatedly urged us to eat quickly. There were no seconds. As each of us finished, we were told to leave the dining area and line up outside. Apparently, screaming and yelling were not the only things one deals with in basic training. Mind games were part of it as well. A word of advice: when someone yells 'Hey you!' don't stop and look back. I made this mistake and was called back by the drill instructor to a table of drill instructors. This area was actually a number of tables placed end to end and was known as 'the snake pit'

"What the fuck were you looking at?!" he yelled. Not knowing what else to say, I spoke as quickly as I could.

"Sir, nothing, sir!"

"Nothing!" he replied. "Were you looking at me?!"

"Sir, no sir!" I answered.

"Are you sure?! 'Cause I swear to Christ I saw you look back at me!"

"Sir, I'm sure, sir!" I replied.

I was impressed with his attempt to stare me down. But, I refused to let him get to me.

"Get out of here!" he yelled.

I turned and walked away, taking my place in line just outside the dining area. In military speak - a language I would become fluent in - this was called the 'mess hall'.

I finally understood the purpose of basic training. It wasn't just about how to wear a uniform. It wasn't just about adopting the military mindset. From that small exchange I had with the D.I., it dawned on me. This was about learning to deal with chaos while remaining calm and clear-headed. Basic training was a safe zone of controlled chaos as opposed to war, which seemed to be neither safe nor controlled. Not that I'd had that experience. However, the reality of this idea would later confirm itself. After everyone was back in line, we were, again, escorted elsewhere. The D.I. tried to get us to walk in unison.
"Left, left, left right left!" he called out.
It didn't seem so much as marching but as forty monkeys trying to build a spaceship. It was pathetic. Apparently, learning how to be a soldier means learning how to walk as well. We were 'marched' to the other side of the building and slowly filed into a room where we had our heads shaved. It wasn't completely down to the skin, but I have to admit it felt quite liberating. I really didn't care what I looked like. After all, it was just hair. But, in the winter warmth of South Carolina, the sudden loss of my hair felt pretty comfortable. After this, we stood in line and prepared to leave. However, adding insult to injury, they had arranged for two strikingly beautiful women to photograph us as we stood in line with our newly

shaven heads. Prompting embarrassment was also part of the game and anyone who so much as glanced at either of them was harassed to no end. After getting our haircuts, we were once again led outside. This time, we were taken to a large paved area and instructed to form into four lines of ten. The D.I. began teaching us how to march in formation. It occurred to me that what we were really learning was how to act as a single unit. No one picked it up right away, and more than a few of us began tripping over each other's feet.
"Jesus Christ!" the D.I. yelled. "I've got to teach you morons how to walk too?! Let's try it again, ladies!"
He began calling out 'left, left, left, right, left!' It was a complete fiasco of clumsiness.
But, even in this display of disarray, we were 'marched' to yet another sterile-looking military building. Here, we were issued our equipment - our 'gear'. Uniforms, combat boots, belts, helmets, a gun holster, everything. The fitting for uniforms was quick and efficient, resembling a conveyor of people and clothing. We were also issued a combat knife. If, at an earlier point, someone had told me that I'd end up carrying a gun and a combat knife, I would have told them to stay on their meds. Yet, there I was, holding 'my' combat knife and holster, which would later carry a .45 caliber pistol. I have to admit, holding these items felt more than a bit

surreal, but during my training, I would become more attached to them than anything I had ever possessed, and from that day forward, they would never leave my sight.

We were again shuffled back to the barracks and told to put everything on our bunks. We didn't know quite what to do until the D.I. walked in.
"Stand the fuck-up, morons!" he yelled. "When a ranking officer walks through that door, you get off your lazy, good for nothing asses and come to attention!"
We were all on our feet by that point, and I did my best to stand at attention exactly as they told us.
"Jesus Christ!" he continued. "What a bunch of pussy-whipped fucks did they send me now?! You are the most pathetic bunch of trouser stains I have ever seen!"
He walked up and down the aisle looking for anyone who seemed uncomfortable. Then, he passed me. He suddenly walked up into my face and started screaming.
"What the fuck are you looking at?!" he asked. "Did I see you looking at me, asshole?!"
"Sir, no sir!" I yelled.
I quickly learned that when answering the D.I., yelling was the appropriate way to do it. He continued staring at me.
"What's your name, private?!" he asked.

"Sir, Clarence Taylor, sir!" I answered.
"Clarence?!" he screamed. "You're different from the rest of these fuck-ups! Why is that?!"

I knew exactly what he was talking about. The idea of going to college is to cultivate one's intelligence. It doesn't make you smarter, but it does change you. This was what the D.I. saw.
"I'll bet you went to college, didn't you?!"
"Sir, yes sir!" I replied.
"I thought so!" he said. "And I'll just bet you got yourself a degree, didn't you?!"
"Sir, yes sir!" I answered.
"So, what did you study, slimeball?!" he asked.
I answered with only a moment's hesitation.
"Sir, philosophy, sir!"
"Philosophy?! You gotta be fuckin' kidding me!" he yelled. "What kind of philosophy?!"
Now it was my turn. I had recently read several books on the philosophy of warfare in order to gain some insight into the military mindset and with staunch military bearing, I listed them off - Sun Tzu's 'The Art of War', the Samurai Code, General Patton's 'Principles of War' and the 'Roman Philosophy of Warfare'.
"And what did the fuckin' Romans think, huh?!" he yelled.

It was now obvious to me that I had been singled out, and it happened as soon as the D.I. saw me. My response was both quick and effortless.

"Sir!" I began. "The Romans believed that the key to victory was in the complete and utter devastation of the enemy, sir!"

I'm not sure if he was impressed or not. He walked around behind me and stood at my right.

"Well, if you're so goddamn smart!" he began. "What the fuck are you doing here?!"

Now, it was time for a more masculine approach.

"Sir, I'm here to kill terrorists, sir!" I answered.

"Is that so?!" he replied. "A philosopher on the battlefield?! Is that some kinda sick joke?!"

"Sir, no sir!" I replied.

"Well, here's a news flash for you!" he continued. "From now on, your name's going to be Socrates! How do you fuckin' like that, asshole?!"

Protesting would not be a good idea. So, I said what anyone in their right mind would say.

"Sir, it's fine, sir!"

He pointed a finger in my face.

"I'd better be!" he began. "Cause you're going to hear it a lot! Got that, Socrates?!"

"Sir, yes sir!" I answered.

I was greatly relieved as he quickly walked away.

"Now, you assholes, listen up!" he started. "My name is Staff Sergeant Frank! You will learn that name, and you will remember it!"

He began walking down the row of new recruits - all standing at attention.

"Now, you may think you are soldiers. You are not soldiers! When I look at you, I do not see soldiers! I see a bunch of pussies who can't even wipe their own asses without their mama's doing it for them! Well, I'm not your mama! I am not here to wipe your ass! Now, anyone who says that they were in this Army because they did a few weeks of basic training is a failure! In this Army, failure is not an option! If you do not finish your training, you will be an even bigger pussy than you are now! You may have noticed that there is no name on your uniform! That is because, at this point, you do not deserve a name! You do not have names because you are nothing! You are pukes! You are the most disgusting, vile, lowest form of life on God's green earth! But, that will change! You will be pushed to your limits! You will experience pain! You will experience hardship! But, you will learn to ignore pain! You will learn to ignore hardship! You will move beyond your limitations! You will become soldiers! You will become men! Right now, each and every one of you are nothing more than a waste of skin! I will reshape you! I will make you soldiers and when I am done, each of you will be a well-oiled cog in the United States Army war machine! You will not waver from the mission! You will not hesitate in battle! Hesitation is the first enemy! If you hesitate, you will die! Your fellow soldiers - your friends - will die! Therefore, you will learn to think quickly! You will learn to react with a calm mind! And when you kill the enemy you will do so without mercy! You will kill them before they kill you! And after you kill the enemy, you will walk off the battlefield with your heads held high, for you will have snatched victory from the jaws of certain death! Now, I am certain that all of you are aware of what happened last year on September eleventh - that this country was attacked by terrorists! There is only one kind of person who gets a hard-on by attacking innocent and unarmed men, women, and children, and that is a coward! Terrorists are nothing more than cowards! Terrorists are not people! They do not deserve to live! They are not worth the putrid, stinking shit they are made of! As the soldiers you will become, it will fall to you to make sure that every one of these cowardly bastards dies! Now, the Army does not want murderers! The Army does not want mindless drones! The Army wants warriors who will stand and fight, who will risk their lives for their country; who will receive and carry out orders without question! If I tell you to jump, you will ask how high! If I tell you to shit, you will ask what color! You will become soldiers! You will become warriors! And when you graduate, you will leave behind the person that you are now! You will be different! People will look at you, and they will know that you are a soldier! You will leave your training as a symbol of freedom and why we fight to defend it! Defending the United States has never been as important as it is right now! Is that understood?!"

"Sir, yes sir!" we replied.

The dormitory - or barracks, by its proper name - momentarily rang with a slight echo as a feeling of pride was felt, filling the room like an oncoming storm. Sure, it wasn't Patton's 'blood and guts' speech, but it worked, and it was those words that acted to reaffirm my reason for being here in the first place. I had reached the point beyond any certainty that this is what I should be doing - right here, right now.

Chapter 9

That day was the beginning of 'hell week' – the first week of basic training. It was the most demanding time of our training due to the stress that was imposed on us for the sake of our transformation into soldiers. We were up at five o'clock every day. After breakfast, we would fall out onto the drill pad for pushups, sit-ups, and marching. It seems like when we weren't doing anything else, we were either marching or running. Everything was performed by a strict set of standards. We learned how to fold our uniforms, how to organize our footlockers, and how to make up our bunks. It all had to be perfect and mistakes were not tolerated. A complete absence of technology was insisted upon with the idea that if you found yourself in the middle of nowhere, it was unlikely that your phone would receive a signal. Orienteering was done by map and compass, finding direction by the hands of a watch, as well as using the stars for navigation.

Sit-ups were used as an introduction to pain. We would be lined up ten to a row and ordered to lift a twenty-foot telephone pole. Holding it into our chests, we were told to lie down on our backs. Like everything else in basic training, the first few attempts were nearly impossible, but it wasn't long before we were moving as a single unit. Once this was accomplished, we were ordered to do twenty sit-ups. They were the most agonizing sit-ups I had ever done in my life, but with all the things that required practice, it got easier over time. This was also the case with the obstacle course. If I've learned anything from these experiences, it's that I was completely unaware of how out of shape I was.

It was during these activities of physical torment that we also began training in hand-to-hand combat. I always thought that knocking someone out required a blow to the head. I discovered, however, that it's far easier than people think. One well-placed blow behind the angle of the jaw is enough to get the job done. The idea of stealth was stressed both strongly and repeatedly as we were taught how to sneak up behind someone, using the combat knife to sever the vocal cords and the carotid artery in a single stroke. In this manner, the enemy can be made to bleed out while being unable to scream. After that, it's just a matter of hiding the body so as to leave nothing for the enemy to find. In basic training, a peculiar mindset is hammered into us.

We are taught to dehumanize the enemy – to think of them as 'hostile targets'. The act of killing the enemy is referred to as 'eliminating a hostile target'. It was difficult to wrap my head around this idea at first. But, the more I thought back to the events of nine eleven, the more sense it started to make, and after enough lectures and thought, I'd finally reached the reality of what I believe to be human. This was not something grandiose or worthy of academia. It was an epiphany on a very personal level and one that I would use later in the grim business of war. I came to the belief that 'human' is a title that falls one step above 'monster' and one step below 'enlightened'. It is a title that must be earned by the sincere admission of one's own imperfections.

The enlightened have evolved themselves to a place where there is everything and nothing, where all imperfections have been fought off by compassion and spiritual awakening. The monster, however, must be made to evolve by being slain, only to be reborn with the potential for reflection. Those comprising the enemy are monsters who would rob the innocent and uninvolved of their lives when there is nothing to be gained by their deaths. It is the enemy who must die, and I will be one of many who slay these monsters.

On some deep level, I awoke to an ideology that somehow brought my life into focus. Not to be dramatic, but I had heard the call and my obligation as a human being had become crystal clear. It wasn't just about killing for my country. It's a noble thought, but it's not enough. I would go to the Middle East – most likely Afghanistan – and I would kill to protect the innocent. I would go there as part of the arm that pulls the monsters out from under the bed and gives them the death they deserve. I also hoped that in accomplishing this, I would not create my own monster.

Chapter 10

It was also at this point that we were issued a key piece of equipment. At another time, I would have simply called it a gun. But the Army, never settling for casual terminology, insisted that we call it a 'rifle'. More than that, it was 'my' rifle. It would become a part of me, never leaving my sight. This was the beginning of weapons training and its introduction was the M-16 rifle, and we would learn the name and function of every single part of this weapon. We would spend a great deal of time on the firing range learning how to fire it, how to sight it in, how to carry it, and how to hold it. There were many nights when we would be ordered to sleep with it lying next to us. In my earlier life, I had been quite uncomfortable about the idea that there were guns at all. I felt that if the founding fathers had possessed two centuries of foresight, the Second Amendment would have been written very differently and that the possession of any firearm was nothing short of a formula for self-destruction. I still feel that way, but now I think that weapons belong in the hands of those who keep the peace and withheld from those who would go to war against society. Don't get me wrong, I don't think that war should ever be considered as a workable option for peace, but should only be considered when diplomacy has failed and confrontation becomes inevitable. Then, there is the response to an attack. The response should be swift -- the objective uncomplicated and free of any political agenda.

Maintenance was a huge part of weapons training. Without cleaning, an M16 would last about three weeks before jamming. After that, it was nothing more than an eight-pound paperweight. I became so proficient at dismantling and reassembling the weapon that I could do it in almost complete darkness. We received a manual of technical information for every weapon we would learn. It wasn't Boolean logic, but there was still a lot of information to learn, and memorizing it came easily to me. The M16, for example, is 39.63 inches long and when fully loaded weighs eight pounds and thirteen ounces. It has a bore diameter of .223 inches with a maximum range of thirty-six hundred meters. The magazine capacity is thirty rounds and a muzzle velocity of thirty-one hundred feet per second. Also, on the list were the Colt M1911 pistol and the grenade launcher. When I fired the M16 for the first time, I anticipated a bone-jarring recoil. To my surprise, there was very little, and as I squeezed off the next few rounds my body was suddenly jolted by a surge of adrenaline. My mind achieved a degree of clarity I had never known. It was an addictive experience that would never be in short supply. Power comes in many forms, but there is a unique feeling of power in firing a grenade launcher. When fired, its forty-millimeter barrel makes a low, hollow popping sound. And it has more than a little kick. If God were to begin intervening in human affairs, I have no doubt that He'd use one of these to make His point. We fired at a stationary tank during practice. I couldn't help but wonder what might be the result of firing it at a person.

Learning to throw a grenade was a uniquely terrifying experience. We started by using dummy grenades as it was important to become accustomed to the feel and weight of something that, if used carelessly, could very graphically end one's life. I had never been so terrified of anything as when I held a live grenade for the first time. Remembering the steps for throwing it was easy when you're guaranteed not to die. But when it came to the real thing, I had to fight my instinct to just get rid of it. After all, it's not exactly normal to want to hold an explosive device for any period of time, and it took a great deal of effort to remain calm while consciously going through the steps. "Don't forget," I thought. "Don't screw it up; know where you're throwing it; squeeze down on the trigger lever; pull the pin; hold it back behind your ear; release the trigger lever; throw it straight towards the target. And never panic."

In my previous life, the thought of blowing something up would have caused me to question my sanity. However, there is something to be said for the experience of creating that kind of damage, and my first throw was right on target. I know it sounds strange, but jokingly, I think I found a hobby.

Chapter 11

I took the next two or three weeks to get to know some of my fellow recruits. But, one person seemed to stand out. His name was Kevin Pendleton and, like the rest of us, he spoke only when spoken to - as was the general rule. Unlike the others, there was something different about him, something quiet. Naturally, I gravitated towards him thinking that he may, at some point, need to talk. I found that he wasn't one for a lot of conversation, and he didn't seem to talk about basic training like the rest of us. In fact, he didn't talk about it all. We were required to write letters home. It was thought that family support, as well as a strong sense of connectedness, was important to morale, but Kevin seemed not only to write infrequently but briefly as well. While the rest of us used notepads, Kevin would write on postcards. I found it hard to believe that someone his age would be short on words. As I look back, he wasn't much on eye contact either. Training continued to be difficult and stressful as we began learning survival skills. Survival is always assumed to be complicated by one important factor - the enemy. Battlefield survival can be slightly compared to woodland survival. But unlike being lost in the woods, there could be someone trying to kill you. We also trained in evasion and camouflage - how to cover your tracks; and how to use the landscape to hide from the enemy.

Water is always the first order of business when it comes to survival. Without it, you will die. Finding it isn't nearly as difficult as making sure it's relatively safe to drink. Then there's shelter- something low profile is usually best, so as to minimize the chances of being seen. The next priority is warmth. In ordinary woodland survival, fire is essential for both warmth and visibility, but in a situation where others may not have your best interests in mind, building a fire is never a good idea. If, however, one is forced to do so, it's always best to build something small.

I once read something written by a Native American of the Navajo nation who said, 'Red man build small fire and sit close; white man build large fire and sit far away'. Conserving resources is critical to survival and anything you find can be used for something. It's all a matter of how creative you can be with your resources. After days of training, we were driven to the other side of the base and dropped off at the edge of a heavily wooded area. We fell into formation and were told that we would be sent in alone for the weekend. They dropped us off at different points so no one had the chance to pair up. So, with little more than the clothes on my back, I found myself alone in a wooded area with the single goal of maintaining my existence. Immediately, I began to spot several kinds of edible plants and some grubs, which I hastily stuffed into my pockets. Rule of thumb: if it tastes bitter, don't eat it. We were told to navigate by compass to a particular heading and stay there, then return two nights later. I successfully started a very small fire using a bow I'd made from a branch and one of my bootlaces. Shelter was not a problem, as there was plenty of material strewn through the woods for a small lean-to. For the purpose of practicing evasion, I dug a small trench about ten inches deep. Over this, I constructed my lean-to, just high enough off the ground that I could squeeze myself underneath. However, I didn't anticipate how cold the nights were in South Carolina. Being from Maine meant getting used to the cold, but sleeping in the woods without fire and little more than a few branches over your head was a completely different matter. You might be asking how we were evaluated after two nights in the woods. We were weighed both before and after our experience. A five-pound weight loss was expected. However, any gain in weight prompted questions from the D.I. with suspicions of cheating. This was hardly the case for any of us, and although we were all tired and hungry, we had to wait for everyone to return. Kevin was the last one out of the woods and I couldn't help noticing the look on his face. His skin color was good, but he looked like he'd come face to face with the devil himself. As for myself, I found the isolation of the woods not only challenging but comforting. Not that I'm one to go communing with nature, but the ear-shattering silence of the woods at night can bring a sense of calm. At least, for me.

Like everyone else, I spent a great deal of time studying. We had been introduced to the UCMJ - the Uniformed Code of Military Justice. It outlines specific crimes one can be charged with in both times of peace and war. Naturally, the laws are far harsher during wartime. However, with all the studying I was doing, I had failed to notice the change in Kevin's behavior. Around the D.I., he hid his quickly surfacing issues well. But, Kevin was falling apart. In the morning, he rose exhausted. A noticeable degree of anxiety led him to become a bit uncoordinated on the obstacle course, and he had developed a nervous tic in his left arm. It was actually very slight but did not go unnoticed. Adding to his stress level, some of the other recruits cruelly dubbed him with the nickname 'twitch'. I tried to talk to him occasionally in an attempt to offer some support, but he gave the impression that there was nothing wrong. He seemed not only to be more anxious over time but grew increasingly resentful of those who insisted on addressing him by his new nickname. I guess I was just trying to look out for him. I had even gone to the extent of trying to get the other guys to back off a bit. Unfortunately, this only seemed to make things worse.

I guess the saying's true: 'damned if you do, damned if you don't'. He approached later saying, "Thanks for trying". I thought this might be an opportunity to have an actual conversation with him - maybe even make a friend. I don't think he resisted the idea. He had simply become distant -- maybe as a way of escape. Apparently, I was not alone in my concern. John Drummond, another recruit, approached me asking about him.
"Hey, Socrates," he said.
Yes, by this time everyone was calling me 'Socrates'.
"Is he okay?" he asked.
"I don't know," I answered. "I think the guy just needs a friend."
He glanced over at Kevin, who clearly seemed to be somewhere else.
"You let me know if there's anything I can do, okay?" John said.

It was nice to know that there was someone else who cared.

They were trying to teach us the idea of becoming 'brothers-in-arms'. The practice of this idea was more difficult than understanding it. At some point, we were forced to take a leap of faith - quite literally. After three weeks of ground training, I found myself standing near the edge of an open tail ramp on a C-130, flying over a clearing at three hundred feet. The ripcord was a static line that clipped onto a cable that ran almost the entire length of the aircraft. Everyone was ordered to stand and clip in as we approached the drop zone. "Go!" the D.I. yelled.
One by one, we stepped up to the edge, crossed our arms over our chests, and jumped. I could feel the static line pull as my parachute opened. As parachutes go, these were designed to get you on the ground as quickly as possible without being killed. I guess it's true, what they say: 'It's not the fall that gets you, but the sudden stop'. We were taught the parachute landing fall. This was one thing no one wanted to screw up.

The idea was to land on your feet, bend your knees, and rock backward toward the ground. It all had to be done in a split second, and there's no undo button on a bad jump. I honestly thought I was going to piss myself as I stood ready to take the leap. But, once my feet left the cargo ramp, I became almost overwhelmed by a very different feeling. I still can't fully describe it, as if that one moment had become stretched out over the whole of time. However, I had to remain in control. I couldn't afford to get lost in the moment. I was, after all, falling out of an airplane and didn't want this to be the kind of impression I wanted to leave on the world.

After landing safely, I gathered up my parachute and immediately started looking for Kevin. If he was having problems with stress, I couldn't imagine his reaction to jumping out of a plane. "Did he remember how to land?" I thought.
He was one of the last to jump, so I had no idea where he landed. But at the edge of the clearing stood a roughly fifty-foot silk-covered Pine tree. I ran to the tree and found Kevin hanging about six feet from the ground. He was visibly shaken, but otherwise okay. The D.I. was the last to jump and wasn't far behind.
"Private!" he yelled. "How the fuck did you get up that tree?!"
Kevin was at a loss for words. The D.I. asked me several questions regarding any potential injuries - neck and spinal injuries were a huge concern. But,

other than a bit of embarrassment and a newfound fear of death, he survived the jump in one piece.

We all came out of it with our nerves a bit frayed, but Kevin's near-death experience only seemed to push his state of mind that much further. Over the next couple of days, he was a bit more tense than usual. I tried to ask him how he was doing after the jump. His hesitation spoke volumes as he quietly revealed his intense fear of heights.
"When I saw the ground coming up toward me," I began. "I thought I was going to shit myself."
We both laughed it off as his tension appeared to ease. But with a sudden tone of seriousness, he turned back to me.
"I thought I was going to fucking die."

Chapter 12

Over the next few days, we spent some time studying explosives, learning about different types of ordinance and their characteristics. We would never actually handle explosives - that was the job of Special Ops and the Rangers. We were simply given an introduction. The day following this training was critical as we were prepared for 'night fire'. The conditions of battle seemed harrowing enough, but the idea of exchanging fire at night is one that no words could accurately describe. Contrary to popular belief, most small-caliber weapons do not produce a muzzle flash. If the enemy sees you at night, it's probably already too late. You'll never see where the shot came from without night vision goggles, and learning how not to be seen at night is just as important as in daylight. The enemy, it seems, has access to the same, if not better technology than us. That being said, there is one tool in the soldier's arsenal that, if used properly, can be honed into a superior weapon - his brain. In many cases, learning to use your brain to gain an advantage over the enemy meant staying calm enough to carry out orders and sometimes, your life depended on it. Learning to keep cool under fire would never be as important as during our first 'night fire' exercise and as we prepared for this exercise in class, a diagram was displayed.

"This is not just another training class!" the D.I. said. "This is a briefing on your first 'night fire' exercise! It is critical that you listen to every single word and do exactly as you are told! If you do something stupid, you will die!"

The idea of 'night fire' is to experience the conditions of a battle at night. The exercise area was approximately forty feet by fifty feet, with four concrete open-top bunkers - one at each corner. Two were for the detonation of ordinance, while the other two were for firing flares. We were ordered into concrete trenches and told that live rounds would be fired over our heads. We weren't told the caliber of the weapons being used, but that some of these would be tracers. These were high-velocity rounds coated with phosphorus. When fired, the heat from the barrel ignited the phosphorus and the round would leave a streak of greenish light through the air. They were used exclusively for aiming gunfire at night. The last thing you wanted was to get hit by one of these.

The idea of getting shot seemed bad enough, but the thought of getting shot with something that would also burn its way through whatever it hit was one that I took very seriously. I'm sure the expression 'ouch' probably wouldn't even begin to describe that experience. On both ends of every trench was posted a drill instructor, each holding a small air horn in the event that the exercise had to be stopped, for whatever reason. With sidearms, rifles, helmets, and bullet-proof vests, we were filed in eight to a trench.

We sat in the trenches for at least ten minutes, so as to experience the anticipation of battle. As luck would have it, I found myself sitting next to Kevin and John. It then occurred to me that if the stress of the exercise turned out to be too much for Kevin, we'd both be there to help him. It felt as though we were waiting forever when suddenly the cool night air exploded. I could feel the ground shaking underneath me as explosives were detonated. The night lit up as tracers streaked their green glow roughly one to two feet over our heads.

During our classroom training, we were told how critical it was to stay as low as possible, but all the classroom time in the world can never be as good a teacher as experience. The 'night fire' exercise was a more than adequate example of that idea and crouched as low as possible, it seemed as though the earth opened up and swallowed my senses. The sound of automatic weapons fire filled my head, while flares lit up as brilliant white orbs that gently fell from the sky. It would have been a magnificent sight had it not been so terrifying. I tried to turn to see how Kevin was doing only to be swiftly harassed by one of the D.I.'s.

"Private!" he yelled. "Keep your goddamn head down!"

We were reminded of this almost constantly. I managed to shift my weight just enough to catch a glance at Kevin. We were all scared, but there was something else on his face - something wild. I still can't put a word to it.

"Kevin!" I yelled. "You've got to keep it together!" But, my words fell on deaf ears and as I focused my attention on him, his face took on a blank expression.

In that instant, I knew that Kevin was in trouble. I quickly dropped my head as an ear-shattering explosion ripped through the air. As I looked back, I discovered, to my horror, that Kevin had suddenly stood up. His demons had taken him over, pushing aside his ability to reason and taking control of his body. The entire event happened faster than I was able to absorb it, and by the time I reached out to grab him by the knees, it was too late. At least one round had knocked his helmet off as shards of bone, blood, and brain tissue exploded over the tops of the trench walls. He'd also been hit by a tracer. It left a burning smell in the air that I would never forget. But in spite of seeing Kevin die, someone or something decided that this was not enough.

Just after Kevin collapsed, John panicked and stood up, yelling for a medic. 'Medic'. It was just one word, but John's voice was suddenly cut off as a round found its way into the side of his neck. A torrent of blood instantly followed as his legs folded underneath him. John was not as fortunate as Kevin and while Kevin had been killed instantly, John lay choking on his own blood as he clutched my hand. It all happened so quickly, yet in my mind, it seemed to slow to the pace of an afternoon sun creeping across a cloudless summer sky, too fast for the D.I. to react quickly enough as he sounded his air horn, bringing the night back to a misty stillness. He rushed down into the trench before I even had the chance to turn on my flashlight.
"Clear the trenches!" he yelled. "Everyone, get the fuck out!"
The D.I. grabbed me by the back of my vest.
"Clear the trench, private!"
I moved quickly out of the trench and off the range while medics swarmed over the area. I could hear one of them yelling into his radio.
"We have one critical and one deceased! We need a medevac at the night fire range, stat!"

They did their best to stem the flow of blood pouring from John's neck as one of the medics tried, unsuccessfully, to place an I.V. in his arm.

But by this time, John had stopped choking, prompting the other medic to start chest compressions. Now, the night air was filled with a different sound as a medevac helicopter made its approach. Its searchlight cut through the darkness like a hot knife, while its rotors beat against the chilly mist. The Blackhawk helicopter had been specially outfitted by the Army as an airborne ambulance. It carried onboard oxygen and suction and could transport six patients with three flight medics. They were known as 'angels of the battlefield', trained to perform, among other things, emergency amputations and tracheotomies. They rolled Kevin's lifeless body to one side and, while holding pressure, slid a backboard under John.

He never made a sound or moved in the slightest as he was strapped down and carried to the Blackhawk. Kevin's body was placed in a wire stretcher and loaded in as well, but before the helicopter's side door was closed, I saw one of the medics cover him with a sheet. I would later learn that John had died in flight to the base hospital. We all stood near the edge of the night fire range.

No one said a word. We were only able to watch as two of our fellow recruits died before our eyes. But, they didn't just die. They died horribly, and their families would be forced to say goodbye without the comfort of seeing their faces.

Naturally, there was an investigation. In my previous life, I'd gone to a few funerals - mostly relatives – and I always found them to be a bit tense. After all, no one wants to go to a funeral, right? But clearly, there is a world of difference between seeing the well-tailored dead lying in repose and watching helplessly as two of your friends bleed out next to you. This brought the reality of war far closer, and I wasn't ready to see it - not that I would ever be comfortable with the sight of death, but I had accepted a personal mission to go to the edge of civilization and destroy those who'd voluntarily surrendered their humanity. I had not yet come to accept what I came to think of as the tragic and ugly by-product of war.

Questions began to emerge upon returning to the barracks, and I wondered if there was anything else I could have done. We were all under a lot of stress. That was the idea of basic training - learning how to handle stress. But suicide? I never saw that coming. Maybe I should have, I don't know. As we sat on the floor of the barracks, the air became filled with an eerie silence. I glanced around at the faces of my fellow recruits. Everyone was stunned. They were, of course, curious about what had happened, but no one seemed to know how to ask.

"Private Taylor, report to my office!"

The odd quiet was suddenly broken by the sound of the D.I.'s voice. I quickly got to my feet and upon entering the D.I.'s office, I came to attention and saluted, as is customary.

"Sir, Private Taylor reporting as ordered, sir!" I said.

The D.I. sat at his desk with my file in front of him as well as a pad and pen.

"Your name's Clarence, right?"

His tone was oddly casual. I guess I expected a lot more yelling, and I was ready for that, but this was something unnerving.

"Sir, yes sir!" I answered.

I continued standing at attention.

"Let's drop the sir stuff, alright?" he said. "Have a seat."

He opened my file and skimmed over its contents.

"Clarence," he began. "What the hell are you doing here?"

I was a bit bewildered, given recent events.

"Um…I thought I was here about what happened during night fire," I replied.

"Yeah," he said. "We're going to get to that. I'm just curious about why you're here. You've got a college degree, so you're not an idiot. Why aren't you in officer training school? You do know you're probably going to end up in Afghanistan, right?"

"I know," I replied. "That's what I want."

I spoke briefly about my reaction to nine eleven and the desire I felt to put right what was obviously a crime no punishment could fit, even if it meant killing. Although one person usually can't change anything, sometimes it only takes one person to raise their voice, point a finger, and say 'No, I will not tolerate this!' I wasn't trying to impress him, but the D.I. was, nonetheless, clearly impressed.

"I wish half these guys had your brains," he said with a nod. "So, what happened out there, Clarence?"

Now that I had to talk about it, I wasn't sure I'd be able to control my emotions and hesitated in my response.

"Clarence," he continued. "It's okay."

The floodgates of emotion seemed to open by themselves as I suddenly broke down in front of the D.I.

"I knew Kevin was going through some stress," I began tearfully. "But, all of us are. I saw this look on his face - just for a moment."

"What look was that?" the D.I. asked.

"I…I don't know," I answered. "It was like he just tuned out, and I think John was trying to help."

"Clarence," the D.I. said. "You listen to me. This was not your fault. We try to prevent these things and figure out who can handle it and who can't and sometimes, people just snap. Now, John had good intentions, but he panicked. These things tend to happen really fast, and sometimes you just can't react fast enough. But I'll tell you right now, Clarence, if you're here to fight terrorists, then you're going to see more of this. I'm not saying that you should get used to it, and I hope you never do. But, you better start accepting it, because it's going to get worse. Now, I know they were your friends, and it's a terrible thing to see your friends die - especially like that. So, I want you to think about this, and you don't have to do it, but I think it would be a good idea."

I listened intently, hoping he would offer some inspiring words that would take away the pain I felt, allowing me to move on. Instead, he suggested that I write a letter to each family, telling them of our friendship as well as my impressions of them as individuals. I would tell

Kevin's family how important it was for him to serve, in spite of what he was going through. I told them about the courage he displayed on his first parachute jump, despite his intense fear of heights. In my letter to John's family, I described him as the person I saw - selfless. He was someone who seemed to be just as concerned about Kevin as I was, but he went the extra mile in helping Kevin without so much as a single thought to his own safety. Yes, John made a mistake that cost him his life, but I wanted his family to see him as someone who was truly willing to give up his life to help others. I wanted them to see him as a hero.

"Now," he continued. "I know this is going to sound cruel, but you're not getting any special treatment. I'm going to ride you just as hard as I did before, just like everyone else. Got that?"

"Yes, sir," I answered.

"Alright," he said. "Time for lights out."

I stood up, saluted, and left his office. The D.I. walked out about five minutes later.

"Alright, ladies!" he yelled. "Lights out! Get your asses in your bunks! 0500's coming real soon, so get some shut-eye! Tomorrow, you will have one day of liberty! You will be going into town in uniform! You will remember who are! You will remember what you represent! And I do not want to get any reports on any of you! If I do, I will kick your sorry asses all the way back to your mamas! Now, lights out!"

Chapter 13

The D.I. was right, 0500 arrived far earlier than I would have liked. For most of the night, my mind raced with images from the night fire range. Like angry ghosts, they charged through my consciousness like war horses clamoring to battle. I would drift into a light sleep, only to be pulled away from badly needed rest by the images of blood and shattered bone. Some facsimile of sleep eventually came but only as the result of exhaustion. As I rose from my bunk, I couldn't help noticing how heavy my body felt. I guess it was good that our one day of liberty seemed to be so well-timed. If it had been another training day, I'm certain that I would have been of little use. After the usual morning routine, we marched to the mess hall for breakfast. As usual, it was brief.

After breakfast, we fell into formation and received another lecture from the D.I. before going into town.
"Listen up, assholes!" he began. "The drinking age in South Carolina is eighteen! This does not apply to you! You will conduct yourselves in a civilized manner at all times! This means that you will refrain from the use of alcohol! Also, because of where this installation is located, the area of

Columbia that you will be going to is known for prostitution! You will not cavort with the prostitutes! The last thing I want to see is one of 'my' recruits coming back to 'my' barracks with some kind of slimy fucking disease! So, do not get the idea that you are going into town to get laid! You will be bussed into town and dropped off at Granby Park! That bus will leave Granby Park at 1600 hours on the dot, whether you are there or not! And I highly recommend that each of you be there on time! Do I make myself clear?!"

"Sir, yes sir!" we answered.

It took forty-five minutes to get to Granby Park. Once we were there, everyone grabbed a map and headed off in different directions. I decided to go to the military museum on Gist Street. I didn't really feel like being around a lot of people, given recent events and I thought that the museum would be both quiet and interesting. But, as I made my way out of the park I heard the sound of footsteps rapidly approaching from behind me.

"Hey, Taylor, right?"

I recognized him immediately. His name was Steve Jacobs. He was from a small town about an hour west of Albany, New York. After basic training, he went on to tech school to become an artillery specialist.

"Uh, yeah," I said. "Just call me Clarence."

"I thought they called you Socrates," he said.

"Yeah, I guess that's what they call me," I replied. He walked next to me for a few minutes.
"So, uh, where are you headed?" Steve asked.
"Well," I began. "There's a military museum just up on Gist Street I'd like to check out."
"Awesome!" Steve replied. "Mind if I go along with you?"
I wanted to be left alone for a few hours, but I got the feeling that he might be trying to offer a bit of sympathetic company.
"Uh, yeah, sure," I answered.
We walked a bit further in something of an awkward silence as I continued studying the map. I knew he was curious - everyone was. I suppose I had to say something at some point. Maybe it was best to just get it out in the open.

"So, how are you holding up? I mean, you were right there, right?"
Without stopping, I glanced over at him.
"Yeah, I was," I answered.
"The other guys in the trench said Kevin just snapped," he said.
"Yeah," I replied. "That's pretty much what happened."
"Did John snap too?" he asked.
"No, he was just trying to help," I answered.
A moment went by as Steve seemed to struggle for words.

"And you were right there," he continued. "Fuck, I don't think I could handle that."

The truth is, I wasn't handling it. I was angry. 'Why me?' I wondered. Why did I have to be the one who just happened to be sitting next to two people, only to watch them die? I know it seems selfish, but it just isn't fair that I have to find a way to move on with my life while two of my friends have, for some reason, been removed from the weight of the world.

"Look," Steve continued. "If you ever want to talk, I'm here for you'. I mean…I can't say that I understand but, you know, if…sorry, I'm not very good at this kind of thing".

"It's okay," I replied. "I get it. Thanks."

I had to give him credit. Everyone else seemed to be too afraid to say anything. Maybe they were afraid of saying the wrong thing. Maybe they were afraid of not knowing what to say, to begin with.

Now, instead of keeping watch over someone who needed a friend, someone else seemed to be keeping watch over me, and I was the one who needed a friend. We spent a couple of hours wandering through the museum. I felt especially drawn to the revolvers. They all looked similar to each other, yet each bore an elegant beauty all their own. I would even go so far as to call them works of art. They had clean lines and graceful curves, unlike the pistol I had become accustomed to carrying. I know it's hard to see a firearm as objet d'art, considering the purpose they were designed for, but the passage of time painted a new picture of these relics, overshadowing their function with form, grace, and yes, a certain degree of beauty. We'd spent about two hours in the museum when Steve walked up to me studying his map.

"Hey, Socrates," he said. "Let's go downtown."

I didn't want to be around a lot of people, but it occurred to me that I'd probably never be in South Carolina again.

"Sure," I replied. "Why not?"

We left the museum and walked back down towards Granby Park. If I was going downtown, I didn't want to wander aimlessly. That seemed like a waste of time, and time was something we did not have in abundance. I looked closely at the map.

"Hey, Steve," I began. "How about this?"

I pointed out what I thought was a place that would be hard to wander away from. Neither of us knew this city, and using a landmark as a reference point seemed like the smart thing to do. Twenty minutes later, we found ourselves standing in front of the Carolina Coliseum. This area was a haven for tourists, with small shops and stores that sold a little of everything. If you were looking for something unique and had enough time, you would, no doubt, find it here. I also felt an urge to

buy something 'touristy' and was drawn to what looked like a 'new age' store. Upon opening the door, I was immediately struck by the overpowering aroma of incense. A middle-aged man stepped out from the back of the store.
"Help y'all with something?" he asked.
"Just looking," I answered. "Thanks."
There were scores of books on everything new age - chakras, crystal healing, astrology, and psychic awareness, to name a few. Then, something stood out to me - something small. It was a green jade Buddha. I picked it up and noticed how cold it was. The store owner informed me that jade is always cold. It didn't seem to matter that it was jade. It could have been made of cheap plastic, for that matter, but there was just something about it that fascinated me. So I paid seventy dollars for the four-inch statue and made my way toward the door. As I left, I noticed Steve near the entrance of the Coliseum. My curiosity peaked as I saw him talking with a rather colorfully dressed woman. But, as I grew closer, I was struck by the odd feeling that this was not a chance encounter.

She smoked her cigarette like a man and spoke in a manner that would put a trucker to shame. Here was a forty-something, flamboyantly dressed woman who introduced herself as 'Nettie'. She had a colorful personality and worked the streets of downtown Columbia as a prostitute, presenting a clownishly humorous image that left me thinking that some things are just too unbelievable to be real. Then again, I had never met a prostitute before.

"Hey!" she said. "You didn't tell me you had a friend!"

She looked me up and down as I glanced around, hoping to become invisible.

"Well," she continued. "Look at you, handsome! The prize pig at the county fair's got nothin' on you!"

I think she was complimenting me. I'm still not sure. I do know that it's difficult to respond to something when you don't understand what's being said.

"So," Nettie said. "You guys lookin' to party? I can't take you both, but I got a friend."

Mental note: prostitutes have friends. She continued looking us over as though we were, well, the prize pig at the county fair, I guess. Now, she began touching the creases of my shirt and straightening my tie while her cigarette hung from her painted lips.

"Fuck," she said. "A man in uniform gets me so fucking horny!"

"So, who's your friend?" Steve asked.

I looked at him as though he had just lost his mind.

"Her name's Dorothy," Nettie said. "She's working right now if you know what I mean." She playfully nudged my elbow as a broad grin came over her face. A moment of tense silence passed, only to be broken as Nettie glanced across the street.

"Hey!" she yelled. "There she is!"

From out of the front door of a rundown apartment building walked a middle-aged woman sporting curly brown hair, a halter top, and tight shorts. Stepping off the curb, she paused to light a cigarette and displayed a flare of temper as a car passed far too close for comfort.

"Watch where the fuck you're going'!" she yelled. "Asshole!"

Nettie greeted her cheerfully as she crossed the street.

"Hey! What's up, bitch?!"

Dorothy didn't seem to be one for conversation, but I suppose it wasn't conversation she was paid to provide. Unlike Nettie, Dorothy gave the appearance of someone whose life had trampled into the ground. Her face was devoid of anything cheerful, as though it had been chiseled by both time and despair.

I couldn't help thinking that at some point in her life, she had once been someone's little girl. Now, the only things she seemed to be left with were anger and a not-so-slight sore near the corner of her mouth. I leaned over toward Steve as she continued cursing about the driver who nearly ran her over.

"We need to get out of here," I said, pointing to my watch.

"So," Nettie said. "I think we got a couple of party boys here!"

She smiled broadly and put a hand on her hip.

"What do you' say, guys, fifty each?"

"Fifty?" Dorothy replied. "You gotta be fuckin' kidding me."

"Oh, c'mon," replied Nettie. "Look at these guys, so sexy in their uniforms."

Dorothy rolled her eyes in resignation.

"Fine," she said. "I suppose so."

I didn't think that paying fifty dollars to have sex with a middle-aged prostitute was necessarily a good deal, nor a good idea. Not that I was considering it, but it did seem like a perfectly good waste of money, and what one would get in return seemed not only unsavory but incredibly unfair.

"Which one do 'you' want?" Dorothy asked.

"Would you excuse us for a moment?" I interrupted.

I grabbed Steve by the arm and pulled him away by about twenty feet.

"Are you nuts?! You're not actually going to do this, are you?! Don't you remember what the D.I. said?"

"Socrates, come on, I'm just messing with them," Steve replied.

"Steve," I began. "It's three thirty. We have to get back to the park."

Steve glanced at his watch.

"Shit!" he said quietly.

As we began to walk back toward the direction of Granby Park, I turned and waved to them.

"Ladies," I began. "It's been nice! But we've got to take off!"

As we left, I couldn't help but overhear them.

"Fuck, I love a man in uniform," Nettie said. "Hey, you want to get drunk?"

"Yeah, sure," Dorothy replied. "You buying?"

"Fuck yeah, bitch!" Nettie answered. "I make more money than you, anyway!"

I looked back with a grin as they continued chattering. I would occasionally wonder what became of them. A city the size of Columbia tends to have a mean streak that takes exception to no one. And like Nettie and Dorothy, if you became one of its many lost souls, chances are you'd never find your way out.

Chapter 14

We made it back to Granby Park with enough time that we could find a place to sit. Most of the platoon was already there, with a few stragglers catching up. We waited for the bus as people around us watched. I'm sure they'd seen uniformed recruits in the park every day. Yet, they seemed to look at us as though we were somehow out of place. We weren't there long before the bus arrived. Its hydraulic brakes hissed as it rolled to a stop. The door opened and the D.I. stepped out holding a clipboard. He didn't say a word but looked at us with an expression that spoke volumes. Boarding the bus, we quickly sat down and remained silent, mostly out of the fear of being harassed by the D.I.

He called out our names alphabetically as each of us answered 'Sir, here, sir!' After everyone was accounted for we started back to the base. Another forty-five minutes passed as the bus made its way through the main gate and as the bus stopped in front of the barracks the D.I. ordered us to fall out into formation.
"Well," he began.
He walked slowly through the rows of our platoon.

"I don't smell any booze, so I am assuming that none of you consumed any alcohol!"

Slowly, he continued his examination of us.

"And I don't smell any pussy on any of you, so I trust that you stayed clear of the hookers!"

This was not entirely true, but since Steve and I hadn't been customers, I thought it best not to bring it up.

"I hope that all of you dick heads had a good time on liberty!" he continued. "Because tomorrow, your training will continue! Tomorrow, I will drag your lazy asses through the dirt! Tomorrow, you will go on your first five-mile run! At least a few of you will puke your guts out! But, you will keep running, and I don't give a flying fuck if you're puking on your shoes, you will not stop running! Is that clear?!"

"Sir, yes sir!" we answered.

We were marched to the mess hall and filed in for dinner.

Upon returning to the barracks, the D.I. did a surprise inspection. Anything less than perfect was unacceptable. Our uniforms always came back with laundry tags stuffed in the pockets. Every one of them had to be removed and if any were found on inspection, each one was a demerit. The D.I. found three among my uniforms. Steve had not been as attentive, and the D.I. recovered twenty-one laundry tags from his uniforms. As a consequence, surprise inspections became more frequent.

Chapter 15

We woke the next morning to the blaring sound of reveille. 0500 - right on time. After the usual morning ritual, we put on our 'battle dress uniforms' and marched to breakfast. Upon finishing, we fell into formation. The D.I. again lectured us on our impending five-mile run. This time, he also reminded us to be wary of the symptoms of heat stroke as well as heat exhaustion. This left me with the impression that it was okay to puke as long as we didn't die doing it. Initially, we started with a half-mile run during the second week of training. Eventually, we were running four miles a day. With half-mile increments, I had managed to avoid throwing up. Now, we were going from four miles to five.

Shortly after we started marching, the D.I. ordered us into double time. My body had become accustomed to the pain of constant strenuous activity, and I handled the first three and a half miles easily. But shortly after mile four, I was struck by a different sensation - one that I was not accustomed to. It started with a bit of lightheadedness, then excessive salivation and a sudden feeling of nausea. I took this as a sign of something imminent and moved over to the side of the group. I knew it was coming and there was no way to stop it. And yet, its suddenness caught me by surprise as most of my breakfast churned up and launched itself out onto the ground. As I found myself grasping my knees, I discovered how difficult it is to gasp for breath and vomit at the same time. From the perspective of comedy, I also found it amusing to see someone vomit. Not in the sense of illness or suffering, but if someone did something stupid, like participating in a drinking contest that resulted in vomiting, my reaction was usually one of disgust. However, somewhere beneath my revulsion, I was secretly laughing. I guess that makes me somewhat twisted. But, there's a world of difference between witnessing someone suddenly coating their shoes and being hunched over the dirt coating your own. It's funny until it happens to you.

I continued dry heaving as I began to catch up with the group. The D.I. glanced back at me with a look that could cut through armor plating. We finally stopped at mile five. Apparently, I had not been alone in my gastric upheaval, as I noticed several patches of grass that had recently been bleached by stomach acid. Steve had managed to keep his breakfast down during the run. But, as he bent down to get the blood moving back to his head, the contents of his stomach decided it was best left elsewhere, and he too proceeded to become ill. There is no question that after running five miles, puking isn't just embarrassing, it's painful. We were allowed to rest and hydrate ourselves, being told not to drink quickly or a lot to avoid water intoxication. Flushing out things the body needs can be debilitating and in a combat or survival setting, this condition can be deadly. I was expecting that we'd be driven back in cargo trucks, but to my surprise, we had run a loop that brought us back to the barracks. We were all in agony. Apparently, the abdominal muscles are the most affected by running. I know this because mine were on fire.

By the time we got back to the barracks, I could barely walk. With two weeks left of basic training, I thought everything else would be downhill. I was wrong. That afternoon we went to yet another class. This one, however, was part of gas chamber training. Now, I know what you're thinking. Most people use these words and think of capital punishment. This gas chamber is designed to expose recruits to the effects of tear gas. I'm not sure why they do this when there are so many other chemical weapons used for war, but I suppose that tear gas is a better option than Sarin. After learning how to put on the gas mask, it was important to 'clear' it. This was done by taking a deep breath, putting on the mask, and exhaling hard enough to open the valves and activate the filter.

Once we were in the gas chamber, we would be told to take a deep breath, remove our masks, and recite aloud our name, rank, and social security number. Upon performing this seemingly simple task, we would then exit the chamber. However, some things are not as simple as they appear and before walking into the gas chamber we were given one piece of crucial information - keep your eyes open. The tear gas will get into your eyes, but if you blink, it will burn. Funny thing about blinking, we do it both unconsciously and frequently. Under ordinary circumstances, it's difficult enough to control the act of blinking. Now, step into a brick building filled with tear gas, and this simple reflex suddenly becomes an inextinguishable fire.

The next day we marched to an isolated area of the base where a small brick building stood benignly near the tree line. It seemed to be nothing more than a box quietly nestled among the pines, themselves swaying in a soft wind. We were again briefed by the D.I. on the process of donning the gas mask.

"When you exit the gas chamber!" he began. "Put your arms out and keep your eyes open while walking into the wind!"

If we managed to keep from blinking, the wind would blow the tear gas out of our eyes and off our uniforms. We were warned about the trees on the other side. If we left the gas chamber with closed eyes, chances were pretty good that we would walk into one of them. I wondered how many people had done just that. A second instructor was there to assist as we were ordered to put on our gas masks. I took a deep breath and cleared my mask. After tightening the straps, I stood at attention with the rest of the platoon and waited. I wondered what was worse - waiting to walk into a tear gas chamber or standing in a tear gas chamber without the protection of a gas mask. I would soon find out.

As the others entered ahead of me, it didn't take long to realize what I was in for. The walls of the small building were not thick enough to contain the sounds of choking and vomiting, but most were able to recite their names, ranks, and numbers while a few made the mistake of inhaling after removing their masks. This was a lesson I had the benefit of learning as I stood waiting to enter and decided that the best way to do this was with a clear head - to think calmly and quickly. Right before going in, I went over the steps in my head. It was only moments until I was standing in a dimly lit chemical fog. There wasn't much to see through the lenses of the mask - only fog and shadows. I could hear my fellow trainees as they recited their names and numbers. Then, I heard Steve. He tried his best but was stopped in mid-sentence by a sudden, burning urge to vomit. Between this and the five-mile runs, I couldn't help but think that the Army was, for some reason, obsessed with the need to make us puke. Now, it was my turn. The D.I. stepped up to my right side. "Private Taylor!" he yelled. "Remove your mask!" I took a deep breath and removed my mask. I began reciting my name, but the one thing I wasn't able to do was to keep from blinking. One thing is very certain, hay fever pales in comparison to tear gas. My eyes were immediately forced to shut as tears streamed down my face. I instinctively reached up to rub the pain out.

"Private!" the D.I. yelled. "Do not rub your eyes!" It took all my conscious will to keep from rubbing. "What is your name, rank, and number Private?!" I quickly recited this information and was promptly ordered to exit the gas chamber. But, there was a problem. I couldn't see and in my haste to leave, I walked face-first into the wall. I was so close. The startle of planting my face into a brick wall caused me to gasp. On the inside, I was

cursing a blue streak. On the outside, I was again retching like a drunken college student.
I suddenly felt myself being pushed out of the building. This was followed by a sensation I hope never to experience again. As Steve blindly rushed toward the exit, he ran straight into me, and after he vomited on my back, we both careened into the nearest Pine tree. Not only had I been up close and personal with a brick wall, but within the space of thirty seconds, I had been left picking Pine bark out from between my teeth while my back was covered with puke. I later came to the conclusion that considering I was still alive, it must have been a good day. Now, I could hear everyone else laughing as we tried to help each other up.

Looking back, it was as funny as it was pathetic - both of us puking while stumbling to our feet. As soon as I was able to balance myself I opened my canteen, forced my eyes open, and began flushing them out. Soon after, the burning was replaced by normal vision and the coolness of the water as I continued pouring it over my face. With outstretched arms, I walked forward as the wind carried the residue of tear gas away from my body. Unfortunately, the only thing that would remove the vomit from the back of my uniform was laundry soap. Steve had also managed to wash out his eyes and clean his face of the burning left by the tear gas. However, Steve wasn't covered with puke. He was doing just fine. As we began to recover, the D.I. ordered us to fall in. He paced up and down in front of us, making sure that everyone was recovering. Then he passed me.

"Jesus fuckin' Christ!" he yelled. "Private, you smell like a barroom toilet on Mardi Gras! What the fuck happened to you?!"

Embarrassingly, I was forced to explain the ugly circumstances of what was a genuinely sticky situation.

Most of us were as white as a sheet, but the D.I. would not make an exception for a platoon of queasy recruits. He gave us half an hour to recover while we ran water over our heads at a nearby row of faucets. After filling our canteens, we were ordered back into formation and marched back to the barracks. Things could have been worse - it could have been July. Before leaving, I tried to rinse the vomit out of my uniform shirt. It didn't smell quite so bad, but it definitely needed to be washed, and I was hoping that the sun would dry it out on the way back. Of course, I couldn't be that lucky.

By the time we reached the barracks, a generous build-up of sweat had added itself to an experience that would forever be branded onto my memory.

After being allowed to change, we attended a class on urban warfare tactics. It had been only about six months since nine eleven, but intelligence sources had come to the conclusion that the U.S. would become a larger part of the United Nations effort in Iraq and Afghanistan. These sources also predicted that fighting would be divided between the streets and the desert. Personally, if given a choice, I would rather be sent into the desert where the enemy could be seen at a distance. At least there would be enough time to take up a position.

We took the next two days putting these tactics into practice, and it was at this point that we were introduced to a new tool - the flashbang. It looked like a small fragmentation grenade but packed a blinding punch. Thrown into a small room, it would stun the enemy long enough to gain the element of surprise. Another trick we learned during this part of training was how to kick in a door. Trust me, it's not done like it is in the movies. If the amount of force necessary to accomplish this isn't applied in the right place, the results could be quite painful. The idea is to use the heel of the foot to deliver enough force just below the doorknob. I once read an old Chinese proverb that said, 'You can move a mountain with one finger, as long as you know where to push'. While this can be true for many things, it's especially true when kicking in a door. If you missed your mark, you probably wouldn't be doing it again. It was demonstrated to us that this technique, when combined with the flashbang, created an element of surprise that could provide a devastating advantage when doing a house-to-house search and as we stood in a small mock village, the D.I. had each of us stand in one of the rooms while wearing ear protection. We were to experience this tactic from the other side of the door. The D.I. picked out the 'tough guys' as the first to be given this experience. A trained assault team carried out the exercise. The first of the 'tough guys' walked into the room with an obvious strut, waving with a grin as he closed the door.

The demonstration was performed after some delay so as to be unpredictable. But when executed, it was done with terrifying speed and despite a cavalier attitude, the recruit who was sent in first could not only be heard screaming like a child but stumbled out of the room wearing pants that had become soaked with urine. As our laughter quickly grew out of control, he looked down at himself with both embarrassment and angry frustration.
"Fuck!" he screamed.
Even the D.I. found it difficult to maintain his composure. Now, I knew what to expect and after

a long wait, I stepped into the ceilingless room, closed the door behind me, and donned the ear protection. There was no way to tell exactly when it would happen and even though I knew it was coming, I practically jumped out of my skin as the assault team kicked the door open and tossed a flashbang into the corner.

As soon as it went off they rushed into the room and surrounded me with weapons drawn, their tactical lasers focused on my chest. I instinctively raised my hands.
"Shit!" I yelled.
I felt a bit foolish afterward, but when you find yourself staring down the barrel of an AK47 after having your senses rattled by an explosion, you quickly learn that it's just a drill. At least their weapons weren't loaded and I didn't piss myself. The doors we trained on simply swung on their hinges. At that point, kicking against such little resistance carried a minimum potential for injury. Besides proper placement, the key to kicking is leaning back to extend the hips. This puts more force behind the kick, instead of leaning into it. For me, the most difficult part was balance and I fell flat on my back just as many times as everyone else. But I have to say, there is something satisfying about kicking in a door - something

visceral. Or maybe, I was in the process of becoming a soldier.

Graduation finally arrived, and my parents flew down from Bangor for the ceremony. They sat in the bleachers and waved as our platoon marched by. As ceremonies go, it was uncomplicated. The word 'tradition' was used by the commander more than once. The military has always stood by a long tradition of pride and ethics, but as I would later discover, pride can sometimes get in the way of ethics.

My father is a man of few words and after the ceremony, he shook my hand and told me how proud he was of me.

"I think I understand, now," he said.

My mother has never been given to strong emotions, but on the day I graduated, she approached me with tears in her eyes, telling me how handsome I looked in my uniform.

"So, are you coming home now?" she asked.

She was obviously so caught up in being a 'mom' that she didn't understand how it all worked. I explained to them that I still had another month of technical school. After that, I would be going back home for ten days of leave.

"Then what?" my mother asked.

I glanced at my father, who expressed an obvious look of concern.

"Well," I began. "That's up to the Army."
That answer was of little help. What she wanted was a firm sense of certainty. But, the military isn't known for giving people control - even parents. I knew the chances of being sent to Afghanistan were very high. I just didn't think it was a good idea to tell my mother that, given her emotional state. I introduced them to my drill instructor. Yes, 'my' drill instructor. By this time, Sergeant Frank had become one of the most influential of my life. He taught us that if we pushed ourselves, we could accomplish anything and that there were no barriers for anyone who wants to succeed badly enough. Granted, he didn't exactly say it in words, but I do think he forced us into realizing it for ourselves. My parents spent the night at base visitor housing while we were assigned to temporary quarters. Basic training was over, but that didn't necessarily mean we were soldiers - not just yet. I had reached the understanding that being in the Army and being a soldier can be two very different things. Yes, I was now in the Army, but was I a soldier? I believed that the only way to find out was to experience battle.

I had read somewhere that in the Marine Corps, fourteen percent of Marines in battle were unable to kill the enemy. Instead, they would fire over their heads. So, in spite of all the training, the lectures, and indoctrination a question lurked in the back of my mind. Could I kill someone? It's a lot easier to talk about doing it than it is to actually carry it out. Having the means to kill, especially on the battlefield is easy - just pick a weapon. But, being able to kill without hesitation is a different matter altogether. War is not a video game. Sure, it's probably easier from a drone console, where the enemy is just a target on a display, but what about when the enemy is standing in your rifle sights when you can see the color of his clothes or the way he walks? Considering what happened on nine eleven and what continues to happen in the Middle East, there is a clear difference between having a human appearance and being truly human. I just hoped that this logic would work in battle. If it didn't, I would likely come back home in a box.

My parents and I got together early the next morning for breakfast. They found themselves in a bit of a hurry, so they could get to their flight on time. My mother again asked when I'd be coming home. I told them that I'd just received orders to Fort Benning in Georgia for technical training.
"Training in what?" my mother asked.
I explained that I'd be going to school for Cavalry Scout and as I described the job, she appeared to

be genuinely interested. My father looked at his watch and quietly interrupted the conversation. It was time for them to leave. After calling for a taxi, we sat at a nearby picnic table. It's amazing how much a person can express while saying so little and my mother was oddly quiet that morning.
"Mom," I said. "I'm going to be coming back home in about a month."
She looked up at me with sullen eyes.
"But then you'll have to leave again, won't you?"
"They're giving me ten days off, mom," I replied. "But yes, I'll have to leave again."
I could see the taxi in the distance.
"I suppose you'll have to carry a gun, right?" she asked.
I think she finally understood. The military, ideally, is a force that acts as the defender of freedom.

However more often than not, the military acts as the pawn of political ideology. Still, we must answer the call to arms. This means putting ourselves in harm's way, for whatever reason. I could have tried to appeal to her sense of logic, telling her that the chances of being killed while crossing the street were higher than being killed in Vietnam. But, I don't think that would have done much good. Being a mom seems to be something that exists beyond the idea of reason, and she was afraid of losing her only child.

"Yeah," I answered. "But, I'm hoping I'll never have to use it."

I don't know if that helped or not.

After the taxi pulled up, I gave her a badly needed hug. She hugged me as though I was never coming back. I helped my father put their luggage in the trunk. He hesitated while putting a hand on my arm.

"You do what you have to do," he said. "Your mother will be okay, but you might want to call a couple of times a week. It'll help her to hear your voice."

As he walked back around to the door of the taxi, he stopped momentarily and pointed toward me.

"See you in four weeks, right?"

I closed the trunk of the taxi and walked over to him.

"See you in four weeks, Dad," I said.

He shook my hand again, got into the taxi next to my mother, and closed the door. As the driver started the engine, he waved at me through the window. I waved back as they pulled away and headed toward the main gate.

My mother is a very formidable woman. As a corporate executive, she is someone never to be trifled with. This was not that person, and she presented herself as almost being a stranger to me. Her emotional state made her appear frail and vulnerable. As someone who was used to being in charge, these were qualities she found as signs of weakness. Perhaps she felt it was better to be feared by those who hated you than loved by those who respected you. Naturally, I disagree, but that was one of those issues we didn't talk about much. Our ideas of what defines power are as different as night and day. I spent another night in temporary quarters and after nine weeks of living shoulder to shoulder with thirty-nine other people, it was good to finally have some privacy. The dormitories held two to a room and so far I was alone. This gave me the chance to reflect on where I was at this point in my life. One of the things Sergeant Frank told us was that when we go back home, people will seem different. But, they will not have changed - we will be the ones who have changed. Later, while on leave, this idea would come to fruition.

Chapter 16

I was awakened the next morning by someone who was making the rounds of all the new graduates. They were handing out large tan envelopes, each containing the paperwork necessary for departure to our various technical schools. Some were stamped with the word 'classified'. When it comes to that particular word, you quickly learn not to ask questions. My envelope bore no such stamp. However, it did contain a stapled stack of paper. Each page was identical. These were my orders to Fort Benning, and every person I checked in with would get a page for administrative purposes. Also included was an airline ticket to Columbus, Georgia, as well as instructions on where and when to meet the next shuttle bus going to the airport. My flight was scheduled at 1530 hours that afternoon, and I was expected to be in uniform. I got to the airport with time to spare. Half an hour later, I was on my way to Georgia. The flight was only about forty-five minutes, so there wasn't much time to sleep. The plane touched down on the tarmac of Columbia Metro Airport after an uneventful flight. I grabbed my duffle bag from the luggage carousel and jumped into one of the many taxis parked in front of the main terminal. It wasn't long before I was being driven through the main gate of Fort Benning. I had instructions to arrive at a dorm near Military Road and Avenue A. Another night in temporary quarters with nothing to do but wait and, like the night before, I was there without a roommate - alone. Not that I minded being alone. I guess I'd just become accustomed to the controlled chaos of basic training. Now, it was the quiet I found unnerving, and I also found that without the constant tension of the unpredictable, getting a decent night's sleep was difficult. In the morning, I checked in with Major Philip Stannard, who was in his third year as commander of the education center of Fort Benning. I waited outside his office until called. Upon entering, I saluted and announced myself in proper military fashion.

"Sir, Private Taylor reports as ordered, sir."

I saw no reason to yell it out. After all, this wasn't basic training.

"Relax, Private," he said. "You only have to say sir once now."

He asked for a copy of my orders and in return gave me a map bearing a circled area.

"Report to this location at 1300 hours for orientation," he said. "And you might want to be there about twenty minutes early."

After a moment's hesitation, he looked up from the paperwork I'd given him.

"Is there something else, Private?" he asked.

"No, sir," I answered.

"Alright," he continued. "You're dismissed."
I saluted again and walked out, leaving with the distinct impression that he wasn't especially fond of having a desk job. Perhaps at one time, he was teaching. But apparently, officers don't teach - they command. I decided to leave for orientation about an hour early, partly because I wanted to get a look around. Fort Benning is enormous, and I could see myself easily getting lost. Following the directions, I found my way to the base orientation center. Upon entering, I met Staff Sergeant Eugene Bolger.
"You're a bit early, aren't you?" he asked.
"I just wanted to get my bearings, sir," I replied.
"Sir?" he said. "Let's get something straight Private, I ain't no officer, so you don't call me sir, got it? It's just Sergeant Bolger."
As the classroom began to fill up, everyone tried to put on their military bearing.
"Alright, everyone, have a seat," he said. "First, relax. This isn't basic training, so we're not gonna get all formal here, alright? Second, welcome to Fort Benning. This is your orientation briefing."

We were all asked to introduce ourselves and tell the class what we were training for. There were a few other soldiers who were training for Cavalry Scout as well. Orientation was about two hours long, and we were given a map of the base, and assigned quarters, and provided directions to our respective training areas. As it turned out, our quarters were at our training areas, and we were told where the commissary, base store, and recreation centers were located. Also provided was a map of the area just outside the main gate. There was a large department store and a strip mall, while off to the right was an apartment tower - probably filled with military personnel. The sergeant passed out weekly meal tickets, good for three meals a day for one week. After it was used up, another would be assigned. I wasn't so much interested in shopping on base as I was curious about what was off base, and it was Friday, which meant I had the weekend to do some exploring. I rose the next morning at 0500 hours and dressed in camouflaged fatigues - more often referred to as BDUs, or 'battle dress uniform'. Over the last nine weeks, I had become very accustomed to wearing these. So, I took the maps with me and headed toward the main gate. Only a few blocks into my walk, I discovered that the base had a bus system. It was only then that I realized just how big Fort Benning really was. I waited for a bus, grabbed a schedule, and found a seat. In roughly ten minutes, the bus pulled up in front of the main gate just in front of Victory Drive. Looking at the map, I decided to go to Avondale. This turned out to be a small, quiet suburb just south of Columbia. The idea of going into the city didn't seem wise, considering I was traveling alone. There wasn't much to see, just a couple of gated communities set on a small rise, with the city of Columbia standing intimidatingly in the distance. After fifteen minutes of witnessing what was a disturbing degree of wealth - reminding me very much of home - I caught the southbound bus back to the base, but not willing to go back to the base just yet, I got off at the mall across from the main gate. I spent about an hour in the department store. There wasn't anything there that caught my interest and since I'd be at Fort Benning for only four weeks, I saw no reason to buy anything. After leaving the department store, I wandered down the strip mall and, passing numerous small shops and restaurants, I came to a storefront bearing a sign that read 'Book Store'. My curiosity had become stimulated by a large curtain that hung behind its glass façade. No sooner than I stepped through the doorway, did I quickly realize that this was no ordinary bookstore. To the right was a long row of video booths with their doorways covered by dark floor-length curtains. In front of me were seemingly endless racks of magazines and paperback books. Each one was adorned with a graphic cover illustrating mostly naked people engaged in what could only be described as some form of deviant behavior. To my immediate left was a large glass case filled with items I am still unable to fully describe. Two things became abundantly clear to me. The first was that I had stumbled into a porn shop. The second was that it was very unlikely I would find anything by Shakespeare. The remainder of the weekend passed uneventfully. I did decide to go to the base store. It just looked like another department store, with nothing that really stood out to me. At this point, if I wanted anything in the way of literature, I'd have to order it online. But, it also occurred to me that there probably wouldn't be a lot of time for reading. Tech school was to begin the next morning, and Sunday night found me still living in temporary quarters. I still had no idea where I was supposed to go, just a piece of paper with a circle on it. After turning in, I found that I was still having difficulty getting used to the odd silence of silence, but eventually, I drifted off. I also discovered that the events of 'night fire' were beginning to replay themselves in my dreams and the next morning, I was startled awake by the sound of gunfire. I looked out of the window and saw nothing. The sound of my dreams had shaken me from my sleep, and I took it as a clear sign that I needed to talk to someone. Struggling to achieve clear-headedness, I'd seen their faces in my mind, heard them screaming, and caught a whiff of burning flesh. It wasn't clear to me whether I needed professional help. Maybe a sympathetic ear was all I needed. At least, I'd be talking it out. I also decided to keep a journal documenting these dreams. Perhaps, I thought, it would be a good way to separate myself from them for the sake of self-examination. At around 0700 hours, I was picked up and taken to my new quarters. Fortunately, I wouldn't be sharing a space with thirty-nine other people this time. Instead, I was assigned a dorm room at the edge of the training area. There were thirty people in the class, so we were all lucky enough to get our own rooms. Tech school training would be led by Staff Sergeant Bruce Whitfield, and it was difficult. Basic training would be a close second next to tech school. When I left basic training, I was convinced that the physical aspect would end as well. I was very mistaken. Everything centered on strength training and heavy lifting. At this point, my six-foot frame carried around two hundred and twenty pounds and not much in the way of body fat. I certainly didn't have six-pack abs, but I had put on a lot of muscle mass. One of the requirements for cavalry scout training was that I had to pass a psych test. An overwhelming characteristic of the job was stress and as a cavalry scout, I would be the eyes and ears of the commander during battle. More than that, I would likely be one of the first at the front line relaying crucial information. The commander would base his orders on that information. The lives of American troops would hang in the balance based on my observations as well as my ability to stay calm and focused, thus, the need for a psych test. Sergeant Whitfield gave an orientation briefing at 1300 hours after everyone had settled into their new quarters. He handed out maps of the training area and provided an overview of the next four weeks. He also informed us that we would not be there if we had failed the psych test. Those who had were assigned to a different career field. The next four weeks centered on both classroom time and field training. The primary duty of the job was reconnaissance, and everything else was a means to that end. There are many ways in which to gain information about the enemy, going on patrol was just one. I was taught how to assist at observation and listening posts, how to track enemy movements, and how to navigate for the transport of equipment and ammunition, among other things. Tracking someone who's traveling by vehicle isn't as easy as it might seem. There's a bit more to it than wheel tracks in the sand. Tracking people moving on foot involves another level of difficulty altogether and there are many variables to consider in determining, for example, the age of a set of tracks, weather, runoff, terrain, and temperature, to name a few. I also had access to military satellite imagery as part of being able to assess enemy terrain and weather conditions. Every speck was vital to the decision-making process when engaging the enemy. We would be on their turf, so the scout was heavily relied upon to find the enemy's weaknesses as well as the paths of least resistance for the advancement of allied forces. And of course, there was more physical training. The runs got longer, and we began carrying heavy wooden poles over our heads. Some of the duties of a cavalry scout involved lifting heavy equipment, sometimes carrying it over long distances. I also became familiar with demolitions and mines. Becoming a cavalry scout was far from being a well-armed messenger boy. I would also learn how to fire antipersonnel weapons, as well as maintain communications equipment and reconnaissance vehicles. There were no classes on weekends, but it was expected and strongly recommended that we study and go to the nearby base gym. With only four weeks of difficult training, it was impossible to develop friendships. It seemed that when I wasn't sleeping, I was either in class, in the field, or studying. But, despite the level of difficulty, training went by fairly quickly, and after a total of thirteen weeks, ten days of leave didn't seem like a lot of time. But, I wasn't about to complain.

Chapter 17

On the last day of training, we were all awarded a certificate of graduation from tech school. I was officially a U.S. Army Cavalry Scout. It wasn't a Master's Degree, but it was something to be equally proud of, if not more so. I would go home for ten days, but I'd also received orders to return to Fort Benning for assignment to the 316th Cavalry Brigade. I was also provided with something unexpected - a top secret security clearance. I guess I really wasn't all that surprised. After all, I was going to be working as a human conduit for classified military information. If I were to be captured, I would either fight my way out or die trying. Later, I would learn things that could never be revealed to anyone - ally or enemy, military or civilian. The only exception was the person authorized to receive that information.

I called my parents that day to tell them that I'd be flying back to Bangor for leave. My mother was ecstatic. I changed flights in Boston with a short stopover in Portland. I'm not sure how indoctrinated I'd become, but I chose to travel in uniform and had actually become quite proud of wearing it. I told my parents when my flight would arrive. They were at the gate, right on time. Most likely, they arrived early. My mother stood trembling with excitement - another side of her I'd never seen. My father, always the patient one, stood next to her, emotionally unmoved. Appearances, however, can be deceiving and as he walked up to me, his face broke into a broad smile and as he reached out to shake my hand told me how glad he was to see me. But my mother, having rushed in ahead of him, threw her arms around me with tears streaming down her face.

It had been raining for three straight days from Boston all the way up the coast. I had forgotten about 'mud season' and as I planted my recently polished boots in it, I'd also forgotten how I hadn't really missed it. But if there had been an Army base in Maine, I would have jumped at the chance for an assignment. By the time we got home, I'd been sitting just long enough to realize how tired I was and after putting my duffle bag down in the living room, I sat in one of two leather recliners and promptly fell asleep. It seemed as though it had been only a few minutes, but after my mother woke me for dinner, I realized that I'd been asleep for the last two hours. It's amazing how exhausted a person can become simply by sitting in the seat of a commercial jet.

As usual, my mother had prepared a flawless dinner, and as usual, my stomach found it a bit too rich. Truthfully, I had grown accustomed to mess hall food and ready-to-eat meals, but with all the hard work she put into her cooking, I just couldn't bring myself to tell her. After dinner, we sat in the living room. My father had retrieved his best bottle of brandy and three large snifters. By this time, I'd changed out of my uniform and into street clothes. Without the uniform, I felt like a fish out of water. I'd also realized that without the sensation of wearing my sidearm, I suddenly began to feel naked. My father began asking questions about what I had been trained for.

"It doesn't seem like a month would be enough time to be trained for anything that intense," he said.

I explained that training for the Army was eight hours a day almost every day and with forty hours of training every week, a person could learn quite a bit. My mother seemed rather comfortable with what I'd be doing. I told them that a large part of the job would be gathering information. Perhaps, this left her with the impression that I wouldn't be doing any actual fighting. I thought it was best to let her believe that.

The next day, I found my father tinkering with a shortwave radio. He had purchased it about the time I left for basic training, thinking that listening to foreign radio stations might broaden his perspective of the world. He spent more than a little time listening to the BBC. I walked into the living room as he was dialing through one of the shortwave bands. Near the end of the band, we heard what sounded like Morse code. It was almost buried in background noise, but it was definitely Morse code. He leaned an ear toward the radio as I sat down.

"Hey, Clarence, what's this?" he asked.

As a reconnaissance specialist, I'd been trained in Morse code. I had become so proficient that I could translate it in my head. I listened to it carefully. It was quick and constant, with no pauses or breaks. It was very likely an automated transmission.

"They're number strings," I answered. "It's from a 'numbers station', probably in or near Russia."

Numbers stations were set up to transmit encrypted number strings. Sometimes it was Morse code, while other stations transmitted automated voice loops that broadcast 'spoken' single digits.

"What does it mean?" my father asked.

He seemed truly fascinated by his new discovery of covert communications. Unfortunately, I wasn't trained in cryptography. Even if I could have decrypted it, chances are it would have been 'eye's eye-only' information.

"To me, they're just numbers," I began. "The signal's probably being intercepted by people who can make sense of it. Cryptography isn't something I'm trained for."

Numbers stations can be hidden anywhere - in someone's cellar, out in the middle of nowhere, even underground. All they need to function is power, and a generator can easily supply that. Some people, both military and civilians, spend years trying to understand what these transmissions mean - trying to crack the code. The military had a legitimate need for this information, but honestly, if you're a civilian and spending a significant amount of time on this, you should probably get a life.

It was at that point, my mother walked in and announced we'd be attending a dinner party.

"Great," I thought. "A dinner party."

I didn't like going to those things - the food was rich, the people thought a bit too highly of themselves, and there were too many of them. It would be the same tired highbrow bullshit. The party was being hosted by Gloria's family. Now, I'd have a chance to, again, be snubbed by one of the most beautiful women I'd ever met. So, I guess the circus was back in town for a one-night-only show. My mother wanted me to wear a tux. She intended to show me off. I hated even the idea of wearing a tux and always believed that it said something about me that wasn't true. There was only one suit I was comfortable wearing - my dress uniform. I insisted to my mother that I would be wearing this. Naturally, she resisted but after what appeared to be a sinister pause for thought, she agreed. I have to admit, I found that one moment to be a bit disturbing. Certainly, she would not have agreed without some ulterior motive. Perhaps, instead of showing off her handsome son, she chose to show off her soldier son. This would almost certainly make her the center of attention and likely drag me into the spotlight as well. I was not looking forward to this event. The dinner party was set for the following night. I got up that morning at 0500 as usual. I wasn't in training anymore, but I felt it necessary to maintain a schedule as well as my physical condition. So, I mapped out a five-mile course through Bangor. This was not a looped course, and I began running ten miles a day. I returned home and started organizing my uniforms. I had tried to pack my duffle bag carefully. But, as I began to hang them up, I realized that everything was in desperate need of ironing. Here at home, any clothes that were to be pressed were taken to a dry cleaner. That would take too long, and the dinner party was that night. Thankfully, I had my own iron as well as a small ironing board. It was just big enough to press all my uniforms.

I decided to visit the university and spent a couple of hours just walking around. It was spring break and the campus was deserted. The buildings took on an eerie appearance beneath a sullen sky, as the continuing rain stained the concrete a darker shade of gray. I found the visit bittersweet. I had a new sense of purpose but still heard the faint call of academia. I caught the city bus and headed downtown. Walking around downtown Bangor, I went directly to the nearest bookstore. After nine weeks of military training, I was in literary withdrawal and half an hour later, I walked out with a plastic shopping bag filled almost to its breaking point. I had taken an interest in some of history's greatest military leaders - Napoleon, Alexander the Great, Genghis Khan, and General Patton. But, I hadn't forgotten about philosophy and picked up a copy of 'The Tibetan Book of The Dead' as well as 'The Fountainhead' by Ayn Rand. At the last moment, I bought an English version of The Koran. This may have seemed like an odd choice for an American in the military, but if I was on my way to Afghanistan, I thought it might be helpful to learn something about their beliefs. It was the first book I read upon returning home, and I wasn't planning on taking it back to

Fort Benning. The last thing I needed was for small-minded people to label me as a sympathizer - especially in the military. Over the next eight or nine days, I read it from cover to cover, with a clear understanding of the Muslim ideas of peace as opposed to the writings of 'Holy War' or 'Jihad'.

The dinner party was at seven o'clock and my mother would, once again, be in her element. She wasn't pretentious by any means, but she did enjoy the social limelight. My father, however, simply put on a smile and pretended to enjoy himself. It had become obvious to me that he'd rather be at home reading or involved in his new hobby. In fact, he had found a website that allowed him to not only listen to shortwave radio but record the transmissions as well, and was now looking for software that would translate the Morse code. I suppose everyone needs a hobby.

We arrived at the dinner party at about quarter after seven. Yes, we arrived 'fashionably late' as per my mother's insistence - always the socialite. The hosts hired the usual help. Most likely, they were paid minimum wage. The coat checker relieved my parents of their coats. Between my build and the uniform, he took one look at me and decided not to ask for my jacket, while at the same moment referring to me as 'sir'. I wasn't trying to be intimidating, but it's very possible that my expression conveyed how much I didn't want to be there. As we walked into the main room, I immediately noticed that it was filled with the usual suspects. These were the people who made it a point to be on the list of every dinner party, and it seemed to me that they either had a need for attention or that they made a hobby out of attending social events. Probably a little of both.

As usual, the hostess received the most attention, until we walked in. I've never felt so self-conscious in my life as everyone's heads turned almost at the same time. It was as though a wave of energy had surged through the room. My mother was quickly approached by the hostess, who obviously felt threatened by the fact that she was no longer in the spotlight.
"Katheryn," she began. "You never mentioned your son was in the military."
"Well," my mother replied. "After all those people were killed in New York last year, Clarence decided to stand up and do the right thing."
"Oh, I see," the hostess said.
The claws were out, and like two cats in the wild, they appeared to be sizing each other up - each trying to anticipate the other's next remark.

"Yes," my mother said, "And we're certain that he'll be going to Afghanistan to defend all those people from terrorists."

As she spoke, others wandered over to listen. My mother was very much aware that she clearly had the upper hand.

It was at this point that the host approached me and, shaking my hand gently pulled me away from the fray.

"So, Clarence, is it?" he asked.

His name was Steven, and he was Gloria's father.

"Yes, sir," I answered.

He turned toward me with a kind face.

"You don't have to be formal with me, son," he said. "In fact, it seems to me that I should be calling you 'sir'."

I found this very surprising, considering the company he kept.

"I've always had great respect for people who are willing to put themselves in harm's way, and I think it's a very noble thing you're doing."

"Uh, thank you," I replied.

I was at a loss for words. I guess I'd mistakenly assumed that most, if not all, people of wealth had a tendency to look down on those in military service as they seemed to look down on everyone else. A tense moment went by as I struggled for something to say.

"This is a very nice dinner party you've put on," I said. "I would go so far as to say that you've outdone yourself."

He grinned broadly as he glanced down at the floor.

"Oh, come on now, Clarence," he replied. "I saw your face when you walked in. You really don't want to be here, do you?"

His perception was extremely acute, and I quickly felt my face flush with embarrassment.

"Oh, it's alright," he continued. "To be honest, I can't stand these things - bunch of pretentious pricks running around all full of themselves. Actually, I probably wouldn't do this at all if it weren't for my wife."

He nudged me a bit with his elbow.

"You know what they say - when the wife's not happy, nobody's happy."

I fully understood what he meant and grinned in acknowledgment.

"Besides, you looked as though you needed rescuing."

We glanced over at my mother and Steven's wife. They were still slugging it out in a civilized battle of wits, where the prize of victory was momentary social dominance. Shakespeare once wrote that upon returning from a victorious battle, Caesar's chariot driver spoke these words into his ear:

'Glory is fleeting'. That would certainly be the case here.

My mother always chose to outsmart her adversaries instead of displaying a temper. She believed that winning an argument through reason and logic was a strong sign of intelligence, and it wasn't long before the hostess excused herself from the conversation. Victory had been won, as the hostess retreated from the field, leaving my mother to mingle while displaying her social supremacy. If the description of this brief exchange seems dramatic, it's only because these particular women tend to be dramatic, at least in social situations.

Turning away from this aristocratic carnage, I discovered that Gloria had appeared out of the crowd and was standing only a few feet in front of us.
"Oh, Gloria," he said. "Have you met Clarence? Clarence, this is my daughter, Gloria".
"I think we met briefly around New Year's," I replied.
She was a striking image of feminine beauty, wearing a shimmering black cocktail dress that hung to the middle of her thighs - her shoulders adorned with spaghetti straps. The dark locks of her hair fell down between the middle of her back,

as though by some divine intent. She stepped towards me as her father excused himself. I barely comprehended her first words, as she spoke with such beautiful eloquence and gentleness. Certainly, this was not the same woman who snubbed me three and a half months ago. She smiled and extended her hand. That moment of physical contact seemed eternal. Her hand was warm, and her skin was soft beyond description. My reaction was respectful and controlled. If I were prone to using 'pickup lines' I might have said something like 'It seems that Mount Olympus has lost one of its goddesses'. But this woman, as with all women, deserved more respect than that.

As she closed the distance between us, I could see her face beginning to flush. It was flawlessly beautiful, and her makeup was perfect to a fault. It was obvious that she had acquired her mother's Greek beauty.

"Clarence," she began. "I remember you from New Year's."

"Yes, we did meet briefly," I replied, as I did my best to politely play the fool.

She looked at me rather quizzically.

"Something's different about you," she said.

"Maybe it's just the uniform," I replied.

She took a couple of small steps back while quickly examining me.

"Well, she continued. "The uniform is very handsome, but it's something else."
The tone of her voice had gone from polite to intimate in a very short period. Another man might have attempted to sound the charge and move in for the kill. As for myself, I was not only enjoying her wonderful presence, but I was also enjoying the game.

I engaged Gloria in a bit of small talk by asking about her law career. As it turns out, she had landed a very well-paying job in a bankruptcy firm. Either she gave in to her father's 'suggestion' or she concluded that it made more economic sense to work in that particular field. Either way, she still had plenty of time to find her direction.
"I'm sorry," she began. "I'm being terribly rude. Can I show you the rest of the house?"
As Sherlock Holmes was known to say: 'The game is afoot'.
"Of course," I answered. "Am I getting a personal tour?"
She looked up at me with a playful grin while taking my arm. We casually made our way out of the dining room while she gave me a quick tour of the house. I knew what she wanted, and the anticipation was killing me.
"Would you like to see the guest house?" she asked as she blushed again.

I had no doubt that she would, one day, make a very good lawyer. But, what she really needed to work on was how to conceal her emotions. Gloria's behavior and responses spoke volumes and I could almost read her thoughts.

"You have a guest house?" I asked almost naively. "I'd love to see it."

No, I wasn't being naïve. I was simply enjoying the game.

I opened the back door for her while gently placing a hand on the middle of her back. I could feel the firm inward curve of her spine through the cocktail dress she was wearing. The air became noticeably warmer as my heart began pounding in my ears. The rain had let up to a slight sprinkle as we walked to the guest house. I opened the unlocked door for her and after stepping through, she commented on how warm it was. Stepping in after her and closing the door I noticed that it wasn't warm at all. She turned around, fanning herself with her purse.

"So," she began. "Are all you Army guys such gentlemen?" she asked.

Removing my cap, I responded, "I hope so".

Smiling again, she reached out and grabbed my hand.

"Come on, let me show you around," she said.

She now spoke in a way that was far more casual and any formalities disappeared the moment she took my hand as she led me through a small foyer and up the stairs.

"I want to show you something," she continued.

The guest house wasn't exactly a sprawling mansion, but it was big enough for a family of four to be comfortable.

"You're going to love this!"

Once upstairs, she led me into the master bedroom. Everything was made of wood. The bed frame, dressers, and writing desk were made of hand-carved mahogany.

"This is beautiful!" I said.

Gloria stepped in close and put a hand on my shoulder, looking up at me with a still-flushed face.

"That's why I brought you here."

I turned towards her and slowly wove my fingers through her black curls. She responded by craning her neck up, reaching out to me with her lips, and as we embraced each other, I kissed her gently as the warm feeling of arousal took control over us. She slowly pulled the spaghetti straps of her cocktail dress down over her shoulders, letting it slide down to the carpeted floor. Her body was firm, yet her skin was as soft as a thinly oiled pane of glass. We embraced again and as I ran my fingertips down the middle of her back, she took a brief gasp of arousal.

She pulled me over to the bed and began removing my uniform. Our bodies continued in their entanglement as we slipped between the bed's white satin sheets.

"What about the door?" I whispered.

Gloria giggled as she wrapped her arms around me.

"I locked the front door when you weren't looking," she said.

There was something strange about making love while leaving the door open. It felt as though anyone, at any time, could walk past the doorway, catching us - literally - with our pants down. My arousal was beginning to get the better of me.

"Slow down," she whispered. "There's plenty of time."

As I kissed her open mouth, we reached towards each other with the tips of our tongues as I slowly brushed the back of my fingers down her right breast, discovering how sensitive she was as she arched her neck back and took in a breath of arousal. Her body shivered beneath me as her breasts became overwhelmed with goosebumps. Giving me a playful grin, she began to sit up while wrapping her arms around my neck. We rolled over together like a well-choreographed dance until she sat astride my hips.

I reached up to her shoulders and gently moved down her arms until our fingers became interwoven. Leaning over toward me, she kissed me on the mouth while sliding her body up towards me. I turned my head, letting my lips brush over one of her warm, supple breasts. Reaching down with some careful manipulation, we both contributed to the joining of our bodies as together we took an abrupt gasp of passion. A sudden glistening of sweat erupted from her skin as she began rolling her hips back and forth while I held her hips firmly and repeatedly locked our bodies together. Some would say that nothing lasts forever. I would disagree. We had both become lost in each other as our moment of passion raced out of control. Gloria curled her fingers into my chest, leaving claw marks on my skin.

As I lay on my back, staring into her eyes, I witnessed in her a release as though a wild animal had escaped from her soul. Now, my arousal peaked as we both achieved release together. Her body arched back as she let out a deep breath, letting her hair hang down to the small of her back. A thin ribbon of sweat slowly made its way down between her breasts towards her navel as though it knew the way. She lowered her body down onto me and shifting her hips, slid over next to me and laid her head on my chest.

"Oh, I'm sorry," she began. "I dug my nails into your chest."

I looked down as the nail marks slowly filled themselves in with blood.

"That's okay," I replied. "I've been through worse."

She looked up into my eyes.

"What you're going to be doing in the Army, will it be dangerous?" she asked.

Her question raised other questions that I didn't dare ask. Was Gloria developing feelings for me? Did she actually care or was she just curious?

"No more dangerous than crossing the street," I answered.

"C'mon," she replied. "You know what I mean."

I understood her question completely, but I wanted to know exactly how she felt. Would this be just a brief encounter, or was there something more - something deeper? Certainly, there is a difference between lust and passion and if it's one thing I value, it's honesty. But, I didn't want to ask her directly. The last thing I wanted was to appear as a love-struck puppy. I've always believed that 'love at first sight' was unrealistic and misleading. I just wanted to know if she saw me as just a sexual playground or as someone she might see as becoming part of her life. I told her that the majority of my job would be gathering information -- reconnaissance. This seemed to satisfy her question - be it concern or curiosity. Not that I was being misleading, I just didn't see the point of going into detail.

We lay in each other's arms for only a few minutes when she slid out from between the sheets and quickly picked up her clothes from the floor she walked to the bathroom.
"Be right back soldier boy," she said.
'Soldier Boy'.
I wondered if this was Gloria's idea of a pet name or if she was just teasing. I got up and began putting on my uniform. I was still a bit confused but within the next few minutes, the answer would be as plain as day. Whatever Gloria was doing didn't take long. She walked out a confident, yet slightly casual step wearing not only the cocktail dress but a pair of black pumps that I hadn't noticed before. I guess I was preoccupied with other things. Seeing them on her now left me believing that they were the sexiest shoes I'd ever seen.
"I have to get back," she said.
Making her way to the door, she hesitated and slowly walked over to me. Her lips fell open slightly as she looked up into my eyes. Reaching up, she straightened my tie as a slight look of concern washed over her face. Gloria took a deep breath as though carefully gathering her words.

"Look, Clarence," she said.

She answered my question with two simple words. Anything more would have only created tension. I put my hands on her shoulders.

"Gloria," I began. "I get it. You just started your career and you don't want any attachments. It's okay."

She tightly wrapped her arms around me.

"Thank you," she said. "Thanks for understanding."

She stepped back and turned toward the door.

"You're right, you know," she replied. "I'm not looking - yet."

She blew me a kiss and winked before quietly disappearing from the room. I smiled to myself, knowing that there was, in fact, something underneath what seemed to be just a roll in the sack. Gloria had made it obvious that there was indeed a small glitter of a spark, in spite of her initial attempt to let me down easy. Eventually, it would need to be fanned into a raging fire, but not yet. A relationship was a bad idea for both of us. She had a new career as an attorney, and I was about to go to war. It didn't feel wrong, it just wasn't the right time for either of us. I suppose it could have been worse. She could've just ridden me like a mechanical bull and walked out, maybe even thanking me on the way, but Gloria had a heart. Not that I would describe her as being completely innocent, certainly not after today. But, she did care. She just didn't want to show it until she felt safe, at a time when she'd be less likely to get hurt.

I walked back to the main house. It was raining again - just my luck. Upon entering, I found that the guests had been seated in the dining room with the usual minimum-wage servants waiting on them hand and foot. Naturally, the hostess was getting most of the attention, as though she was the Queen of England. At least, she seemed to think she was. Then, I was struck by an oddly humorous thought. I walked in resenting people like her for seeing the less fortunate as the bottom feeders of society. Then, I slept with her daughter. I'm not proud of this but at that moment I saw it as a twisted form of poetic justice. It was a feeling that might be best expressed with the words 'fuck you'. Either way, it was just an afterthought that had nothing to do with Gloria. My father approached me. He was very good at reading people.
"You and Gloria go out for a walk?" he asked.
He knew exactly what had happened.
"Yeah," I began. "She wanted to show me around."
"Uh huh," my father replied. "Did you see anything that particularly caught your eye?"
A pause went by as we both stood watching people being seated.

"More than I ever imagined," I answered with a slight grin.

"So, when you're here on leave, I guess you'll be attending more of these dinner parties, huh?" he asked.

He knew I couldn't stand dinner parties, and he knew why. Now, he felt that I'd be a bit more motivated to attend them in the future.

"Without a doubt," I said quietly.

From the moment Gloria left my side, I was unable to take my eyes off her, and after she sat down, she looked at me with a slight grin.

"I think someone wants your attention," my father said.

He didn't miss a thing.

I walked over and sat in the chair next to her. It was obvious that she was holding it for me. A servant pushed my chair in as I sat down. I wasn't used to being waited on by servants and found it to be very uncomfortable. As usual, the food was decadent, and, as usual, my stomach didn't agree with it. Conversation began as dinner was being served. Immediately, I noticed that Gloria's demeanor had returned to its previous degree of formality. At some point during dinner, a tuxedo-clad middle-aged man got my attention from across the table.

"So, young man," he started. "What do you make of your military career thus far?"

"Well," I replied. "It's very challenging."
He looked at me with a slight nod.
"Really," he replied. "And what do you find most challenging about it?"
Obviously, he had never served. All the same, it was a difficult question to answer.

With Gloria sitting next to me, I chose to refrain from any discussion about the night fire incident or gas chamber training. Some stories just shouldn't be told.
"I think that would be survival training," I answered. "It was a good exercise in resourcefulness."
He paused dramatically while picking up his wine glass.
"Yes," he said. "I imagine it would be."
I dealt with this brief exchange in a friendly, respectful manner. But in my mind, the words 'pretentious asshole' played several times. He then began talking about how his father fought at Normandy Beach and lived to tell about it.
"How did he survive?" I asked.
He paused in a dramatic moment.
"If I remember correctly..."
His wife suddenly interrupted.
"Oh, Geoffrey," she said. "These lovely young people don't want to hear about such terrible things."

I honestly did want to hear it, but she was right. It wasn't really appropriate dinner conversation.
"Now, Gloria," she continued.
She changed the conversation to what could only be called 'girl talk' - leaving her husband quietly grumbling.
"As a woman, don't you find a man in uniform to be the most handsome thing you've ever seen?"
She looked at Gloria with a knowing expression, as though she had seen everything.

Gloria did not cower from the question, nor the way in which it was asked.
"Well," she began.
She put an elbow on the table and leaned in slightly. Her other hand went directly to my knee. I tried to contain my reaction as the woman's husband grinned faintly. He knew exactly what had just happened.
"As a matter of fact, I only recently discovered my appreciation for our servicemen. It seems there's a great deal more than just the uniform."
Her response stopped the woman cold as her hand made its way up the inside of my thigh. I'm sure that my blushing face lit up the entire room as my forehead broke out into a hot sweat. The entire experience could have easily qualified as an act of torture and while I was able to retain my self-control, I was not able to control what my body

was doing. Gloria's touch brought on a physical reaction that I can only describe as furious, one that completely consumed me. I reached my hand down to pull my chair in another two or three inches and immediately moved Gloria's hand back to my knee. It wasn't that I minded her touching my leg - in fact, I deeply craved it. But in a crowded dining room, I found it both teasing as well as arousing.

But, Gloria wasn't quite finished playing as she gently ran her nails across the inside of my knee. The women continued talking as every hair on my body stood on end and now that we were more than a bit familiar with each other, I decided that participation in 'this' game was absolutely necessary, and I reached down to adjust my chair again and moved my hand over, deftly stroking her knee with a single touch. Withdrawing my hand just as quickly, I felt her grip tighten as she shivered slightly and squirmed a bit in her chair. The gentleman across the table gave me a quick wink and a slight nod. He obviously remembered what it was like to be young, and we both knew what the other was thinking.

The dinner concluded without any further teasing from either of us. But in all honesty, I wish there had been more. The gentleman across the table finally got the chance to tell his story about how his father survived the invasion of Normandy Beach. His wife wasn't nearly as impressed as I was, and she had to have heard it at least a thousand times. Gloria disappeared about fifteen minutes before we left, missing the chance to say good night. As my parents retrieved their coats, she walked up behind me. Even before I saw her, I caught a whiff of her perfume. The aroma was an intoxicating blend of the splendor of Paris and the soft, flawlessness of her skin. I felt myself becoming slightly dizzy and warm as she put a hand on my arm.

"My parents' dinner parties can be quite boring," she began. "But I hope you enjoyed yourself."

I looked into her eyes and leaned towards her ear.

"You have no idea," I whispered.

She stepped in closer and took my hand.

"Actually, I do," she replied.

Gloria retreated into the crowded dining room, glancing back over her shoulder with a smile. She left in my hand a folded piece of paper. Without opening it, I slipped it into the inside pocket of my jacket. Whatever was written on it was certainly something personal, and I would read it another time. This was definitely 'eyes only' information.

Chapter 18

The rain had let up to a pale mist as the valet pulled up with the car. A valet, really? I guess the wealthy had their own rules and, obviously, one of them was that you weren't allowed to walk to your own car. Valet parking is great for a hospital, but it's a bit too much for a dinner party. On the other hand, maybe it's just me. At any rate, we got home just in time for another downpour. The sky was as black as ink, while the air felt cold and still. I had a strong suspicion that these would be the conditions for my entire ten days of leave. After changing, we gathered in the living room. My father started the gas for the fireplace. He picked up his copy of the Portland Press and casually looked over at me, noticing how relaxed I was.
"You seem fairly relaxed," he began. "Usually you can't stand going to these dinner parties."
"I'm just glad it's over," I replied.
That wasn't exactly true, but I didn't think he realized that I had slept with Gloria.
"So, what do you think of Gloria?" he asked.
He had opened his newspaper and was skimming through the national section.
"Well," I began. "She certainly is beautiful and very intelligent. She seems like a woman who knows what she wants."

My father glanced at me from over his newspaper, nodding slightly.

"And what do you think a woman like Gloria wants?" he asked.

I took a deep breath and dug for an answer that wouldn't be too revealing.

"Well, definitely a career," I answered. "No one goes to Stanford without prioritizing for a career."

His eyes remained in his newspaper.

"I suppose you're right," he responded.

Ah, success! He didn't suspect a thing. Could it be that I had just outwitted my father? He turned to the next page.

"She does seem to be more than a bit interested in you," he said.

"I don't know. Maybe it's the uniform," I replied.

He looked up over his reading glasses and smiled slightly.

"I don't think that's it at all," he said.

"I noticed how she looked at you just before we left. Trust me, Clarence, it's not the uniform."

He still had no idea. If he did, he never let on. My mother, on the other hand, quietly sat drinking a cup of tea, her gaze lost in the flames of the evening fire. It had been a long day and I found myself especially fatigued. By eleven o'clock, I had turned in for the night. There had been no further conversation about Gloria. I found this to be a bit uncomfortable. Did he know or not? It wasn't as though I could just walk up to him and ask.

As I walked up the stairs, I glanced back out of the corner of my eye and saw him smiling as he continued reading the paper.
"Son of a bitch," I thought.
Was there anyone at this dinner party who didn't know that I had slept with Gloria? I began to feel self-conscious about the whole thing, not that there was anything to be ashamed of. The question now was: did her father know? Not that I thought he'd come kicking the door in -- we were both consenting adults, after all. The rain stopped a day or so later, but the cold April air remained with its frigid grip, holding firmly against all hours of the day. At night, one could step out beneath the bleak, steely sky and clearly see their breath hanging in the darkness. It wasn't much of a reprieve, but I'd rather be cold than cold and wet. About a day and a half later, any blue that had appeared in the sky had become blotted out by an angry sea of clouds as the April rain returned. I cut my morning runs down to four miles and dressed in layers. I would soon be returning to Fort Benning and as much as I would miss Maine, I would not miss mud season. There wasn't an opportunity to do much of anything considering the weather, so I spent much

of my time reading the Koran as well as doing some online research.

It seems that every religion is based on the miraculous or some great realization. Islam began around 500 A.D. and culminated with Mohammed's ascension to heaven. The core beliefs of Islam are the same as the other major religions -- compassion, universal acceptance, and forgiveness. So, what happened? Islam was born to an oppressive culture in a place that has never known peace. The details of the Islamic faith fostered more oppression, especially towards women, and were eventually used for conquest and political fanaticism. Much like the Bible, the devil is always in the details. Both religions have been used by fanatics who believed themselves and their religion to be superior, acting with divine counsel. A violent fundamentalism was created by each and used to wage war against the other -- Islam vs. Christianity. This conflict of fanaticism would go on for centuries, and nine-eleven would serve as a constant reminder to the world that we have always fought this war of ideology. It's likely that Christians and Muslims will continue locking horns -- probably indefinitely. And who's really to blame? Everyone. We have all spent so much time and resources using ideology as a weapon that we've lost sight of our similarities, the fact that the core beliefs of all faiths are the same, and they all bear the same goal. Not that I'm being preachy. I'm just calling it the way I see it.

A week and a half can go by pretty quickly. But during mud season, everything comes to a standstill. It wasn't exactly the best timing for ten days off, and before I knew it, nine days had gone by. I'd picked up a leather garment bag, so I could avoid having to iron my uniforms again. All my books went into my duffle bag except one. I have my copy of the Koran at home. Taking this with me seemed as much a bad idea as waving a copy of the Communist Manifesto around at a Republican. I never saw Gloria again during my ten days of leave. She was busy at her new job and honestly, I'm not sure it would have been a good idea anyway. We both knew our own feelings. At least, I knew what mine were. But, I had the feeling that this was not the end. I looked for the folded piece of paper she slipped into my hand at the dinner party. It was still in the inside breast pocket of my uniform jacket and having retrieved it, I sat down on the floor against the wall. I didn't unfold it. I just sat and stared at it. Would its contents change anything, or was it just another part of the game? I decided I wouldn't read it just yet, but I felt that when I did, it would be something wonderful or something disappointing and now was not the time to take that kind of risk.

My parents drove me to the airport and, as usual, they waited at the gate until I boarded. My mother gave me a hug. She seemed a bit stronger this time, but she was still not completely happy with the choice I'd made. My father, once again, shook my hand.
"Stay out of trouble," he said, with a grin.
The flight seemed longer this time. At least, it felt that way. I was struck with a feeling that I'd left something important behind, as though I'd forgotten something. I knew I had packed everything and tried to remember if there was something I'd overlooked. But, there was no point in being concerned about it now. If I had forgotten something, I'd ask my parents to send it down to me. Looking back, it was clear that I'd been in denial of my feelings for Gloria. She was what I'd left behind. I could never reveal my feelings to her. It just wouldn't be fair. Besides, love and war rarely get along. One is usually a distraction for the other.

Later, that night, the plane touched down on the tarmac of Columbus Airport. The sky was clear, but the air was heavy and warm. I took a cab to the main gate of Fort Benning and, again, found myself in temporary quarters. As much as I'd become accustomed to being moved from place to place, I had grown to hate even the idea of temporary quarters. It was too quiet, as opposed to assigned quarters where there were more people to talk to. I was never a social butterfly, but having people around to talk to meant there would be a certain degree of distraction. The next day, I reported in uniform to the commander of the cavalry unit I'd been assigned to. There, I was given another map with directions to my assigned quarters and the name of the Sergeant in charge. The Sergeant ordered me to see the quartermaster for the issuing of weapons. I signed for a standard .45 caliber pistol with three extra magazines and holsters. Instead of the M16, I'd trained with, I was issued an AK47. As it turned out, it was less expensive and required less maintenance so, it wasn't as likely to jam. If the enemy was advancing, the last thing you wanted was a jammed rifle. I was also issued a combat knife and sheath. There would be scheduled runs and a required exercise program as well as mandatory time at the base gym. I was told that the terrain where I'd likely be going was rugged and mountainous, so it was important to stay in shape. Otherwise, there really wasn't much to do.

I decided to make exercise a full-time job and developed a regimen that encompassed a six-hour workout plan. This made the time pass quickly and when I wasn't running or in the gym, I was reading - another distraction with the added benefit of learning. A month after I arrived at Fort Benning, our unit received orders for deployment to the base at Kabul. We were flown by C-130 cargo planes to the naval base at Norfolk, Virginia. I had packed everything - uniforms, boots, and books. I made sure to slip the note from Gloria between the pages of my copy of the biography of 'Alexander the Great'. Until I got to Kabul, I knew the note would be safe. I had also begun putting a lock on my duffle bag.

We left on the USS Ross, an Arleigh Burke class destroyer stationed at Norfolk. I was amazed at how enormous it was. One could easily call it a floating city, and I quickly realized why they were called destroyers. I was told that the hull was composed of four-inch-thick steel, with canons and anti-aircraft guns mounted on each end and side. In my civilian life, I'd spent more than a little time on boats, so making the adjustment to walking on a rolling deck came rather easily. This was not quite the case for most of my fellow soldiers. Those whose stomachs were especially sensitive to motion were responsible for cleaning up their own mess. By now, you might be asking yourself how anyone could sleep on a rolling ship. As it turned out, the Navy had installed hammocks for the entire crew as well as any troops that were in transport. They were hung pointing toward the ship's bow and simply swung in the direction the ship was rolling in. Sleeping in a hammock was a lot more comfortable than I expected, but some of my fellow soldiers didn't find the experience quite as pleasant. They had an especially hard time getting into their hammocks. Most found it easy, but a few quickly became prone to obscenities when upon climbing in they just rolled over it and onto the hard steel deck. The only injuries were a few bruised egos as everyone laughed at their expense. In mind own twisted mind, they looked like clowns attempting the high jump for the first time. It just wasn't working.

It took five days to cross the Atlantic and during that time, I took advantage of the ship's gym and read through most of the battle strategies of Napoleon. I still hadn't read the note. It wasn't that I didn't want to. I guess I was afraid of what it might say. Maybe Gloria revealed something about her feelings that I just wasn't ready to confront, something that would pull me deeper into my own emotions. Or, maybe I was reading into the fact that she gave it to me in the first place, and I was hoping for something that wasn't there at all. I suppose that the real world has little to do with the heart's flights of fancy.

Our first stop was Spain. More specifically, the Rota Naval Station at the northern end of the Bay of Cadiz. Due to the urgency of matters in Afghanistan, it was decided that we would stay aboard the Ross as she refueled and no one was allowed to leave without direct authorization from the captain. Two days later, the Ross weighed anchor and cruised through the Strait of Gibraltar. We were allowed on deck just before entering the Straight. The warm Mediterranean air carried a slightly sweet aroma I had never experienced before. Unlike the waters off the coast of Maine, the ocean in this part of the world was somehow different. It could have been the types of trees or, it could've been something about the air itself. Either way, some experiences are beyond description. As we passed into the Mediterranean, Gibraltar stood off the ship's port side as a majestic guardian, 1,398 feet high. The people of Tibet believe that Everest possesses a living soul that can be easily offended. Standing on the deck of the Ross, I let my gaze drift to the grandeur of the Rock of Gibraltar. I wondered if the Tibetans were right. What might this rock think of a warship passing before its mighty presence? But mountains, like the rest of the planet, are devoid of consciousness, right?

At its widest point, the Strait of Gibraltar is about eight miles wide and 2,624 feet deep. But despite these factors, it was necessary for the ship to slow to a crawl. Its forward sonar was used to map the bottom for any changes in depth, and course corrections were made for the ocean floor's terrain as well as tidal changes. Although we were in friendly waters, all precautions were made to ensure the safety of the ship and her crew. Once the ship made its way through the Strait of Gibraltar and into the deeper waters of the Mediterranean, we all felt a sudden forward tug. After feeling a bit alarmed, we were told that the Captain had ordered to proceed at half speed. The next day found us at the island of Crete, just south of Greece.

The Ross was moored in at the naval station at Souda Bay. When the ship was finally secured, we were allowed to disembark. If it can be said that one can see the beauty of a country by looking at its people, then Crete must be the most beautiful place on earth, as the only thing more stunning than Crete were its women. Each was a true work of art, with flowing black curls and a face that was reminiscent of the ancient beauty of Greece. Even the older women still retained the vibrant beauty of girlish youth. I was, without a doubt, in the land of the immortals.

While many in our unit found this to be an opportunity to drink, I found it as a chance to explore, and I decided that even though Crete is an island, it's just too big to explore thoroughly. So after checking into temporary quarters, I went into the nearest town. Because of the money being brought in by military people, Crete had developed an impressive tourist industry, mostly small restaurants, bars, and tourist shops filled with handmade crafts. The people were devoutly religious, mostly Greek Orthodox, so crime was limited to a few drunken brawls on the weekends and there wasn't one prostitute to be seen. It was refreshing to see people who practiced what they preached. Perhaps, as island people, they had not become nearly as poisoned by the world as the rest of us. It seemed that even womanly virtue could be found here.

The town of Souda was nearest to the naval station and even though it looked a bit touristy, one could still see its ancient beauty among the town's facades. The Greek style of architecture was everywhere. I didn't think it would be wise to explore beyond the town, so I spent what little time

I had wandering around downtown, and after eating in one or two of the local restaurants I came to the conclusion that Americans really don't know what Greek food is. Sure, they go to nearby restaurants for what they think is Greek food, but it pales in comparison to an elderly woman's recipe, handed down to her through generations of family cooks. I've never been one for heavy drinking, but one shot of ouzo nearly knocked me on my ass. Crete, like all ancient countries, is a living museum. You can learn more about Greek history here than in any textbook unless you happen to be in Athens.

Souda had only one bookstore, and I was disappointed when I discovered that it carried mostly American novels. It did, however, have both folklore and religious books. I never considered myself to be a Christian, but I knew that the New Testament was, at one time, written in Greek, so I couldn't pass up an opportunity to buy a Greek New Testament in Greece. I also ended up buying a few books on the island's folklore. Fortunately, these were in English. They reflected a certain mystique about the island with tales of ancient heroes, the battles they fought, and the ghosts of history that still wandered the island in search of rest.

After two days on the island, I was awakened by the roar of four C130 cargo planes. Our ride was here. Our country had been given permission by Greece to use the airport at Souda. The islanders knew that this was mutually beneficial. It was of strategic value to us and economically valuable for them. Loaded with troops and gear the C130's left the tarmac at 1730 hours. We were on our way to Afghanistan and would soon be doing a job that we believed had to be done. A northerly route was taken to avoid countries that were seen as hostile to the United States. Being shot down by a trigger-happy anti-American regime wasn't anyone's idea of a good day. Taking a longer way around also meant a longer flight. I don't think it would have been so bad on a commercial jet but, on a military cargo plane, there is no such thing as comfort.

Between the almost constant bumps and the deafening roar of four prop engines, a C130 is definitely not the best way to travel. Finally, we crossed into Afghani airspace. We were nearly there. Our course took us parallel with the southern slopes of the Hindu Kush Mountains. Unfortunately, there are no windows on a cargo plane and the cockpit was off-limits. We touched down on the runway at Kabul but before leaving the aircraft, we were told to strap on our helmets, secure our body armor, and make no eye contact with the locals. Afghanistan was a powder keg of potential uprisings against Americans. Even though their military was in shambles, there were still well-armed splinter groups everywhere, and they followed a strict idealism of Jihad, based exclusively on political fanaticism. They believed that the reward of heaven awaited those who were willing to kill for God by any means possible, even at the cost of their own lives. This isn't much different from the Crusades, but fanaticism, in any form, is still dangerous.

The airport terminal had been deemed a security risk, even though the Afghani government allowed us to use it. A direct attack on the building would have resulted in almost certain death for anyone inside. Once the cargo bay doors opened, we were told to move quickly around the perimeter of the terminal. By this time, we were carrying live rounds for both our rifles and side arms. I have to admit, carrying a rifle loaded with a magazine of live rounds seemed to give it a different feel. I can't explain it any other way. Maybe it was just me. There was a line of cargo trucks and armored personnel vehicles waiting near the front of the terminal and as we climbed into them, I heard a voice shouting.
"Where's your scout?!" the voice yelled.

The C130 pilots could not shut down their engines and needed to be back in the air as quickly as possible. The less time they spend on the ground, the less likely they would become targets. So, we had to yell in order to be heard.
"Here, sir!" I answered.
I followed the voice to the staff sergeant in charge.
"Well, get over here Private!" he yelled.
I ran over to him and saluted.
"Private Taylor reporting, sir!" I said.
"Got a first name, Taylor?" he asked.
"Clarence, sir!" I replied.
"Alright, Clarence! I have two requests for you! First, drop the formal shit, this ain't basic anymore, and I'm not an officer! Second, don't even think about getting on one of those cargo trucks, your job is too important! You get your ass in one of those APVs, got it?!"
"Yes, sir!" I answered.
I climbed into the nearest Armored Personnel Vehicle and buckled myself in as the Staff Sergeant continued to get everyone into the trucks as quickly as possible.
"C'mon, we're burnin' daylight! Everyone in the trucks! Let's go!"
He glanced at his watch and climbed into the APV, buckling himself in across from me. I leaned over towards him.

"Sir, why am I the only one sitting in the APV?" I asked.

"Are you shitting me?!" he said. "You're the only scout this cavalry unit has! Each one of these guys knows how important your job is!"

Like any other soldier, I was trained to do a job, but it became fully obvious to me now that my job made me a valuable resource, one that warranted this degree of protection.

We were forced to travel at a slightly higher speed than the roads allowed in order to avoid coming under fire. Reports of roadside bombs streamed in daily and getting from the airport to the base was a crap shoot. Today, we were lucky. There were no side windows on the APV and while I was not allowed to sit up front, I managed to get a view through the windshield. I had been warned about culture shock. I had seen pictures on the internet of their cities and towns as well as how the people lived but what I saw left me in complete disbelief. Children played near burned-out cars and urinated along the roadsides. Burka-clad women knelt weeping next to the shattered bodies of those who'd come to a pointless demise.

Afghanistan had become occupied by countries that were part of the U.N. effort, whose goal was to keep some semblance of order among warring clans. We were there for the same reason. However, our agenda was slightly different. We were there to hunt down those responsible for bringing death to American soil, the masterminds of nine eleven. The government held a firm stance against racial profiling, but it's human nature to be suspicious and the military suspected everyone of something, with the idea that the enemy was everywhere, and it was often the case that people were picked up and questioned for 'appearing' suspicious. Whatever that means.

Our military wagon train slowed as we approached the joint military installation in Kabul, lying just far enough from the city to avoid a direct assault. The Army Corps of Engineers was always working to expand the base, constructing new quarters, defensive sights, and roads. They had recently added another airstrip and two more helipads. The hospital was of a construction I'd never seen before, appearing like Quonset huts but made of heavy rubber with inflatable walls. Once fully inflated, they were as solid as steel. As long as military personnel continued to arrive, the base would continue to expand and within the next year, it would, essentially, become nothing less than a militarized city for American troops.

I climbed out of the armored personnel vehicle and within minutes of planting my feet in the sand, I looked around at what I would soon think of as home. We were assigned quarters in one specific location. These were not temporary quarters, and we would occupy them for as long as we were here. No one knew how long that would be, but for now, they were more than sufficient. The base was run like a well-oiled machine. Everyone worked together with a single vision - to fight terrorism. President Bush referred to the 'War on Terror' and it didn't take long for everyone to follow that perspective, forcing the mission and its goal into sharp clarity. A day or two after settling in, I was ordered to attend a mandatory briefing. I suppose that in the military, all briefings are mandatory.

As part of Operation Enduring Freedom, everyone was required to become intimately familiar with the enemy. The people we were looking for worked directly for an organization known as Al-Qaeda and according to intelligence sources, it was developed by Osama bin Laden in Peshawar, Pakistan around 1989. They believed that the Judeo-Christian world was conspiring for the destruction of Islam. The spiritual aspects of the Koran forbidding the taking of a life were ignored to allow suicide bombings of innocent civilians. At some point, this organization merged with other terrorist groups, like the Taliban and the Mujahideen, proclaiming jihad, or 'holy war' against America and its people. Then, on September eleventh, 2001, nineteen Islamist militants associated with Al-Qaeda carried out an attack on the World Trade Center in New York City.

During the next month, the U.S. set into motion a series of attacks against Al-Qaeda and the Taliban. The military response carried out by the U.S. was named Operation Enduring Freedom, whose mission was to capture or kill most if not all, high-ranking members of Al-Qaeda. The ultimate goal was to capture bin Laden and bring him to trial for the attack of nine eleven. Bin Laden, himself, turned out to be a wealthy Saudi prince who used his business profits to organize and fund his terrorist enterprise. He was stripped of his Saudi citizenship in 1994 due to his continued protests against the regime of that country. Now, here's the part that wasn't in the briefing. Bin Laden organized logistical support against the Soviet invasion of Afghanistan during the mid-eighties. The U.S. had no military presence in Afghanistan for fear of a Soviet response. However, for Al-Qaeda to carry out its mission to support Muslim fighters, bin Laden would need specialized training, and he got it from the CIA. This aspect of

Al-Qaeda's activities was never up for discussion by the American military and the American public knew little, if anything, about it. No one in Washington seemed to want to admit that the U.S. government could, in any way, be even fractionally responsible for the existence of an enemy that appeared to be everywhere, yet hidden in plain sight.

The briefing was two hours long. No one was allowed to take notes and there were no handouts. It was preferred that written information be non-existent for the sake of security. A paper trail of any kind would not be tolerated. A week later, our unit would be briefed for our first mission. Last December, just four months after nine eleven, the battle of Tora Bora took place. This is a small mountain range along the southern edge of the Hindu Kush Mountains near Kabul. It was peppered with caves and man-made tunnels. This area was referred to as the Tora Bora cave complex. A cross-section of some areas oddly resembled an underground apartment complex, and some of these caves had been in use for centuries, while others were created during the Soviet invasion of the early eighties. The December assault was carried out in order to clear the caves of Al-Qaeda and Taliban insurgents, as well as weapons and booby traps. Any information in the way of documents that were deemed as having military value was turned over to intelligence. The Sixth Space Operations Squadron had been focusing its attention on Afghanistan since before nine eleven. The reason why has never been disclosed.

The military, however, had exclusive rights to purchase images from the commercially owned IKONOS earth observation satellite. It could photograph any area in sharp focus down to one square meter. Any images acquired depicting countries hostile to American interests were evaluated for their strategic importance and with the discovery of terrorist training camps in the U.S., heavily wooded areas of this country were also photographed. Based on infrared images taken at night, it was believed that insurgents may have been trying to reoccupy the cave complex. Making a comparison between these images and those taken over previous time frames, I discovered that there was, indeed, traffic along an unmapped road. The infrared, or heat signatures, were impossible to miss. As a result, we would be sent out to investigate the complex and map out any thermal hot spots in preparation for an air strike.

Before the end of the briefing, we were given the authorization to engage any insurgents who might show themselves to be 'trigger-happy' and would leave for the complex in three days, making our approach under cover of night. While the darkness would conceal our presence, it would make it nearly impossible to see any booby traps or trip wires. So, we were all outfitted with night-vision goggles. A mission review would be held only hours before leaving for the complex and two days later, our unit met under the briefing tent. It was 0800 and every unit would be briefed separately on their part of the mission. Our primary goal was reconnaissance. We were to get in, map every thermal image, sector by sector, and see if anyone was home. My job was to map out areas of activity for our assigned sectors. Since every unit had a scout, the collection of GPS data from this mission would be critical in planning the air strike or any assaults in the near future.

Tora Bora was in the Pachir Wa Agam district of the Nangarhar Province. Politically, it was a sensitive area, as the northern and southern slopes were divided by the Pakistani border, and under no circumstances were we to cross into Pakistan, as this could not only bring about a military response and jeopardize the mission but would certainly create an international incident. And no one was to fire a single shot unless either fired upon or observed by the enemy. Being invisible was the key to the success of the mission, and the last thing we wanted was a Pakistani air strike. We would be taken by CH-47-2 Chinook transport helicopters to the Logar Province, just west of the Pakistani border. It had been decided that instead of monitoring the southern slopes, even from a distance, we'd be hiking through a pass in the southern panhandle of the Logar Province. We would comprise fifty percent of all the units going to the Tora Bora Mountains. The rest would be choppered to the eastern part of the Nangarhar Province, about twenty miles west of the Khyber Pass. They would head west while we moved northeast through the pass at Logar and east along the northern slope. If everything went according to plan, we would meet somewhere in the middle and after spending roughly ten days to two weeks in the field, we would be extracted by helicopter.

With equipment and troops loaded, we began the six-hundred-mile trip to the southern Logar Province. It took four hours to get to the drop-off point. We camped about twenty miles from the southern end of what is now called Logar Pass. The Chinooks left before dawn the next morning, so they provided us with cover for the night. Whatever you've been told about the desert, you should know one more thing. The desert gets very cold at night and unfortunately, I had left my winter cap at home.

Because it had determined that we were in enemy territory, in spite of the fact that we were not in Pakistan, guard duty would be done four men at a time in two-hour shifts. Perhaps I should mention here that falling asleep on guard duty is a serious court-martial offense, especially during a time of war. We began making our way through the pass, traveling in small groups to avoid becoming one large target, and as we moved along the northwest slope, everyone's eyes were on the mountains. They surrounded us on each side, leaving us exposed to anyone who might be hiding and in possession of a sniper rifle. This degree of exposure had been anticipated during the planning stage of the mission, but it had been determined that the potential information coming from the mission far outweighed the risks. We had to know if Al-Qaeda was moving back in. The units moving towards us from the Nangarhar Province covered most of the northern slope. If there was a problem, they could fall back into the desert toward the north. If we encountered a problem, we'd be trapped. Before moving out, I made a decision that made me more than a little uncomfortable. Since I was the person gathering information, I became a valuable target for capture. So like everyone else, I loaded my magazines with live rounds, inserting one into my rifle and the other into my pistol. However, I put one forty-five caliber round in my breast pocket. If push came to shove and I ran out of ammo, I would use this last round to destroy any and all information left in my possession. It could not be forced out of me if my brains were scattered all over the rocks, and being tortured was not my idea of a party. I'd rather die instead. Our pickup point was sixty-five miles in front of us, but the distance we had to walk was not important. We were there to do a job and would be moving about fifteen miles a day. Investigating the cave complex required a slow pace. There were no speed records to be set on this mission.

Throughout the night, we worked in shifts, making observations with night-vision binoculars and rangefinders. Night or day, any movement in the mountains was plotted as a GPS heading and recorded on a digital map. The laptops we carried were custom-designed with quickly removable hard drives. They were primitive and a bit clumsy but served their purpose. In the event we were overwhelmed by hostile forces, the hard drive could be slipped out and destroyed. In order to minimize our visibility, they had been set up to display green characters and outlined graphics on a black background. As locations were plotted on the map, the program automatically saved it to an encrypted file. The Department of Defense claimed that this encryption could only be broken after roughly ten years of constant work.

The mission was simple to the point of elegance and backup plans had been accounted for, should the need for data destruction arise. Of course, the last backup plan was tucked away in my breast pocket. The CIA had been looking closely at Al-Qaeda for about the last five years. Their intelligence reports revealed that bin Laden had been buying weapons and equipment from Russia and Iran, and it was unlikely that the Soviet government was knowingly selling arms to terrorists. They believed that Al-Qaeda was almost certainly getting them through the Russian black market, and Iran was probably selling them outright. What the CIA couldn't tell us was what Al-Qaeda actually possessed. So, we went into the mission with the assumption that they had, at least, the same weapons and equipment as we had, and it was this assumption that kept us on our toes. It was agreed that if Al-Qaeda members were moving back into the caves, they probably had just as much ability to see us as we did to see them. This thought made all of us feel a bit spooked, especially at night. Having anticipated this, we were each carrying a thermal blanket. These were often used by hikers, campers, and hunters to stay warm by reflecting their body heat and were large enough to cover one person. Not only did they keep us warm, but also concealed our thermal signatures from anyone using night vision.

Later, we would learn that even the infrared camera on the IKONOS satellite was unable to detect us. As far as 'it' was concerned, we had simply disappeared. The early morning sun struck the mountain slopes with cloudless rays, giving them a warm steely hue. The air was sharp and cold. The rocks were covered with a sparse hint of snow. Most people believe that the desert is a hot, harsh, and forbidding place. But, the desert is as cold at night as it is hot during the day and one can easily become a victim of either extreme. No one came out from under their thermal blankets right away without getting the 'all clear' from the sentries. To get up and walk out blindly would almost certainly invite trouble without first maintaining a secure perimeter. This was another reason for working in shifts.

The calm morning air suddenly grew tense as cautious whispers came from the sentries. A small reflection had been spotted among the rocks somewhere nearby on the mountainside. Whoever it was made the mistake of facing into the sun, giving away their position. We were ordered to maintain cover until it could be investigated. A spotter had determined that we were being watched was that the reflection was intermittent and moved along what was believed to be a defensive trench. The solution was simple. We brought a sniper. Armed with binoculars, I was in a unique position to view this quiet glint among the rocks, as well as the untimely fate of whoever was behind it. The sniper and spotter got into position to assess how the shot would be set up. I was close enough, under my thermal blanket, that I could hear every word of their conversation. The target was about half a mile away. Many people might think that half a mile is a pretty good distance, right? Well, not really. As far as the battlefield is concerned, half a mile is an alarmingly short distance. If a thief is chasing you through your hometown at that distance, you probably have nothing to worry about. But, if an enemy division is advancing on you from that distance, you have a great deal to worry about and as the morning sun continued to rise, the sparkle among the rocks became more pronounced. The spotter confirmed that, indeed, there was a dark-haired man watching us through a pair of binoculars and was likely assessing our troop strength. He also appeared to be alone.

Army and Marine Corps snipers used the MD50 rifle, firing a fifty-caliber round. If you got hit with one of these, you probably wouldn't even hear the shot. Paired up with a good spotter, a sniper could hit a target at a mile and a half. Among other variables, in order to assess a shot, the rotation of the earth would sometimes have to be taken into consideration. The shot rang out, echoing through the mountains. What I saw through my binoculars was as graphic as it was impressive. The entire event passed within only a moment as the dark-haired man's head exploded into a cloud of blood. His demise was sudden and without a doubt, painless. By all appearances, death by sniper seemed like a fairly humane way to go.

The spotter made a careful sweep of the surrounding slopes and determined that, for now, there were no other eyes among the rocks. However, it was now assumed that we had attracted unwanted attention and of course, the easiest way to avoid this was not to fire a fifty-caliber rifle. But, there's no undo button on some things, and shooting our lone observer was a calculated risk. The best thing to do now was to pack up and keep moving. Having plotted the sniper's kill, we proceeded northeast through the pass. There were no more targets staring back at us from the rocks, but we did detect several more heat signatures. One looked like a small campfire. The rest appeared to be moving, and no wildlife had been observed in the area. Each hot spot was plotted as we made our way through the pass.

By the time we arrived at our pickup point about eight days later, I had plotted roughly seventy-two thermal signatures. This information was used to map out a series of precision air strikes, and the coordinates would be transmitted from the pickup point by mobile satellite uplink to SATCOM's Kabul division. The digital map would later be used as confirmation after the initial planning phase of the air strikes. We met with the other half of the reconnaissance team in the western Nangarhar Province. The exact location of our pickup point had been classified, but once we entered the Nangahar Plain, we radioed our location by way of a secure frequency and awaited orders. When both units had reported their locations, we were ordered to proceed to the predetermined coordinates. The data was sent, and we were quickly airlifted out.

Chapter 19

The next day, I asked to see the unit commander. I still felt haunted by Steve's behavior and wanted to find out if he was okay. I told him which province he was in and asked if there had been any casualties reported. I was told that the patrol mission he was on was classified and that I knew better than to even think of asking. I informed the commander that Steve wanted me to be the 'go-to' person in case something happened.
"I know," the commander said.
"I'm sorry, sir," I began. "It's just that he wasn't doing very well when he left."
"How so?" he asked."
Well, sir," I answered. "He thought he was going to die. He gave me a letter to send to his girlfriend in case he didn't come back."
"Private," he replied. "For as long as there have been wars, soldiers have made those same arrangements. Sometimes it's a letter; sometimes just a name and address. This wouldn't be the first time, and it probably won't be the last. As far as your friend's state of mind is concerned, the only thing I can tell you is that we all feel fear. I've been there. And even if his mission wasn't classified, there's no way to know which sector he's in. I'm

sorry, Private, I can't help you, but if I hear anything, I'll let you know personally."
"Thank you, sir," I replied.
"You're dismissed," he said.

I left the commander's office feeling a little angry with myself. I don't know what I was thinking. Did I really expect him to tell me anything? I felt like an idiot. More than likely, Steve would be fine. He was as new to this as I was, so I understood why he reacted the way he did. As much planning that goes into fighting a war, there is a certain degree of unpredictability. You go to war knowing there's a good chance that you won't come back. It occurred to me that if the outcome of any war was certain, warfare would be made obsolete. After all, who in their right mind would fight a war, knowing they were going to lose? Upon returning to my quarters, I discovered a letter had been slipped under my door. It was nothing more than a sheet of paper that had been folded into thirds. It was, however, marked 'urgent'. According to the letter, a mission briefing had been scheduled for 0900 hours tomorrow. No other information was included.

I woke early the next morning and after the usual morning ritual, I went to the mess hall for some breakfast then straight to the briefing tent. I arrived early enough that I could find a chair near the front. Everyone stood at attention as the commander walked in.

"Alright, everyone," he began. "Have a seat." We sat down as he started the briefing. It turned out that this mission would also be politically sensitive and strongly connected to our last reconnaissance mission in the Tora Bora Mountains. Intelligence reported activity along the Khyber Pass, and we were ordered to go there and verify it. Military intelligence sometimes keeps strange bedfellows, in that it's only as reliable as the people providing it and most of the time, it came from locals who were being paid for information. How true their stories were was a different matter, but in spite of that, we had to either verify or dismiss the reports. And the first step was always satellite imagery.

The recent air strike in the Tora Bora had been declared a success. Now, the question that needed to be answered was twofold. Was there any activity in the Khyber Pass and if so, in which direction? The Khyber Pass lies east of the Tora Bora and runs northeast through the Spin Ghar Mountains. It was once part of the 'Silk Road' used by medieval merchants and is believed to have been part of the route taken by travelers who brought the Black Death into Europe as well as the

Mediterranean. Torkam was a village that lay within the Afghani side of the pass, and it was believed that if the Taliban or al-Qaeda were coming back through the pass, they'd probably be hiding there. If that was the case, there would be a stockpile of weapons as well. We were to go into the area in small groups at roughly five to ten miles distance. Radio silence would be critical to the success of the mission, and it was assumed that if there was a weapons stockpile, then there would also be communications equipment. Terrorist groups are highly organized, and their outposts are always within communications range of each other. Their logistical support network operated at the level of any highly trained military force, and we would be monitoring the area over the course of a week, looking not only for movement but also for any vehicle traffic or signs of weapons smuggling from across the Pakistani border. Naturally, being the scout, I would be the principal set of eyes for the mission. So, I would have to get as close as possible and from the right vantage point so that I see both the village and the route into the pass. Finding an elevated area would be essential to gathering accurate information.

The remainder of the briefing outlined our transportation to and from the mission site. We were to be dropped at a small military outpost five miles from Chenar Kalay by helicopter and would camp there while performing surveillance and reconnaissance within the target area, working in shifts both day and night. I would also be joined by another scout. Typically, each unit had its own, but another was assigned to the mission, so we could work in shifts. With the additional scout, we would have our eyes on the target area twenty-four hours a day. Again, I assessed the current satellite imagery. The images did show some traffic moving in both directions through the Khyber Pass. What they couldn't reveal was if any weapons were being transported. There was no question that we had to go there to find out.

Later that afternoon, there was a knock at the door of my quarters. I had been working with Kabul's SATCOM division monitoring the Khyber Pass and was waiting for any updated images. It was critical to stay on top of the current intelligence coming in as part of mission support. I opened the door and found the commander standing in front of me with a deep look of concern.
"Sorry to bother you, Private," he said.
"It's okay, sir," I replied.
He paused a moment and glanced at the ground with a deep sigh. I knew exactly why he'd come.
"Fuck!" I thought.
This was not what I wanted to hear.

"How did it happen, sir?" I asked.
Sometimes the truth about a soldier's death is never revealed due to the nature of the mission, or because of some political sensitivity. In this case, the commander gave me the entire story. Steve was one of a small handful of soldiers patrolling a sector near Gossam, in the Nari district in the Kunar Province. They were inspecting a road for recent signs of activity when he stepped on an IED. He was killed instantly.

Usually, improvised explosive devices leave an impression around them, as their edges tend to displace the ground they're placed in. But, the wind blew sand over its edges and evened out the ground, making the device undetectable. Several more were discovered afterward, probably saving more lives. Normally, the idea of sacrificing one life for the good of the many is one I find acceptable, but it's very different when you know the person whose life was taken. This seemed to take utilitarianism from being nothing more than an idea to something that felt like a kick in the stomach. Of all the places to bury a bomb, what were the odds of it being right under Steve's foot? At least, it was quick. I suppose that was better than having to deal with the pain of being shot. I've heard soldiers and marines talk about that experience and how much it burns. They say it feels like they're being branded.

His remains arrived that evening by helicopter. He had been placed in a standard, olive-drab military body bag. I stood at the edge of the chopper pad as the flight medics lifted him out and into a transport truck. He was taken to the base morgue and placed in an airtight stainless steel casket. This was put into a walk-in refrigeration unit. It would be flown to Germany for processing and then Steve would be taken home. Because of the condition of his body, I was not allowed to see him, and it was likely that his family wouldn't either. Naturally, the Army would print a letter informing his family. It would be exactly the same letter that so many other families get - standard, automated, and impersonal.

As promised, I would send Steve's letter out to his girlfriend, but I wanted to do something more so, I sat down to write to her myself, telling her about my friendship with him and the kind of person I saw him as. This is what I wrote.

Dear Trisha,

I wish I didn't have to write this letter. My name is Clarence, and I'm currently serving in Afghanistan.

Steve wrote you a letter and made me promise that I'd send it to you in case something happened. He came to me with it right before leaving for a patrol mission. Most of the time, things go okay, but while he was out on patrol, Steve accidentally stepped on a roadside bomb. There was no way anyone could've seen it. His parents will probably get a formal letter, but he thought you deserved better. And I agree.

We first met in basic training. I was going through a rough patch and Steve was there to listen. About two weeks ago, we ran into each other here in Kabul. Our conversations often went on for hours and without knowing it, he helped me to forget the things that make war ugly. Recently, he showed me your picture, saying that he wouldn't know what he'd do without you. I can't imagine how painful this must be, and it would be wrong to tell you that everything's going to be okay, but eventually, you will feel better.

If there's one thing you should know, it's how much Steve loved you. You were the light of his life. No good person deserves to die, and Steve was a genuinely good person. Please know that I am truly sorry for what you've lost. I know that I will never meet anyone quite like him again, please don't feel that you have to write back to me.

The only thing you should be concerned with is letting yourself heal. With this letter, you'll find the one Steve wrote. Again, I'm sorry for what you must be going through. I wish there was something I could do to make this easier for you. It seems that the only thing I 'can' do is to write this letter. Please take care of yourself. And remember, you are never truly alone.

Sincerest Regards,
Clarence Taylor

I tried to be brief but still sensitive without getting too personal. I made it a point to let her know that she did not have to write back. And honestly, I really didn't want her to. I know that sounds harsh, but the last thing I wanted was to be a long-distance counselor for a young girl whose boyfriend had just been killed. It would have been a wrinkle in my life that I just didn't need. I put both letters in an envelope and dropped them into the mail. A military carrier would pick it up that evening. Chances are, she'd get the letter a week or two after being told by Steve's parents of his death. People's lives can't be fixed and hopefully, Trisha would not be on her own with her grief. She would have to find a sympathetic ear and eventually a way of moving on, and I had to find a way of letting it all go. I never heard from her.

The mission review was that evening, and we'd be moving out to the Khyber Pass in the morning. We surveyed the maps and satellite images, looking for any elevations in the terrain from which to make our observations. This meant we would be taking the risk of exposing our positions, as there would probably be a number of lookouts posted. This method of acquiring information always carries a very real risk of attack, but we were all determined to get the job done. I took my usual precaution in order to avoid capture, putting a forty-five caliber round in my left breast pocket. Ordinarily, I saw suicide as a product of mental illness. Other times, I saw it as an act of cowardice. Death is usually the easy way out. Most people don't see shooting yourself in the head as a means of serving the greater good. However, most people will never find themselves near the Pakistani border gathering critical information on terrorist activities. I think the difference is very clear. Would I be able to blow my brains out in the event we were overrun? I honestly don't know. I guess that's one of those things you find out when the time comes. As much as I believed I could do it, I would, fortunately, never have to.

The mission review was given in the morning. There were no snipers on this mission and we would have no air support. Officially, this had not been classified as a covert mission, but it was obvious that was what we were doing. It was at the mission review that we were given information on exactly where we were going. We were previously told that our drop point would be at an outpost near Chenar Kalay. In addition, we would be hiking to just below the summit of SlingharMountain. We'd make camp there and use the summit as a temporary observation post, being careful not to stray across the Pakistani border. The two platoons of Marines assigned as support would hold a position near the base of the mountain to minimize our visibility. Hopefully, we wouldn't need them.

By the time we landed at Chenar Kalay, the Marines had already arrived. They had gone in the night before to secure the area we'd be camped at. According to every map available, Slinghar Mountain was on the Afghani side of the Pakistani border. However, it was strongly suspected that if our presence was detected, the government of Pakistan might make the claim that the mountain was within their border and use it to start an international incident. War is never without politics.

We waited at the outpost until nightfall. The most important part of the plan was to be invisible. The meteorology division at Kabul had forecast a windstorm for that area. The wind-driven sand would make things miserable, but it would also cover our tracks. Strategically speaking, the conditions would be perfect. We'd be able to move like ghosts in the desert. SlingharMountain is near the easternmost tip of the Tora Bora Mountains and overlooks the Khyber Pass. We would be observing from the western side of the summit in order to get an unobstructed view of Torkham. We were using high-powered, night-vision binoculars mounted on tripods. To eliminate wind vibration, small sandbags were hung from beneath the top of each tripod. All we needed to do was watch, take pictures, and remain invisible. We would be there for no longer than a week.

Chapter 20

Our observations confirmed that not only was there traffic going through the Khyber Pass but there were also wooden crates being unloaded from trucks. We had also seen people carrying weapons across their shoulders. This was the information we needed. The reports and photographs would be examined by military intelligence and a plan would be put together. An air strike would be politically risky. Torkham sat almost exactly on the Pakistani border, and an air strike would certainly be interpreted as an act of war. Instead, a blockade would be established between Torkham and the Tora Bora. Any lines of travel west and south of Torkham would be cut off. The Taliban and Al-Qaeda would be forced to abandon the trafficking of weapons or divert their route south and cross the Tora Bora Mountains on foot. From the photographs, it would also be assessed that some of these weapons appeared to be Russian, but that was only a guess.

We began pulling out six days later. The first platoon of Marines moved out ahead of us to clear the way of any resistance we might run into. The second platoon would be at our backs in the event of a surprise attack. We would be walking back to the outpost and choppered back to Kabul. Extraction from Slinghar Mountain by helicopter was out of the question. We'd be returning during early daylight hours, and a fleet of helicopters would be certain to attract attention. In order to maintain the lowest visibility possible, we traveled in small groups of two or three. The Marines, however, were ordered to travel in larger groups. I had been paired up with the sergeant in charge of the unit. His name was Ryan. He was pretty easygoing, but it was obvious that he felt the full weight of responsibility when it came to his job. The last thing he wanted was to lose someone under his command.

It was 0800 hours, and the desert sun was already beating down on us. As we walked through the sand, I saw something I hadn't noticed before. There was a small settlement about half a mile west of our location that didn't show up on any of our maps. We had no information on it at all, and it had been overlooked on the satellite images. From a distance, it was nothing more than a small arrangement of shelters whose walls had been carved from rocks brought in from the mountains, each seemed to be the size of a modest walk-in closet. Many of these small settlements had been constructed centuries ago and had seen many tenants over time. In these isolated places, the idea of time was nonexistent. The past, present, and future were irrelevant to the people living in these places. For them, life was an ongoing struggle to survive. We stopped to survey the small settlement and noticed there was no movement.

"Why didn't we see that before?" the sergeant asked.

I stood next to him, sweeping the area with a pair of binoculars.

"Maybe we just weren't looking for it," I replied. "It's not on any of the maps."

The early morning sun slowly rose over the mountaintops, casting long shadows of our shapes across the sand. It was hard to tell how big the settlement was from half a mile's distance, but I had the distinct feeling that it was not as empty as it seemed.

"I don't know," the sergeant said. "What do you think?"

I continued to scan the settlement.

"I think it's worth a look," I replied. "There could be a weapons cache down there."

It was at that moment we heard the crack of a gunshot. We suddenly raised our rifles and dropped to our stomachs.

"That sounded like it came from the settlement," I said.

Another shot rang out from the stone shelters.

"I think you're right, Private," the sergeant replied.

This shot was followed by the sound of a crying baby.

"Private," the sergeant said. "We need to get down there."

I nodded in agreement.

"Sir," I said. "If we're going to do this, we should have more people."

A third shot suddenly brought silence to the sound of crying.

"By that time," the sergeant said. "Everyone down there's going to be dead. We need to get down there now."

"I'm ready whenever you are, sir," I replied.

We both got up and ran toward the settlement, taking cover behind the occasional rock. What we were doing went against everything the Army taught us. Never go in alone, and always make an accurate assessment of any given situation. What drove us in was the sound of the crying baby and glancing over at the sergeant, I could see the anger etched on his face. At that moment, I believed that this was the reason I had joined the Army. All the training and hard work seemed to culminate into that one moment. I felt that my purpose was crystal clear, and I became filled with rage at the idea that someone - anyone - could stoop so low as to kill a defenseless child. My sense of reason escaped me and in its place was the monster, the thing that, without warning, can rob us of our humanness. It had taken over so quickly that I had suddenly stopped being a soldier and became a mindless killer, devoid of any degree of conscience. I was driven by the adrenaline of rage and as we neared the settlement, I quickly realized it was somewhat larger than it first appeared.

We slowed our approach as the sergeant tapped my left arm and pointed off to the right. I moved quickly to the corner of the building that lay to the far right, while the sergeant took up a similar position on the far left of the settlement. We'd circle around and meet at the rear of the settlement's perimeter. Everything we did was by the book, with one possibly fatal mistake. There were only two of us, and an area this size required two or three squads in order to fully cover the area. But, neither of us was thinking clearly. Looking back on it, I believe that a fair assessment of our actions could be summed up by saying that we were trying to fight madness with insanity. I rounded the corner and headed for the back side of the building as another shot was fired. It was preceded by the sound of a woman screaming and followed by yelling. The voice spoke in English and sounded vaguely familiar. I rounded the next corner to find the ground littered with dead. They all appeared to have been in a sitting position, and all of them had been shot in the head. Each body bore the same entry wound -- the middle of the forehead. They had not simply been shot. They had been executed. But, it was the exit wound that left the deepest impression on what little remained of my faculties. Blood and brain matter had painted the stone wall as the dead lay sprawled with eyes open and mouths agape. The backs of their heads had exploded with such force that skull fragments had left themselves embedded in the wall behind them. Had I been in possession of any degree of sanity, I would have certainly become violently ill.

Working my way down the row of slaughtered men, women, and children, I cautiously approached the rear of the next building. What I encountered was beyond my mind's ability to fully absorb, as the monster inside me began to roar. I recognized him immediately as the marine I stood up to in Kabul. He was obviously from one of the platoons that had been attached to the mission. Unfortunately, he found the settlement before we did and had begun lining up its people and executing them with a single shot to the forehead. "What the fuck are you doing?!" I screamed. He didn't seem too surprised and paused while aiming his sidearm at the head of an elderly woman. She was sitting with her back against the wall, her knees tucked up into her chest while holding her hands out in an attempt to protect herself.

"Hey!" he yelled. "I know you! You're that asshole that told me off back in Kabul!"

The elderly woman began crying as he continued to aim his pistol at her head.

"Shut the fuck up!" he screamed.

He turned back to me with a grin.

"Excuse me a second. Let me deal with this pig so we can talk."

He turned back to the woman while cocking the hammer on his pistol.

"Wait!" I screamed. "What are you doing?!"

I stepped forward in an attempt to stop him, but he fired before I could get close enough. The back of the woman's head exploded against the wall as he casually dropped his arm.

"What am I doing," he said. "I'm doing my job. You know, killing terrorists."

He removed the magazine from his sidearm and discovered he'd run out of ammo.

"Shit!" he yelled.

He holstered his pistol and brought out his combat knife.

"Guess we got to do this old school."

"These people aren't terrorists!" I screamed. "Jesus fucking Christ! You can't just start killing innocents!"

He turned to me with a puzzled look.

"Innocents?" he began. "No one's innocent!"
He pointed behind me with his knife.
"You see that kid right there? Now, it's more than likely that he would've grown up to be a fucking terrorist. All I did was stop him. Problem solved."
If war does anything successfully, it is to test the sanity of those who face the chaos of battle, and both of us had failed miserably.
"Are you out of your fucking mind?!" I yelled.
He walked towards me at a startling pace and pointed his combat knife at my face. His eyes suddenly became wild and angry.
"Listen, grunt," he said. "That's what they call you Army types, right?"
In spite of the fact that he was still pointing his knife at my face, I held my ground with vengeful resolve.
"Now," he continued. "You can help, or you can die."
He suddenly became disturbingly calm and let out a slight giggle. During the next moment, he had quickly become overtaken by rage and frustration as he turned away, walking only a few feet from me. He crouched down in front of an old man who had also been sitting against the wall. Hardship and time had robbed him of his voice, but he sat unafraid, with an expression of resolution etched on his stony face. He pointed his knife at the old

man and spoke to me without taking his eyes off him.

"Now, this one," he began. "I'll bet this fucker's killed a lot of people."

He leaned forward into the old man's face and began screaming.

"Are you a fucking terrorist!? Do you know what your motherfucking people did to us?!"

As he continued screaming, I quietly unclipped the strap on my holster and slipped out my sidearm. He grabbed the old man by his clothes and pulling him forward, putting the knife against his throat. The old man was unmoved by the threat against his life.

"So," he started. "Should I cut his throat, or just pull out an eye?"

He looked up at me to discover that I was pointing my sidearm at his head. He snickered slightly as he momentarily dropped his head and then, just as quickly, looked back up at me with a grin.

"Are you fuckin' serious?" he began. "You'd protect 'these' people? They're not even people! They're animals! Look at this shithole! They fucking live like pigs, and you'd kill me to save them!?"

He shook his head in disgust.

"You're pathetic."

He dragged the old man out from the wall and forced him to his knees so they were both facing me.

"You know how this is done, don't you?" he asked.

He angled his knife, placing the point down against the man's windpipe.

"Down through the carotid artery and into the vocal cords, right?"

I stood, continuing to aim my sidearm at his head, as my thoughts started to become cloudy.

"Marine!" I yelled. "You will stand down, or I will be forced to fire!"

His face broke into an angry grin as he spoke through clenched teeth.

"Grunt, you don't have the balls," he replied.

He glanced down at the man's neck and teasingly broke his skin with the tip of his knife. The old man winced in pain as a small pool of blood gathered on his skin. I cocked the hammer back on my pistol.

"I said stop!" I yelled.

My finger immediately made contact with the trigger.

"I don't think so, asshole," he replied.

The old man took a sudden gasp of pain as the marine pushed his knife deeper into his flesh. My mind had completely separated itself from my emotions. The monster leaped forward through the barrel of my .45 as I unknowingly squeezed the trigger. The crack of the discharging round was a sound I would never forget. It would break into my waking thoughts and take up residence in my nightmares. My mind would never be released from that sound.

The back of the marine's head exploded as his body crumbled to the ground, while the old man quickly crawled back to the wall and held his hand against his wounded neck. The sound of the shot drifted away and vanished into the morning desert air. But, the silence was broken by another sound, one that I found difficult to place and after hearing it a second time, I decided to follow it. I was led down along the wall, passed the dead as well as those who were lucky enough to remain unharmed. I discovered the sound somewhere along the back of the next building. A second marine was photographing the dead. He had been posing a corpse with his pistol in the hand of a young man who'd also been shot in the head. I recognized him as the marine I'd pissed off with the 'cheerleader' remark back in Kabul. In actuality, I guess I'd stood up to both of them. I was still a pretty good distance from him when he picked up a crying baby by the arm.
"Where's the Sergeant?" I wondered.

As much as I wanted this to stop, I also wanted someone to tell me whether any of this was real. I walked towards him as quietly as possible.
"Shut the fuck up!" he screamed.
I approached him with my sidearm aimed at his head.

Somewhere in the back of my frozen mind, I had the idea that I would, and could, save as many of these people as possible.
"Jesus Christ!" I yelled.
He turned toward me as if he'd already known I was there.
"Hey," he said. "I know you."
He dropped his arm, lowering the infant to the ground.
"You're the asshole that called me a 'cheerleader' the other day."
He held the baby back up, still clutching it by the arm.
"Well, first I'm going to deal with this, then I'm going to deal with you."
"Look," I said. "We can settle this, alright? Just put the baby down, please. That kid hasn't done anything to anyone.
"He could hear the desperation in my voice as a broad grin came over his face.
"Oh, you want me to put the baby down?" he asked tauntingly. "This baby?"

"Stop fuckin' around!" I yelled.

He glanced down at the ground where a rock lay partly exposed while bringing up his other hand and holding the infant under its arms. All that time, the child had been screaming helplessly.

"Fine," he replied. "I'll put it down. I'm not much into kids anyway. Oh, by the way, your Sergeant's dead. He got in the way of the mission."

He began to raise the infant over his head as his grin twisted itself into an expression of rage. It happened so quickly and by the time I squeezed the trigger, he already had the infant over his head. The round entered an area near the middle of his face, causing his nose to split. The round tumbled through his head and exploded out through the base of his skull. He was dead before he hit the ground. Had I not hesitated, the baby might have survived.

Falling from above, the marine sent it to the ground faster than I could move to catch it. Sand isn't as forgiving as you might think, and the child was quickly silenced upon impact with the hot, dry earth. I ran over to the infant as it lay on the hot sand, its face bathed by the morning sun. Its eyes were only half open as its mouth had fallen into a faint smile. I sat in the sand next to it, stroking the top of its head. I didn't know the child's name. I didn't even know if it was a boy or girl. I just sat and talked to it as it quietly passed into whatever lay on the other side of its last heartbeat. Then, I cracked. I couldn't hold it back anymore. The ghosts that had been haunting me had finally broken free of their chains. Everything had come to the surface, escaping through a torrent of tears and pain.

Others in the settlement had survived, so why wasn't I able to save this one child? As I looked around with tears flowing down my face, I saw some of the settlement's survivors staggering toward me. I realized that they would not remember us for our intentions, but for our actions and the sight of a U.S. soldier sitting next to the body of one of their children would be branded on their souls forever. It never occurred to me what their reaction might be if they suddenly saw me as a target of revenge. I looked up at them again to see them slowly backing away as their eyes had become fixed on something behind me. I turned around to find myself surrounded by several marines, all aiming their weapons at me. Their sergeant stepped up to my right side with an assault rifle aimed at my temple.
"Private, get on your feet," he ordered.
I got up with no intentions of resisting and, having been relieved of my weapons, I was led out of the settlement.

"You're being taken into custody," the sergeant continued. "You'll be turned over to the MPs once we reach Kabul."

Once we returned to the outpost, I was placed under heavy guard. It wasn't as though I was going anywhere, but they had to follow procedure. I suppose they could've just shot me.

That being said, I was surprised that they took me into custody in the first place. In the middle of the Afghani desert, no one would have known, and I would have simply been added to the MIA list. Their sergeant, accompanied by three guards, woke me early the next morning to board the first helicopter back to Kabul. The helicopter landed just moments after I stepped out of the tent. Maybe they expected me to put up a fight, or at least struggle a bit, but I was determined to remain calm and would not give them the satisfaction of becoming difficult. There was no conversation or eye contact on the way back. About twenty miles outside Kabul, the pilot radioed our ETA and informed air traffic control of my arrest. My mind went blank as the memories of the incident became hazy.

About fifteen minutes later, I found myself stepping out of the helicopter and faced with what must have been a dozen MPs. I don't really remember how many there were. The sergeant in charge ordered me to get on my knees and place my hands behind my head. I felt the ratcheting of cold steel around my wrists as I was handcuffed and escorted to a waiting vehicle, where I was driven across the base to the security center. It was only after being allowed to sit that I realized how exhausted I was. Sleeping in the desert is hard enough. Sleeping while surrounded by armed guards authorized to use deadly force is impossible. I hadn't noticed it before, but while waiting to be processed, I looked down and discovered the brownish-red stains of blood spatter on my uniform. As cloudy as my thoughts were, the realization that I'd spent the night with someone else's blood on me crept into my consciousness, but I still believed that what I had done was right.

Chapter 21

I was charged with violation of at least four articles of the Uniform Code of Military Justice. This included article fifteen, non-judicial punishment. You can be charged with this simply by allowing yourself to be sunburned to the point of requiring hospitalization. I suppose that maintaining order can't be accomplished through compassion. In addition, I was charged with two counts of murder and two counts of assault with a deadly weapon. I was read my rights and ordered to change into an orange jumpsuit. Everything I'd been wearing had been confiscated as evidence. My boots and underwear had been taken as a means of preventing me from committing suicide. I had no plans of ending my life, but I understood it was procedure.

Shortly thereafter, I was interviewed by the officer in charge of the investigation.
"Do you understand the charges against you?" he asked.
"Yes," I answered.
I was still exhausted and had no doubt that he would use that to try to obtain a confession. In the civilian world, a confession was nearly worthless, as it could easily be challenged and in many cases

thrown out. And even though you were given the same rights in the military, a signed confession could very well be your undoing.

"Are you aware of what the consequences could be?" he asked.

Apparently, this was his idea of a scare tactic. Of course, I knew. I could spend the next twenty years of my life in prison if I was lucky, and I was willing to accept that considering the number of lives I'd saved. But I was still exhausted, too exhausted to answer a lot of questions.

"Look," I said. "I just want to sleep, alright? Can't we do this later, sir?"

"Private," he began.

His voice was stern and impatient.

"You're due to be shipped back to the States for trial in two days. Even without your case, I have a mountain of paperwork to do. So, let's just get on with it, okay?"

I decided that if I was going to start answering questions, I needed to be awake and alert.

"Alright," I began. "I'm not answering any more questions without an attorney."

The officer scribbled a note in the file that he'd compiled for my case.

"Fine," he replied. "We'll get you a lawyer."

He glanced up at the guard and shook his head in frustration.

"Alright, get him out of here."

The guard escorted me to a holding cell where we were joined by two more as the door to my new quarters was opened.

After stepping inside, my handcuffs were removed, and I was finally allowed to sleep. I awoke later that afternoon to the sight of a meal tray that had been slid under the door. I ate so quickly that I hadn't given myself time to see what was on the tray. Sliding the tray back under the door, I spent the next few minutes absorbing my surroundings. My cell couldn't have been more than eight feet by ten feet and by the looks of it, the walls were made of cinder block that had been painted a stark white. I had been sleeping on a cot that folded down from the wall, while across from me was a stainless steel sink situated beneath a recessed metal mirror. At the back wall was a stainless steel toilet. There was no window to the outside, just a heavy wooden door with a small barred window and a slot at the bottom, large enough for a meal tray. This was where I spent the next two days.

All my possessions had been inspected, inventoried, and packed up in preparation for shipment to my family. God, my parents. Back at Fort Benning, my mother had been nearly inconsolable when she realized where I'd be going, but her only child being in custody for what might turn out to be a capital crime would kill her. Then, there was my father. He always believed that you should stand by your principles, that your word was your bond and should be of more value than any signed document, but I wasn't so sure he'd understand this. He was usually a strong and somewhat stoic person who never seemed confused about the direction his life took at any given moment. I became afraid that his strength may not be enough to get them both through this and realized that, regardless of the outcome, what they were about to experience would most certainly be with them for the rest of their lives. First, they would get a letter from the Department of Defense. It would be a simple computer-generated form letter, bearing a DOD form number and probably sent by delivery confirmation. One of my parents would have to sign for it. The letter would inform them that I had been taken into custody pending formal charges and would also instruct them to contact the Judge Advocate General's office for information on where I'd be held once I arrived back in the States. It would not provide any details of my case.

Two days later, I stepped off a C130 cargo plane and led out in chains by four armed guards. I had spent the last forty-eight hours in silence as investigators continued their attempt to question me. Now, I found myself carefully walking to a waiting cargo truck at the Army's Regional Confinement Facility in Mannheim, Germany. Most military cases were handled on base through a department called 'Social Actions'. They dealt with a lot of minor offenses that usually didn't go to courts-martial but still resulted in confinement as well as some form of counseling. Because of the nature of my case, I would be sent to the States to face trial, and in less than a week, I would be escorted aboard a Navy destroyer where I spent five days in the ship's brig. I still refused to see my actions as a crime. I joined the Army not only to kill terrorists but to also protect the innocent from them. The problem in war was that it could be difficult to tell the good guys from the bad guys, and by this time, I was beginning to wonder which one I'd become. Perhaps we possess both; the principled and the monster; the saint and the sinner. Maybe this is what defines us as human. Maybe it's just a matter of achieving a balance between them. Or maybe, we're just born killers, living our lives with a subconscious agenda for personal survival. Yeah, I had a lot of time to think lately. Or, maybe it's all just bullshit. I would later discover that thinking can sometimes be a bad idea.

The ship dropped anchor in Norfolk and once again, I was escorted off in chains. The hardest part of this entire process was hearing the rattling sound they made. The links were made of thick welded steel that even Houdini had no chance of escaping from. Their sound dredged up all manner of dark images, and being forced to wear them could easily rob a person of both hope and humanity, bringing them down to the level of an animal. I spent a great deal of time-fighting against that particular transformation. If I lost my strength, I would lose myself and everything I was would be gone. I would not allow the shattering sound of the chains to break me. While in what I believed to be temporary confinement, I was notified that my case would be tried in Norfolk.

While in my first week there, I received a phone call from my parents. I would have rather carved my own cell out of solid stone with my fingernails than take that phone call. I was escorted to a row of booths where, in each, a phone had been installed. They were all supposed to be private lines, somewhere along the way, I had learned what a tapped phone line sounds like. As I put the receiver to my ear, I detected the telltale clicks created by the presence of a third pair of ears. I began shaking as I tried to find the right words. Sometimes a simple 'hello' just isn't the way to begin a conversation, especially when talking to your parents from within a military detention center.

"Hello, Clarence?"

It was my father. His response was a mixture of shock, deep concern, and disbelief.

"We got a letter saying that you'd been arrested," he said. "What's going on?"

I hadn't fully realized what was happening to me, but my next words would push me closer to that realization.

"Dad," I replied.

My voice became strained as I uttered the words with a trembling voice.

"I've been charged with murder."

The silent response was both surreal and painfully long as he tried to gather his thoughts without becoming emotional.

"Clarence," he said. "Have you been answering any questions? Have you signed anything?"

I told him that I had done neither.

"Good," he replied. "Don't say anything."

He didn't ask for an explanation, but instead, told me not to go into any details over the phone. He also told me that they would both be flying down to Norfolk, bringing with them a private defense attorney and that I was to refuse military counsel. My father didn't exactly have a tremendous amount of faith in the government and believed that my case might be jeopardized if I was represented by the same organization that was putting me on trial.

Chapter 22

Within only a few days, the facts of my arrest had reached the media and became a high-profile case. This meant that my parents' entire social circle would become aware of my circumstances. Knowing these people as I do, I was sure that they'd form their own opinions and judgments. After all, the jury of public opinion can often be far harsher than any court and, of course, the media would run it into the ground. By the end of the week, my parents had arrived at Norfolk with an attorney who specialized in military law from one of the top firms in Manhattan. A guard came to my cell to tell me I had visitors. This was not the way I wanted my parents to see me, dressed in an orange prison jumpsuit and hobbling out in chains. I stood up as the guard opened the door. His name was Allen. We had talked a bit over the last couple of days, and he quickly got the impression that I wasn't the kind of person who would give him a hard time. He instructed me to face the back wall as he entered the cell and as he walked up behind me, he spoke quietly.
"Your family's here," he said. "I'm not going to put the ankle chains on you this time, okay? I don't think you'd want your folks to see you like that."
I turned my head toward him slightly.

"You have no idea how much I appreciate this," I replied.
So instead of ankle chains, he wrapped a heavy leather belt around my waist and looped the handcuffs through a large 'D' ring in the front.
"This is the best I can do for you'," he said.
"Thanks, Allen," I said. "I owe you one."

He walked me down a hallway lined with private rooms and stopped at the third or fourth door from the end. I would rather have been killed horribly in battle than face my parents like this. Allen opened the door. Its hinges made a creaking sound that filled the hallway with an almost unearthly shrill. The room was lit by a single fluorescent ceiling light. A wooden table sat beneath it, bolted to the floor, with several chairs placed around it. I entered the room with several short steps, as had become my habit, given that my legs had grown accustomed to being shackled. Sitting directly across from the door, my mother suddenly brought her hands up, cupping them over her mouth. Her eyes welled up immediately as her expression fell into one of shock and emotional pain. My father, who always seemed to be in control over his emotions, sat looking at me with an expression that I can only describe as 'grave'. Allen closed the door behind me as I sat in the remaining chair. I had no idea where to begin and stared down at the

table for a moment while slightly shaking my head. My eyes filled with tears as I looked up at my parents. There are moments in life that exist beyond what any words can express. The moments of birth and death are certainly among them, but the agonizing depth of shame is, without a doubt, an experience that seems to lay beyond description, much less any words of apology.
"I'm sorry."
My voice choked as I quietly began sobbing. Unable to raise my hands, my head began drifting toward the table as my mother placed a hand on my shoulder in an attempt to comfort me. I had no more words. There was only despair that struck me with the suddenness of a tidal wave. My father reached over and put a hand on the back of my neck.
"Clarence," he said. "We're going to get through this, alright?"
I could only nod my head as I continued sobbing. The last thing I ever wanted to do was hurt my parents. Now, I had deeply scarred them and the pain they were being left with would never release them, and I had caused it.

My father continued to talk to me and eventually, I calmed down enough, so I was able to think straight.
"Clarence," he continued.

He motioned toward the man across from me.
"This is Randall Oliver. He's going to be representing you."
He stood up and leaned over the table, extending his hand.
"Just call me Randall, okay, Clarence?" he said.
I stood and put my hand out as far as the handcuffs would allow.
"Thanks," I replied. "I'm sorry you have to go so far out of your way."
He shook my hand firmly.
"It's not a problem, Clarence," he said. "I'm going to do everything I can for you."
I found both his words and confidence comforting. I just wasn't sure his best effort would be enough. My mother still had her hands over her face and had begun slightly rocking back and forth. Her formidable qualities had been replaced by the pain at seeing her only child brought down to such an agonizing existence. In her mind, things couldn't possibly get any worse, as she feared that my life would ebb away in an eternity behind bars.

Randall had obtained a copy of my case file and, opening the folder, he skimmed over the charges as well as the list of items and reports being held as evidence.

"They want to charge you with a war crime?" he said. "That's a bit extreme. We can have that thrown out for lack of evidence."
He continued reading the evidence list.
"Let's see," he said. "What else are they trying to get away with?"
He turned back to the list of charges.
"Murder one? I don't see how they can prove that."
"I don't understand," I said. "If you kill someone, isn't that murder?"
He looked up at me with a slight smile.
"Actually, murder is a legal term. Bringing someone to trial for murder requires proof of intent. They have to prove it was carried out according to some predetermined plan. Without witness statements, the only evidence they have is circumstantial at best. I'm going to file for a mental competency exam."
My eyes widened in disbelief.
"I'm not crazy!" I said.
"Clarence," my father said. "Just listen, okay?"
How do you respond to the words 'mental competency exam'? I found myself deeply threatened by these words. Wasn't it enough that my life had spun out of control? Would I now have to deal with the possibility that I had lost my mind as well?
"Clarence," Randall said. "That's not how it works. You have to be competent to stand trial. Now, it's

possible that we could plead not guilty by reason of insanity. They can't try you if your actions were the result of some kind of mental lapse. The problem is that it's almost impossible to prove."

"Alright," my father said. "What's the next step?"

The only person who seemed to know what was going on was Randall. The rest of us had become observers to a process we would never begin to understand.

"We can plead down to involuntary manslaughter and try to avoid a life sentence," Randall began. "I know that twenty years is a long time, but you're young enough that you'll be able to get your life back on track."

I couldn't believe what I was hearing; twenty years in prison? How would I survive that? I looked at my father, as though he might have some brilliant solution that would clear all of this up.

"Clarence," he said calmly. "You'll have your inheritance. You'll be able to start over."

I fell back in my chair with a deep sigh of resignation.

"So, if I'm going to prison anyway," I began. "What's the point?"

Randall looked up with sudden concern.

"Clarence," he said. "The military court system tends to be a lot harsher than civilian court. My job is to protect your rights and make sure that you get the lightest sentence possible. On paper, military law is very fair, but just like the government, damage control, and image seem to be their biggest priorities and I don't want to see you turned into a victim of the military's 'good ole boys club', alright?"

He closed the folder and slid it into a black leather bag. I had run out of words. The idea of spending the next twenty years of my life behind bars had effectively robbed me of my ability to understand it in the first place. I felt the floor tilt suddenly as the reality of my situation began to sink in.

My father stood up and called to me.

"Clarence?"

He put a hand on my shoulder in an attempt to steady me.

"Clarence, are you okay?"

"Yeah," I answered.

I was far from okay and felt as though I was witnessing the end of the world. Or, maybe, it was the end of my world.

"I'm fine."

Randall dug into his inside breast pocket and fished out a business card.

"If there's anything I can help you with, or if you just need to talk, call me," he said. "And reverse the charges, alright?"

I reached out and took the card from his fingers and stared at it for a few moments. It seemed odd

that, at any point in my life, I would be in need of a criminal defense attorney. It just didn't seem real.
"Okay," I answered quietly.
I knew I wasn't a murderer, but would the military try to cover up what really happened in that settlement? Would they try to turn me into someone who had simply snapped? I suppose that many people crack under the stress of war, but most of them don't start shooting people in the head just because their principles had been violated.

My father looked at him with a puzzled expression.
"So, that's it?" he asked.
"For now," Randall answered. "His pre-trial hearing has to be scheduled. The important thing is to keep this from going to trial. So, we have to come up with a plan for a plea agreement. The Army isn't going to want to spend a lot of time on a lengthy trial, especially when they don't have a witness."
My father nodded his head as I sat at the table, my mind still spinning from the reality that continued to tighten its grip on me.
"So, what's the next step?" my father asked.
"Well," Randall began. "I have to file some paperwork, and I'll have to get access to the evidence. It's going to take at least a couple of

weeks to prepare for pre-trial, but I can do all of that from my office."
My father stood up and shook his hand.
"Thanks for doing this, Randall."
"Hey, no problem," Randall replied. "I'll get back to you in a couple of weeks."
He turned to me, speaking in a reassuring tone. "Clarence, try not to worry, alright? And don't talk about your case with anyone, got it?"

The door creaked again as he left. My father was very confident of Randall's legal skills and described him as someone who could present any argument as though it was the word of God. The door closed behind him, leaving the room filled with an ear-shattering silence. I was so tired. The last ten minutes left me physically and emotionally exhausted, and all I wanted was to sleep. Maybe I would wake up at home and realize that this was all just a bad dream. I would get up, go to class, and try to impress Gloria at the next dinner party. But, the feeling of cold steel against my wrists pulled me back from the doorway of denial. My mother's face had drawn itself down into an empty, lost expression. In truth, I'd never seen her look so old. My father was still at a loss for words, and his expression had shifted from one of deep concern to one mixed with a degree of hopelessness. My mother reached out and grasped my hand. Her grip was gentle and warm, but there was something else I hadn't noticed before. Her skin had become thin and fragile, leading me to think that she might be getting old before her time. I did not doubt that my situation was doing neither of them any good, and I started to believe that I had failed my parents. There would never be a chance to make this right, to turn back the clock and start over, to make a different decision. While grasping my hand, she glanced down at the handcuffs.

"Can't they take these things off for a little while?" she asked.

My father looked at her with deep concern. He didn't like to see her in pain and knew what my incarceration might do to her.

"No, mom," I answered. "They can't take them off."

She began weeping again. She couldn't stand seeing her only child chained up like an animal, and I wasn't about to tell her that my ankles were normally shackled as well. I held her hand as she continued crying.

"Mom," I said weakly. "Everything's going to work out, alright?"

She sat, looking down at my restrained hands while hopelessly shaking her head. None of us could be certain of the outcome of my case, but it was certain that I was not going to simply walk away. Every act carries consequences, but not knowing what those consequences are is the hardest part of going through the criminal justice system, and waiting for those consequences can be as brutal as it is lengthy. But, I had plenty of time to wait.

As I tried unsuccessfully to comfort my mother during what was certainly the most painful moment of her life, my father interrupted with a gentle voice.
"Clarence," he said. "I should your mother back to the hotel. I think a little rest would do her some good."
She slowly began to stand as I did my best to help her up. But as distraught as she was, she refused to leave and clutched my arm with both hands.
"Mom," I said. "You have to let go, okay?"
I looked up at my father helplessly, unable to release her grip. Leaving as I remained in custody violated her deepest maternal instincts, and my father was forced to gently pull her away as she continued sobbing. "We'll be back tomorrow," he said.
He opened the door and slowly walked her out and down the hallway. I stepped through the doorway to watch them leave, only to be stopped by the guard. As they continued walking, I could hear my father trying to calm her.

"Randall knows exactly what he's doing. He's the best there is."

The only thing I could do was watch. There wasn't anything that anyone could say to console her. If you think that being behind bars is hard, let me tell you, it's a lot harder for those on the outside - the people who care.

I slept for the rest of the day as well as that entire night. Not that I was that tired, I just needed to escape. As important as sleep is, being asleep for so many hours a day does not afford one any measure of existence, and blotting out the world, regardless of how troubling it is, allows only for the symbolic reflection of dreams, the hazy mirror of the tragic reality that had become my life. But, dreams do not bring amnesia from intolerable circumstances. They hold us captive in the theater of our minds, playing out our wrongdoings and misguided deeds, turning our brains into a far more permanent prison, one that is truly inescapable. Rarely are things as bad as they seem. At other times, however, they can be unimaginably worse. It was this I was trying to hide from.

My parents arrived the next day. Randall had flown back to New York to begin working on my case. My mother was a bit more collected this time, but she had not yet accepted the reality of my

situation. I was, again, escorted to one of the private rooms where my parents were already waiting. Allen had, once more, spared me the humiliation of shackled ankles. All the rooms seemed to be the same; one ceiling light, one table, bolted to the floor, and three or four wooden chairs. There were no windows and the walls were light beige. I sat down to, again, face my parents. I turned to my mother with a concerned expression. "Mom, are you okay?" I asked.
What a stupid question. She wasn't okay, and chances were pretty good that she would never recover from my probable imprisonment. By this time, it was safe to say that we all had a good idea about how this would end.

There wasn't much in the way of conversation. We just sat there saying nothing.
"I've been doing some thinking about this," my father said. "If there were no witnesses, how could they prove that anything actually happened?"
There's a common saying in the military: If it didn't get documented, it never happened. I wondered if that might happen here. Maybe Randall could find a loophole or a precedent, something that might cast enough doubt on the military's case to warrant an acquittal. At this point, walking away on a technicality would be

just fine with me. I looked up at my father curiously.

"That's true," I replied. "What do you think they'll do?"

My father gave it a few moments' thought.

"I don't know, Clarence," he answered. "I don't know a lot about the legal system."

I had a friend in college who was studying pre-law. He once told me that trial law and the real world rarely have anything in common and that anything can be made to seem true. An argument can be complete bullshit and yet be flawlessly logical. He said that this was called 'good lawyering'.

My mother raised her head and looked at me through reddened, tired eyes.

"Clarence," she began. "What happened over there?"

Her words were quiet and conveyed a continued degree of exhaustion. My father's eyes suddenly shifted to her.

"Katheryn," he said cautiously. "We talked about this, right?"

Her quiet tone suddenly turned to a piercing, yet muffled anger.

"Don't patronize me, Donald," she said. "I have the right to know what happened!"

She was never one to raise her voice, but the look in her eyes was as frightening as it was demanding.

The thought then occurred to me that my mother may have reached an emotional tipping point. It would be tragic to see someone as strong and willful as my mother suddenly fall over the edge. My father, trying to contain his frustration, said, "Randall told us not to talk about it - especially here. If someone hears that conversation, it could jeopardize his case."
My mother wasn't happy to hear this, but she knew he was right.
"Katheryn, we could have the upper hand here. We have to be careful and do exactly what Randall says, okay?"

My mother looked away toward an empty corner in silent protest. I understood how invested she was, but there are some things even a mother has no right to do. Interfering with her son's criminal case is definitely one of them. And in a military detention center, one never knows who else might be listening. My father looked back at me while trying to maintain his composure.
"Is there anything we can send you?" he asked.
"Yes," I began. "Did the Army send my things back to you?"
"Yes," he answered. "We got them about four or five days ago. Was there something specific you wanted?"

The Army had sent everything back to the States except my dress uniform. I would have to wear that when I appeared in court.

"Can you send the books back to me?"

"Sure," my father answered. "Which ones?"

I wasn't so much interested in reading all of them, but the note from Gloria was stuck between the pages of one of them, and I couldn't remember which.

"All of them," I answered.

"Sure," he said. "Will they let you have books?"

Up to this point, all they allowed me to have was a few magazines, but with good behavior comes rewards and allowances. I could now read anything I wanted. However, all incoming mail was x-rayed for the presence of 'restricted items'. Not that I was expecting to get a file disguised as a book, but the rules are in place for a reason.

"Yeah," I answered. "I can read whatever I want now."

I tried to stretch things out by asking a few trivial questions, anything to get them to stay, but the room had grown quiet to the point of being painful. We spent most of the time we were given glancing down at the table. My father, at some point, looked up at me and said that Gloria had been asking about me. This was before I had been taken into custody.

"Please, Dad," I begged. "Please don't tell her about this."

"Well, what should we tell her?" he asked.

I hadn't thought that Gloria might start asking questions, given that I really didn't know what her feelings were.

"Tell her that what I'm doing is classified," I answered.

Yes, what I had been doing was largely classified. I just wasn't doing it anymore.

"Tell her I'm fine. I don't want her to know what's going on."

Gloria wouldn't be asking about me if she wasn't thinking of me, to some degree. I guess it was nice to know that, but she would eventually find out that I was likely on my way to prison. I had no idea if she should know now, or find out on her own. If the media ran my case into the ground -- and I was certain they would -- it would be all over the internet and was probably already being picked up by news stations. It wouldn't be right to let her find out that way. I just didn't know how to tell her.

Time dragged on as my father glanced at his watch, then over at my mother, who looked back at him with tired eyes.

"Clarence," he began. "We have a plane to catch in the morning, so we should probably go."

I swallowed hard and tried to hold back my emotions, but my eyes gave me away as they welled up, sending tears down my face. I just wanted all of it to go away.

A philosopher once asked, 'Are we the dreamer of our dreams, or merely the dream of another?' I don't remember who said it, but I was beginning to question my sanity. The only thing that seemed to anchor me to the real world was books. But, sometimes that wasn't enough, and occasionally, I'd feel my thoughts become cloudy. Maybe my mind was simply looking for a dark corner to hide in, far from the cell I was forced to occupy. Now, just as the day before, my parents left in a state of emotional ruin. My father looked back as though he would never see me again. My mother was, once again, beyond consoling. They promised to write often, although I was certain they would be at a loss for words. After all, what does one say to someone who's spending time behind bars? The words, 'Hope you're doing well' seems ridiculous under the circumstances, but they tried, nonetheless, to keep their words light and brief.

During the following week, I contacted Randall by phone, asking him to send me a copy of everything connected with my case. Not that I was planning on representing myself, but my mind needed something to do other than reading books, and I thought that being a bit involved might help to keep me grounded to reality. Up to this point, everything taking place, legally speaking, was being done by phone, but it wasn't long before my arraignment date arrived. I stood next to Randall in my dress uniform as my case was called by docket number. I was not aware of it previously, but in spite of having a private attorney, courts-martial proceedings required that I have a military defense team assigned to my case. However, Randall was the one who made the decisions. I was not to say a single word or express any emotions. My parents had also arrived and sat directly behind me as the charges were read. A plea agreement was expected, and Randall asked the murder charge be thrown out in exchange for voluntary manslaughter. The military prosecutor would have nothing to do with it and wanted me tried for murder on the grounds that the gunshot wounds that killed the two marines resembled an execution. It was, however, discovered that the round found in the sergeant's body had come from one of the marine's sidearm. I guess I wasn't being blamed for everything. A trial date was set, and I would be brought before courts-martial and charged with first-degree murder, manslaughter, conspiracy to commit murder as well as several assault charges. Randall contained his reaction until we could meet privately. I was terrified.

We sat across from each other in a private room back at the detention center. My parents sat listening intently.
"I don't know what they think they're doing," Randall said. "Clarence, they can't prove any of this."
He sat studying my case file.
"The best they can hope to do is manslaughter."
"What does that mean?" my father asked.
"Manslaughter means that there isn't the intent to kill,"
Randall answered.
"I'm going to file another petition for evidence. There's something about this that doesn't make sense. Realistically, based on the evidence, you should be released."
Randall was beginning to wonder if the prosecution was withholding critical evidence, and planned to petition directly to the judge.
"I'll bet they're holding something back," he continued. "The prosecution knows that we can only build our case on the evidence we have. You'd think they'd know better."
"I don't understand," I said.
Randall paused and looked up at me from the pages of my file.

"Okay, let's say that they're holding back evidence," he replied. "They could bring it up at the last moment and use it to manipulate the jury into a guilty verdict. Now, we can't call evidence into question if we don't have access to it and if they present it without giving us a chance to examine it first, then we can move for a mistrial. That would mean a retrial, and the military doesn't like to have its time wasted."

My parents tried hard to understand, but none of us knew anything about the legal system, much less trial law.

"So why would they do that?" my father asked.

Randall let out a deep sigh as he considered the possibilities.

"Maybe they just want a conviction. Reputations are built on success and any lawyer wants to have a good track record. Or, maybe it's political. Our fearless leader just got us into a war. They may be trying to make an example of you to keep everybody in check, as a means of control. The military overseas has internet access too, and they're going to read about this. Who knows? Maybe the military wants to use this case as a warning, to scare people into following the rules. All they need is a guilty verdict and 'murder' is a very strong word."

"What do his military lawyers think of this idea?" my father asked.

"Well," Randall answered. "I'm in charge of his defense team, so I have to confer with them. But, I'm going to handle the petition for evidence myself. They won't like being kept in the dark about this, but I don't want to end up doing damage control because one of them might not be able to keep their mouth shut. I guess I just don't trust these guys."

Later that day, Randall met in chambers with the judge as well as the lead prosecutor. His plan was to appeal directly to the judge, forcing a confrontation with the prosecution in order to prompt them to share any evidence they may be withholding. His instincts were right on target. The prosecution had been holding back evidence they planned on presenting to the jury. What they had could have changed the entire direction of my case and each member of the prosecution team received a documented reprimand for attempting to subvert justice. The judge was furious and warned them of the consequences of a mistrial. Randall was able to secure a photograph taken at the settlement shortly after I had been taken into custody. A forty-five caliber round had also been recovered from the skull of one of the dead marines. The rifling marks on the round matched the barrel of my sidearm. The photograph showed a row of Afghani settlers lying dead along the back wall of the stone building. It was exactly as I remembered it. One of the marines lay stretched out on his back, a stream of blood running away from his head and across the sand. The infant, its skin having turned a dingy yellow, lay half-clothed with its eyes staring lifelessly at a cloudless blue sky. In the background were a few survivors cowering against the wall, their faces etched with terror and grief. I only saw the photograph at a glance during my meeting with Randall. It's amazing how much detail you can see in such a brief period of time. But, it still wasn't enough for a murder charge. There was no escaping a conviction, but what Randall wanted was a conviction on the less serious charge of involuntary manslaughter and redesigned my defense, accounting for this new evidence. A trial date was set. All I had to do was wait. My parents would undoubtedly be there for moral support, but in the end, it would be between Randall and the jury. He would have to convince them that I had no plans to kill anyone.

Chapter 23

Weeks went by as I waited in my cell. I tried to keep myself distracted by reading. My parents sent me the books I had asked for and while inspecting them, I found Gloria's note still stuck between the pages of the book on Buddhism. For a moment, I wondered what she might think of my actions. Would she understand that I was only trying to do what I thought was right, or would she react with disgust? I didn't know her well enough to assume one or the other but holding the note brought back a flood of memories from the night when our souls mingled beneath waves of passion and sweat. I was trying to put Gloria behind me, but I still wanted the note. Maybe some part of me refused to let go - probably the same part that refused to accept my circumstances as reality. I knew I'd never see her again, but at least one of us would be able to move on. She would, no doubt, establish a career as an attorney, find someone, get married, have a family, and as the saying goes, live happily ever after. I honestly hoped that, given enough time, she would forget about me. There was no sense in both of us being miserable, but I kept the note anyway as a trap door of escape, into a life I should have been living. It was the only thing that connected me to my sanity.

Chapter 24

Randall arrived the day before my trial and again, we met privately with my parents as he told me what to expect. He also advised my parents not to become emotional, as it could send the jury the wrong message. I tried hard to focus on what he was saying, but I was at the point where emotional exhaustion had become a daily occurrence. In short, I felt like shit. One of the last things Randall said was, "Just let me do the talking".
Okay, I can do that.
The next day, I went through my usual morning routine. I wasn't allowed to use an iron for my uniform and I clearly understood why. After all, who in their right mind would give any prisoner an iron? My uniform was brought out of storage, laundered, pressed, and given to me by one of the guards. After changing, I checked myself in the mirror. The only thing I saw that resembled a soldier was the uniform, but not the person in it. Not too long ago, the uniform was a large part of who I was - a soldier. I was proud to be a soldier, to be part of something greater than myself. At least, I thought I was a soldier. I sat back down on the cot and waited, trying not to think too much about what was happening, but it wasn't working very well. I was about to go to trial for murder and

in spite of Randall's confidence, I knew that my fate ultimately lay with the jury. I don't really know how long I sat there. It seems that the passing of time changes dramatically when you're behind bars. I don't know why, but I found myself thinking about Steve. I started to feel almost envious of him. He didn't have to go through this; he wasn't facing twenty years in a military prison. At this point, I would have traded places with him in a moment. You know how bad things are when you become jealous of someone just because they're dead. No, I wasn't thinking about doing anything stupid. I just wanted a calm, predictable life. Unfortunately, life doesn't come with an undo button. We simply practice it as we live it. It really doesn't seem fair that to develop good judgment, we must first have poor judgment and the results of that can be irreversibly life-altering -- sometimes fatal. But, what happened to Steve was not his doing. Sometimes, shit just happens. My situation, on the other hand, was of my own making and perhaps, the result of a string of bad decisions.

I was suddenly jolted back from my moment of reflection by the sound of the cell door opening. Standing next to the guard was Randall. He was dressed in a three-piece business and carrying his black leather bag.

"Ready to go, Clarence?" he asked.
I stood up and walked towards him.
"No, not really," I answered.
He looked at me with sympathetic concern and put a hand on my shoulder.
"C'mon," he said.
On our way to the courtroom, he reminded me about what I should and shouldn't do.
"Alright Clarence, whatever happens, you don't say a word, got it? I am here to protect your rights, but if you start talking or display any lack of emotional self-control, my job becomes that much more difficult, understand?"
I didn't know what else to say, in court or not as I was still surrounded by a fog of emotional exhaustion.
"Clarence," he continued.
His voice was still firm as he reiterated his instructions.
"I need you to understand how critical it is for your case that you follow my instructions to the letter. You will not say a word, and you will not, under any circumstances, testify on your behalf. The prosecution can cross-examine you and trust me, if they get the chance, they will bury you. Do you understand, Clarence?"
The forcefulness of his words acted as a sharp slap that brought me into complete focus.
"Yes," I answered. "Not one word."

"That's what I wanted to hear," he replied. "And don't fall asleep. That can be just as bad, if not worse, and it's the easiest way to piss off a judge." His approach was organized, strong, and confident. I was truly impressed and quickly came to the belief that if anyone could keep me from a life sentence, it was Randall.

We were escorted by armed guard into the lobby of the Norfolk legal building. My handcuffs were removed just before entering the courtroom.
"One more thing," Randall began. "Your parents will be sitting right behind you. Now, I've already spoken to them. During the trial, you will not speak to each other. We don't need a display of emotion, okay? So, face forward and don't go looking around the room, alright?"
We walked through the double doors and down the center aisle. The prosecution team sat behind a table on the right next to the juror's box. We sat at the table on the left with two military defense attorneys who had been briefed by Randall. They were only there to assist Randall and would not be arguing my case. It wasn't long before the judge entered the room. Everyone stood as the courtroom was called to order.

The jury was composed of twelve officers from each of the four branches. It was my understanding that to reach a verdict, the jury had to vote unanimously and by secret, written ballot. In the military, there is no such thing as a hung jury. The judge took his seat behind the bench and my case was presented as The United States v Private Clarence Taylor. I won't pretend to know how the legal system works and to be honest, much of the trial seemed to be nothing more legalese gibberish. However, the prosecution argued in favor of murder, based on the match between the sidearm I was carrying and the rifling marks on the recovered round. They also pointed out that the shot had been fired at close range and appeared to have been carried out as an execution. But, there were certain elements missing from their argument, and Randall was quick to expose them. In my defense, he argued that the idea of motive had never been brought up, and they were still unable to demonstrate intent.

He also brought up an interesting idea that, in a war zone, everyone possesses the means and opportunity to kill. These are necessary elements of war. We go to war with the means to kill the enemy, as well as the will to create the opportunity to do so. Means and opportunity can take on a different meaning for murder in, say, Los Angeles, but in these circumstances, the prosecution couldn't possibly prove murder without intent. The results of my psychiatric exam were presented, and The prosecution outlined everything, trying to prove that I had been on a personal mission to save innocent lives at the expense of American troops. Randall stepped in, appealing to the judge that this was nothing more than speculation, and asked that their remarks pertaining to my psych test be stricken from the record. The judge refused on the basis that it was Randall who had requested the examination and, as evidence, could not be excluded. Instead, the judge demanded that the prosecution prove intent or drop the murder charge. It didn't take long for their lead attorney to withdraw the charge and, in doing so, avoid a formal reprimand. But at the same time, it became possible that the credibility of their case could have been damaged. I felt very relieved that I would not be convicted of murder.

They still wanted to use the results of my psych test against me and after momentarily regrouping, the prosecution decided to pursue the charge of involuntary manslaughter. The jury had been convinced that I had been holding my sidearm when the shot was fired and that the recovered round came from that weapon. The only issue to be argued was how it happened. But, if the prosecution wanted to use the psych results, so would Randall, and he argued that being an educated, principled individual who enlisted right after nine eleven, I was morally incapable of voluntarily committing the crime I had been charged with. That being said, the location of the gunshot wound had to have been a chance event and the result of an accident or misfire. The prosecution was quick to point out the flaw in Randall's argument and presented the report that had been filed by the sergeant who had taken me into custody. The report stated that I had been found on my knees crying over the body of a dead infant. They argued that it was my principles that, under those circumstances, pushed me into a heightened state of emotion, causing me to act out of rage. Randall argued that this was purely speculation, but when the jury was reminded about my degree in philosophy, a few of them suddenly became noticeably more attentive. Seeing this, the prosecution offered what they believed to be a probable timeline of events leading up to the gunshot. It all came down to personal ethics.

After closing arguments were made, the jury was released for deliberation. All we could do was wait. It was just a matter of what the jury would find me guilty of. Randall said it could go either way. There was no clear evidence, and both arguments were largely hypothetical. It seemed that whatever I would be convicted of depended almost entirely on who was best able to manipulate the jury, but I guess that's what the courtroom comes down to. It's not a matter of who's right, but who's more right. Morality, it seems, doesn't even come into the picture and the only thing that's important is protecting the interests of the client. Is that justice? Probably not, but it's the only thing we've got.

Chapter 25

I was escorted back to the detention center, where we were shown to a private room. I had been handcuffed just before leaving the courtroom. The only times they came off were when I was in my cell or in court. The four of us sat at the table as the agonizing wait began, and there was no way of knowing how long the jury would be in deliberation. Randall quietly reviewed my case file as my parents sat staring at the table. The only other thing Randall would do was to prepare an argument for my sentencing trial. Everyone was exhausted as time crawled to a near standstill.
"How long should this take?" my father asked. Randall shook his head slightly.
"It could take an hour; it could a day," Randall answered. "But, we want them to take their time. The jury has to vote unanimously, and the longer they take, the more uncertain they're going to be."
"What if they can't decide?" I asked.
"If they can't make up their minds, then a mistrial is declared, and we start over again," he answered.
I immediately decided that I could not go through another trial, and I certainly didn't want my parents going through it again. I just wanted it over. I would have been glad to do the twenty years, as long as it meant that I wouldn't have to go through

this again. A little more than two hours went by when there was a knock at the door. Our apprehension was immediate as Randall got up and walked the short distance to it. Upon doing so, he was met by two armed guards, who informed us the jury had finished its deliberations and that court was reconvening.

Ten minutes later, we were once again standing while the judge took his seat at the bench. The jury soon followed, taking their seats right after the judge gaveled the court to order. According to procedure, one of the jury members had been assigned as foreman. This was the only person who could deliver the words that would mold my fate. The judge silently requested a handwritten note from the foreman. Upon receiving it, he skimmed its contents and handed it back. The courtroom grew silent as he called to the foreman to read aloud the jury's decision. The charges of war crimes and murder had been previously thrown out. Now, without a shred of emotion, the foreman announced that they had found me guilty of involuntary manslaughter. My parents had been sitting right behind me as my mother began weeping loudly. My mind started spinning with shock and denial as the voices around me began to sound muffled and distant.

Knowing the charges and hearing the words are two completely different experiences. Now, they were set in stone. My life would continue as a tangled mass of tragic, personal defeat. Sitting next to Randall, I could feel my soul transform into a cancer as I realized that the next twenty years of my life had been forfeited by only a few minutes of uncontrolled rage. Death would certainly be easier. Before my case was closed, the judge announced the date of my sentencing trial. In civilian court, there would be a hearing and the sentence would be handed down by a judge. A defense attorney would ask for leniency, but the final word would rest with the judge. In military court, sentencing was decided upon by a jury through a written, secret ballot. I would wait another three and a half weeks to receive my sentence.

Chapter 26

Again, I tried to busy myself with reading but at some point, I had lost my interest in anything that had to do with war or military philosophy. Instead, I immersed myself in history and ancient religions, finding both equally fascinating. But, this would not provide a complete escape, and the real world had begun catching up to me through the surreal passion play of my dreams. Everything came back to me, colliding into a handful of immeasurable moments where images and emotions became fused. I soon realized that as one may continue to run from their mistakes, the faster one is pursued by them, and no one can run forever. I would often find myself sitting on the edge of my cot at night, my skin soaked with sweat, as images and sounds from that small settlement ran around in my head like a caged animal. The smell of the morning desert; the sound of gunfire and the screaming of an infant who, by now, lay long dead in the hot sand, its earthly form likely consumed by nature. I faced twenty years behind bars, but a lifetime in a prison of my own making. Even if I managed to survive my sentence and start my life over, my actions would always be there, staring me down like a wild dog. My dreams would be my ultimate undoing. I would be pushed over the edge of my sanity by something I could not control and if I couldn't trust sleep to give me even a temporary peace, I would certainly slip into madness.

I saw my upcoming sentencing trial as nothing more than a formality, thinking that it would be such a relief to get this entire matter over. Having gone through this, I can safely say that the process of being tried in criminal court is as frightening as it is stressful; perhaps more so than being locked in a cell for twenty-three hours a day. You might lose your mind behind bars, but at least your day would be predictable and given the length of time I would likely be incarcerated for, maybe I could start doing a bit of writing. If I got to the point where I could no longer handle the real world, then perhaps I could create my own through pen and paper.

The day of my sentencing trial arrived, and I was, once again, joined by Randall and my parents. We went to the same courtroom, sat at the same table, in the same chairs. Just as before, my parents sat directly behind me. Everyone stood as the judge entered. On the surface, the only thing that was different was the judge, and it occurred to me that in order to maintain the objectivity of the court, a different judge should be appointed. The jury walked in and took their seats as well. One might think that at this point, I would be terrified, but knowing what to expect, I was actually pretty calm. My parents, on the other hand, were nowhere near calm. For them, this was the moment of truth.

The prosecution reviewed my case to the jury and asked them to consider the harshest possible punishment based on the premise, as had been determined during the trial, that I'd chosen to allow myself to lose control. I'm still not sure how that works. How does someone 'choose' to lose control? The prosecution also asked the jury to consider the death penalty. The death penalty!? I wasn't sure that I actually heard the words, but it didn't take long for them to sink in. I suddenly turned to Randall in a state of panic.
"Death penalty?!" I yelled.
The judge struck his gavel and ordered me to remain silent.
"You didn't tell me they could do that!"
The judge struck his gavel repeatedly.
"Counsel, control your client!" he yelled.
Randall turned and quietly tried to calm me.
"Clarence," he said. "Sit down."
I brought my voice down, but I still wanted an explanation.
"Clarence, listen to me. I'm not going to let that happen, okay? Now, sit down."

He turned towards the judge as I slowly lowered myself back onto the chair. To say that I was in shock would be an enormous understatement. In every sense, I was at a profound loss of what to think or how to feel about the request that had just been made to the jury. Would they really do that? My parents were shocked into complete silence.

"My apologies, your Honor," Randall said. "This will not happen again."

The judge nodded and allowed the prosecution to continue. After they finished their argument, Randall stood and requested a five-minute break. The judge granted it and, pulling me off to one corner of the courtroom, Randall quietly gave me an explanation.

"Look, Clarence," he began. "I didn't tell you about this because I wanted you to stay calm."

"Did you tell my parents?" I asked.

"No," he answered. "I couldn't afford to have anyone get emotional. Clarence, I'm on your side, remember?"

There was no time for lengthy conversation and I took my seat having all but given up. Later, he told me that during a time of war, as declared by the president, the death penalty can be imposed for any capital crime, and it was all up to the jury. Twelve men and women would decide whether I lived or died.

Now, it was up to Randall to convince the jury that I did not deserve to die. He argued that considering my education, I could still be of service and strongly suggested that I could counsel other inmates, assist with social programs, and help teach classes, that ending my life would be a waste of promising potential. As far as my crime was concerned, he presented me as someone who held great respect for life and that I had joined the Army after witnessing the events of nine eleven. "All Private Taylor wanted was to do the right thing," he said.

He pointed out that my actions were, indeed, an act of passion, but we participate in war to kill as well as to defend, and sometimes, the line between killing and defending becomes blurred by the necessity to accomplish both, not realizing that we can't always have it both ways and that is often why civilians get killed in war because as human beings, we are sometimes incapable of separating those two ideas. If we were able to, war would either become a lot more complicated or would become obsolete altogether. Yes, we have the rules set down by the Geneva Convention, but rules are not an adequate substitute for clear, ethical judgment, and he argued that I had not willfully crossed the line from defending into killing, but had become trapped between the two. I had stumbled into a place that could not be resolved through reasoning or the rules; a place where there was no moral high ground. Randall presented my actions as an unconscious utilitarianism, that the good of the many outweighs the good of the few. He argued that I had acted on the instinct to preserve as many lives as possible and that sometimes doing the right thing means having to make compromises. He further stated that making these compromises, whether consciously or not, in no way acts to rob life of its dignity, but it is the compromise that represents the price of doing the right thing. Furthermore, he continued that I should not be put to death for the lives that were lost - as regrettable as it was - but that my life should be spared for those who survived because of my actions. Randall wanted the jury's decision to be as difficult as possible. He felt that if he could force them out of the single-mindedness that seemed so typical of the military, he might be able to prompt their humanity. He wanted them to decide with their hearts, not their uniforms.

The sentencing trial seemed to end as quickly as it started as the jury was excused for deliberations. We were escorted back to the detention center and, once again, sat around a table in a small private room, waiting. Randall explained the approach he used with the jury, saying that they needed a unanimous vote in favor of the death penalty and the more difficult it was for them to agree, the more likely it would be that they would vote for imprisonment. If they could be forced to think with their hearts, then they might want to do the right thing as well. Or, at least, be prompted to make a safe decision, one they would not question later.

The wait was agonizing, and my parents were without words as they sat with me in the detention center. They had stuck by me through the entire process and the stress it created etched itself on their faces. My mother was exhausted to the point of appearing gaunt. Her eyes had developed dark circles and her face appeared to hang loosely as she continued to be consumed by events she had no control over. My father appeared to be lost, not in thought, but simply lost. How does one begin a conversation, any conversation, with two people who already seemed to be grieving with the knowledge that their only child could be taken away from them right before their eyes? Randall was no longer pouring over my case file, and I wondered if he had given up, or maybe there was simply nothing more to be done.
"So, this is it, huh?" I asked.
"Not necessarily," Randall answered. "There is an appeals process. If the jury decides on the death penalty, the appeals process is automatic, and I'll be handling that too."

My father looked up at him with a curious expression.
"So, who actually has the final say in all of this?" he asked.
Randall hesitated a moment.
"The death warrant is signed by the President," Randall replied. "That makes it final."
"Are you kidding me?!" I yelled. "The President!? Our President!?"
I was stunned to realize that the person who occupied the Oval Office could, essentially, end my life with nothing more than the stroke of a pen and asked myself if certain politicians might use the President's decision to make a political statement, or if they might remain silent so as not to risk their credibility. My conviction was the result of what I can only describe as misguided personal ethics, but would my life end as a result of party politics? There was no clear answer to this question, and trying to explain how Washington thinks seems to be similar to the idea of navigating by the stars during a hurricane. The only thing one can agree on is that both are ruled by chaos. We had been notified that the jury had been sequestered for the night. Randall said this was a good sign in that difficult cases seem to take more time. As there was no point in continuing to wait, my parents and Randall left for their respective

hotel rooms and would return the next morning. A guard escorted me back to my cell.

Sleep proved elusive that night, as the anxiety of the next day's events hovered over me like a ravenous vulture. My mind had been scrambled by a decision that I could not participate in. Issues of life and death are usually seen as distant and academic unless they're your issues and as far as issues go, I would gladly have traded with anyone. As the night wore on, I found that I became increasingly unable to maintain any mental clarity. My mind became a jumbled mass of disconnected thoughts crawling around in my head like a nest of spiders. Morning found me curled up on my cot, still awake, still waiting. Prison or death. Did it matter anymore? As far as beliefs are concerned, I had many questions and even more doubts. I was never one to put stock in the idea of faith. I guess I had come to a place where I was too afraid to live as an inmate and too scared to die by the hand of the organization I was once so proud to serve.

My parents arrived by mid-morning, with Randall following soon after. By this time, I'd finished my morning routine and sat in my cell waiting to be escorted to yet another private room. My mother's face was pale and deeply unsettled, as my father sat across the table looking at her with grave concern. She had literally become sick with worry and grief, and I was suddenly struck with the realization that what I had done could be her undoing. I sat down at the table as Randall was paging through the transcripts from the trial. Except for the appeals process, there was nothing left for him to do. I don't know how long we were there, but at some point, there came a quiet knock at the door. We all looked up at each other, then toward the door, as an officer entered and informed us that court was convening. The jury had reached a decision.

Once again, we stood as the judge walked in and sat behind the bench. Once again, he gaveled the court to order. The room seemed to carry an odd stillness. Maybe it wasn't the room, but the terror I felt of what the next few moments would bring. The judge called the jury in and, with expressionless faces, they took their seats in the juror's box. The judge, without uttering a word, held his hand out to the foreman, who stood and gave him a handwritten note. Reading the note, he turned towards me. Randall stood up and motioned for me to stand as well. I don't exactly remember getting to my feet, but I do recall the feeling of floating near the ceiling.
"Private Taylor," the judge began. "For the crime of involuntary manslaughter committed during a

declared time of war, this court sentences you to death by lethal injection. This sentence will be carried out on..."

It's funny how things sound just as you're losing consciousness. The overwhelming reality of my now imminent death hit me like a brick wall.

When I opened my eyes, I found myself lying on the courtroom floor looking up at the ceiling. A med tech sat at my side, shining a penlight into my eyes. My head spun as I tried to get to my feet, only to be assisted by Randall and an MP. My father sat with his head in his hands while my mother had begun trembling, as tears rolled down her face. Randall steadied me as I stood and continued to face the judge.

"Private?" the judge continued. "Do you understand the nature of your sentence?"

I looked at the judge through a mental haze of confusion and fear.

"Um, yes," I answered. "Yes, sir."

The words seemed to come out with an almost complete lack of thought and seemed to be simply a mechanical response to a simple question. Did I understand that I was going to die? Yes. No. I wasn't sure, to be honest. I mean, everyone dies, right? Some die sooner than others, and others live longer than some. Then there are the few who are told by medical science that they have 'x' amount of time to live. But normally, death is as uncertain as life, and no one is born with an expiration date - unless you're given one. For the record, the judge also needed to be certain that I was aware of when my sentence would be carried out. So, with his focus on me, he repeated the date. My life would come to an end in almost two months.

I really thought that I had dodged the bullet and that I'd spend the next twenty years locked up behind bars. One can do a lot of reading in twenty years' time, and probably write a few books as well. However, I'm not sure what's worse, twenty years rotting away in a military prison or slipping beneath the cold, still water of death. I don't even remember walking out of the courtroom and although Randall later told me I needed one person on each arm to help me stay on my feet. My mother needed help as well.

I regained my wits shortly after being poured into a chair at the detention center. My parents were in a private room where a med tech was examining my mother. I can't imagine what it must be like to outlive your only child. And right now, my mother was not capable of describing the experience. The guard gave me a glass of water. I drank all of it with the sudden realization that, in a few months, there would be no water. It's strange how you can come to an appreciation of even the simplest things, only as they're being taken away from you. And in that one fleeting moment, as the last few drops trickled down my throat, I decided that there wasn't anything better than the taste of water.

Chapter 27

In military law, if a death sentence is handed down, the appeals process is automatic. On the plus side, this means that one has a chance to avoid execution. The downside is that it lengthens the wait for something that's probably inevitable anyway. Randall made sure the military filed the paperwork, but this meant that my sentence would be pushed back until the death warrant was signed. Now, I question entered my mind. If I had a choice, would I prefer death or the torment of incarceration? I had no idea. Our instincts drive us to survive, but they also help us to avoid pain, physical or otherwise. It becomes a difficult choice, given that you're provided with one, to decide between two things that contradict what our instincts demand. If I had to make the decision myself, I'd be between a rock and a hard place. But, I wouldn't have to do that. Considering there was no other alternative, maybe it was better that someone else make the decision for me. Besides, and I know it sounds strange, but I had other matters to deal with. My mother was becoming increasingly ill, yet she insisted that she continue making the trip down to Norfolk. Her maternal instinct wouldn't have it any other way. Randall appeared from around the corner and motioned me to a room where my parents were waiting. The med techs had just finished treating my mother. They wanted to take her to the base hospital for observation, but she adamantly refused. I did, however, notice that she looked better. As it turned out, the med techs gave her a very light sedative, just enough to take the edge off.

After the med techs left, Randall explained that he'd be taking my case to the military's court of appeals. The goal was to have my sentence overturned in favor of imprisonment. If he succeeded, I would at least, have some small measure of a life, even if it was little more than an existence, it would still be enough that I could still contribute something, instead of simply gathering dust behind bars.
"I can't tell you not to worry," Randall said.
I quickly raised my head, reacting before I could think.
"No shit!" I said loudly.
I had run out of patience. I was tired of everything. I was terrified, lonely, and felt as though I was rapidly losing my mind. Worse than that, my mother was beginning to look like she belonged in a nursing home. So, yeah, I was angry.
"The fucking Army just sentenced me to death!" I continued. "My parents are going through hell; my mother had to be sedated, and you have the

fucking balls to tell us 'I can't tell you not to worry'?! Are you fucking kidding me?! You were supposed to keep this from happening in the first place! This is my fucking life, not yours!"

My parents looked at me in complete shock and Randall was speechless.

"When all of this is said and done, you'll go back to your office in New York and my parents will have to bury their only child! I'll be dead, so they're the ones who'll have to suffer, not you!"

Randall's response was calm and controlled.

"Clarence," he began. "This isn't over yet, okay? I understand that you're angry. Anyone in your situation would be."

"Oh, you think?!" I interrupted. "Don't sit there and tell me that you understand! You don't understand shit! Do you think it's easy to be locked up in that cell? Do you think I enjoy seeing my parents go through this?! Did you know that every time I come to one of these rooms to see my parents, the guard gives me a break and just puts on the handcuffs?! Normally, I have to wear a five-point harness. Do you know what that is?! Do you?! Besides the handcuffs, I have to wear leg irons that loop over a chain that goes around my waist! That's what they do with people like me! So, don't tell me about being angry! You have no fucking idea!"

I have to say, Randall handled my outburst pretty well. My parents, however, looked at me as though I'd suddenly grown another head. Some people might think that I'd been more than a little harsh and I suppose I was, but this had been building for a long time and I really needed to get it out of my system. At least I didn't call him an asshole.

Once the appeal was scheduled, my sentence was postponed. It would not be rescheduled until the appeals process was complete. So, my parents left for Bangor and Randall flew back to New York. I felt bad about how I'd spoken to him and wrote him a letter of apology. Several days later, I spoke to him by phone. He told me not to worry about it and that he'd experienced this kind of situation before. I thanked him for his understanding, but his words didn't seem to make me feel any better.

By this time, another emotion had begun to raise its head, as though the terror of possibly being put to death wasn't enough. I had been going through this entire process in, more or less, a state of shock and hadn't stopped to consider what I had actually done. I had killed two people. They had each been someone's son, someone's brother, someone's friend. Why is it that we never think about the lives we take? It's only when we feel guilt when we think about those we cannot bring back, and it was guilt that slowly began to dismantle my sanity. I had found a way to remove myself from the existence of a locked cell, but guilt had dug itself a hole in my brain, and only a hardened psychopath could escape from guilt. The rest of us are forced to carry to our graves.

Reading started to become difficult. I had read all the few books I had, and my attention span was lacking as I became increasingly agitated. I was beginning to pace the length of my cell, having run out of things to occupy myself with, and not knowing how long the appeals process would take left me with an uncertain amount of borrowed time. I decided that even from a detention cell, I could still do something productive and with my chances of going to prison still uncertain, I decided to start writing while I still had time. I started where any piece of writing starts - the beginning. I wrote down everything - college, nine eleven, Afghanistan; everything that brought my life to its current state. It started as a journal, but at some point, it turned into something far more personal. If there was someone else out there who was in the midst of a life-altering decision, they might read this and choose more carefully than I did. I thought that if my father was eventually able to get it published, I would have, at least, accomplished something.

I shortly found myself on a personal mission as I sat for hours a day writing out my thoughts, feelings, and recollections. I suppose that considering the path I seemed to be headed down, I might achieve some small measure of immortality. If I was put to death, my journal might give me a continued voice. I could still survive, if only to those who read these words. I know it sounds grandiose, but it quickly became an obsession. I felt an urgent need to leave something of myself behind because the idea of dying as a number became far more frightening than simply dying. I came to the conclusion that there is a greater sin than living a wasted life; to die having done nothing. I'm not one to believe that we are born with some grand purpose, but that we are obligated to create ourselves by forging our own path, simply by virtue of being allowed to exist at all.

Writing allowed me to completely immerse myself in something other than my imminent demise, and I was provided with notebooks and pens, as well as access to a computer. I would write up to six hours a day, or until I could no longer keep my eyes open. But, I also began to feel hurried. I didn't know how long the appeals process would take, so I quickly fell into a race against time, trying to avoid the idea that this was a race I might lose, that my life may well come to an end before finishing what I believed was my dying statement. I became obsessed with setting down every thought, regardless of how trivial it might be. Occasionally, I would surprise myself with something that was not only profound but written with such grace that I thought it must have come from someone else. On a good day, my pen would flow like an artist's brush. On a bad day, the words would come out with the anger and force of a sudden storm. I found it surprising how vengeful one could be with nothing more than pen and paper, and it was the pen that had quickly become my weapon of choice.

I learned through Randall that the government was providing the media with only limited information on my case. The world knew nothing of the innocent people who'd been killed by two of our own troops. The only thing they had been made aware of was my crime. It seems that the government is in the habit of presenting its version of the truth for the benefit of damage control, as well as to maintain a noble face. It wasn't bad enough that my life would end; it would end with a lie. So, if the government wasn't going to tell the entire story, I would. Mental note: never piss off the guy with the pen. However, at some point, I began to think that a half-truth was better than a complete lie and that some truths are best left in the darkness of government archives. I guess that's part of the military mentality. The truth can be a dangerous thing, but dangerous to whom? In order to keep what I was doing from being confiscated, I made arrangements with Randall to personally give him sections of the rough draft as I finished them. Telling the whole story could very well be seen as a security risk.

About two weeks later, I received a letter from home. The address was written in an almost calligraphic style that I recognized immediately. It was from Gloria. The postmark was dated roughly four weeks earlier. As I held it in my hand, I began to reflect. I thought I had dealt with my feelings about her. Not that I had put her behind me, but my situation forced me into establishing a more urgent perspective. I let it sit off to the side for a couple of days. I guess I was afraid of what it might say, or maybe what it might not say. Sometimes, when faced with a fear of the unknown, denial can be of great comfort, and a large part of me was quite comfortable with the idea of not reading the letter at all. However, there was a voice in the back of my head that I could not escape, and it quickly became a nagging reminder of the necessity to read it. So one night, before light's out, I gave in to the voice that had been constantly nudging at me, and with a single reading light casting its dim beam from over my shoulder, I sat in my cell and opened the letter.

Dear Clarence,

I was drifting off late at night about two weeks ago when I woke to the sound of your name. I had left my TV on as the national news was airing. Someone must have made a terrible mistake. Please, Clarence, tell me you didn't do this. You are the kindest, gentlest man I have ever met. Please tell me this was someone else. The man I made love to in my father's guest house could never do something like this.

Your father doesn't seem to want to talk about it, but your mom appears to be the one in need of a sympathetic ear. I have never seen anyone so distraught. She told me you are being held in Norfolk. Can I please come down to see you? I need you to tell me that this is all a mistake. I need to hear it from you.

The media is trying to make you look like a criminal. They don't care whose lives are ruined, as long as they get their story. Clarence, I don't want to hear about this from the news. Please tell me what happened. You are a good person, and

I'm sure that if any of this is true, you must have a good reason. I've lived a very sheltered life and am still confounded by the idea of war. I just don't understand how killing can lead to peace.

I know that military law can be very harsh, and I can only guess that things may not be as you hope. I can't imagine the state you must be in by now, but if we never get to see each other again, I still want to be there for you. If you don't want me to come down, would you call me instead? I would love to hear your voice again, and I will always be there to listen. I don't know what direction your case is going in, but whatever happens, I will always be in your corner.

Gloria
P.S. You will always be my soldier boy.

On one hand, I appreciated the fact that Gloria cared enough to write to me. On the other hand, I wondered why she didn't express these feelings before. But, it was the postscript of her letter that sent my emotions spiraling out of control. It drifted towards the floor as I raised my hands to my face and, sobbing uncontrollably, several thoughts ran through my mind. I realized how deeply in love I was. Certainly, I had been attracted to her from the first moment I saw her. But, it wasn't until I first placed my nervous hands around her waist that I felt the epiphany of a passion that can only result from the joining of two souls. I had looked into her eyes that night and found my guardian angel - the woman I 'should' be spending my life with. Now, a handwritten letter was all I had. It wasn't fair! I couldn't stop crying, as I realized just how much I missed her and how much I wanted her.

Then, I was overtaken by a sudden wave of anger. I was angry that it had taken Gloria so long for her to tell me her feelings. I was angry at myself for having spent so much time locked away from my own emotions. The mistakes that brought me to this cell had become crystal clear. Sometimes, enlightenment can come at the price of regret and as I began to feel the walls of my cell closing in on me, I became fully aware that there was no going back. And regardless of the visits from Randall and my parents, I now realized that I was truly alone, and I was probably going to die. I had become aware of my circumstances with frightening clarity. And now, somewhere in my desperate, terrified mind, escape became an option. But, I knew it wasn't a realistic option and I decided that I wasn't going anywhere.

Like anyone else, I wanted my life back, and my emotional turmoil held me as an unwilling witness to the mess I had made of my life. Up to this point, I was convinced that Randall would be able to pull me away from death's door. Now, all I had were doubts. I quickly discovered that sitting down for a good cry can often be therapeutic, but only when you know that you will feel better afterward. I once heard someone say that death is an existence without hope. I guess if I used that statement as a standard, my life had already come to an end. I drifted off that night in a state of exhaustion. Real sleep had become a rare commodity, as my dreams had become far harsher than reality. Even if I could somehow escape my cell, my dreams would keep me under lock and key. They always played the same images to me. The night fire incident from basic training still haunted me, and the images of the dead lying in the sand of that small Afghani settlement intruded on my sleep with little warning. I could still smell the aroma of gunfire. I could still feel my hand gripping the cold steel of the pistol that had been used to convict me of an act that I thought I was incapable of. And I could still see the lifeless face of the child whose death I was unable to prevent. But, something inside me decided that I had not seen enough and that I needed one last push into the ocean of insanity.

Chapter 28

Sometime during the night, my dreams were interrupted by the feeling that I was being watched. It was both sudden and intense enough that I felt compelled to search the hallway outside my cell. The window of my cell door was smaller than shoulder width, about twelve inches square, and lined with a steel frame that bore three one-inch-thick tempered bars. Squeezing any part of one's body between them was impossible, but if I got close enough, I could see for some distance in both directions. Maybe one of the guards was doing a cell check. But when I pressed my face against the bars, the only thing I saw was darkness. I was certain that someone was there, watching me from the cold emptiness that lay just outside the door of my cell. Maybe it was nothing, just one of the ghosts that had taken up residence in my mind, sneaking up in my dreams and tapping on my shoulder. My attention to the silent call that drew me to the darkness quickly fell away as I turned and leaned my back against the door. I let out a sigh of exhaustion and paced to the back of my cell, putting my hands on the cold, painted brick wall as I tried to clear my thoughts.
"Fuck," I whispered.

Stepping back from the wall, I turned toward my cot. I needed to sleep and in spite of the nightmares I was having, it was the only chance I had to avoid thinking - about anything. But, there was someone there whose presence jolted me into speechless disbelief.

She was more beautiful than I remembered as she sat gracefully on the edge of my cot. Her long black curls flowed down her back as she beamed at me with a warm smile.
"You can't be here," I whispered.
I found myself torn between the fear of having crossed over into the psychotic and the maddening passion that suddenly overtook me. She got up and stepped towards me, wearing the same cocktail dress from the evening we spent in her father's guest house. Even by the dim reading light of my cell, Gloria shimmered like an angel in the sun.
"Hey, soldier boy," she whispered. "It's okay. I'm here now."
She stepped in close and put her hands on my chest.
"I told you I'd be there for you."
She pulled me towards her and gently kissed my lips.
"I'm here now."
My hands quickly found their way around her waist as our eyes met in the darkness of a place

that had suddenly fallen to nothing. The world had slipped away as our bodies melted into a fire that would soon burn out of control. I felt a fleeting twitch of boyish nervousness as my hands slowly made their way down to just above the hem of her dress. My attention was firmly held by the gaze of her deep, brown eyes as she quietly kicked off her shoes while teasingly licking her lips. She shivered slightly as my hands disappeared beneath the hem of her cocktail dress, only to discover that the dress was all she was wearing. Gloria bent her head back, taking a deep, momentary breath of arousal. I moved my hands up her body and slipped her dress off over her head as she raised her arms in an act of willing surrender. Again, putting my hands around her waist, my eyes slowly followed down the gentle curves of her body and back up to her eyes as she let her lips fall slightly open.

In a flurry of passion, Gloria began stripping my clothes off with such blind enthusiasm that several scratches had been left on my skin. Their sting was momentary, as a palpable film of sweat welled up on my skin. With our bodies and souls laid bare, we made our way down to the cold, cement floor. We both felt the rush of arousal as we began to touch each other's concealed places. The heat of sweat and passion quickly blanketed us as Gloria wrapped her legs around my hips. Kissing her deeply on the mouth, our tongues collided with uncontrolled fury while she provided a guiding hand, allowing me to gently push myself into her supple, willing body.

We became joined as a key in a lock while the rhythm of our bodies played out like a Toccata of raw passion that nearly matched the frantic pounding of our hearts. It had been so long since I had felt the arousing caress of Gloria's touch. Now, I was overwhelmed by it. Desperately, I tried to maintain my self-control, but Gloria would not allow me to pace myself as she grabbed me firmly behind my hips and pulled me in repeatedly. Her appetite knew neither mercy nor boundaries as our synchronized release became imminent. I felt my toes curl as a sudden outpouring of sweat coursed over my body and in the same moment, Gloria gave way to a divine rage of erotic chaos as her body arched up toward me, her fingernails gripping the cold concrete floor, and as the tigress leaped from the cage of Gloria's soul, her body's tension evaporated as she let her arms fall to the floor. Her breasts rose towards me and fell away, while her breathing continued in its quickening state.

She reached her hands up and ran her delicate fingers through my hair. With a broad smile, she

kissed me on the lips and drew her head back slightly, looking into my eyes. The connection between our souls was complete, and we became lost in our own world. Outside the boundary of what had now become one, there was only a vast ocean of emptiness. Our souls had achieved a perfect pitch, dancing 'round together to an ethereal waltz of the moment.
"My soldier boy," she whispered.
She continued looking into my eyes.
"I love..."

Chapter 29

The morning light screamed into my mind as the loud click of a switch illuminated the hallway. I awoke to find myself curled up in a corner, my skin running with thin ribbons of sweat. I had spent the night clutching Gloria's letter. Opening my eyes to the glare of a world I had come to know too well, I got to my feet and rushed to the barred window.

"Where is she?!" I screamed.

I pulled my face to the bars with enough force to split my bottom lip.

"Where did she go?!"

The guard quickly approached the door of my cell.

"Private, what is it?" he asked with urgency.

"Did you see her?" I replied. "She was here last night!"

I knew she had been there. I had touched her skin, tasted her mouth, and felt the onslaught of her passionate release. Her presence had been more real to me than anything else.

"Private," the guard began. "There wasn't anyone here last night. It was just a dream. Now, relax. I'm going to go get some help, okay?"

The guard vanished down the hallway. It couldn't have been a dream. Dreams are only a vague reflection of what's real, a nocturnal picture book of sorts, and I refused to believe that the fire that had burned between us had simply been the product of a weary mind.

My hands continued to grasp the bars as the images of that night faded into transparency. Gloria could not have left because she hadn't been there, to begin with. I flew into an emotional outpouring as my body slid down to the floor. The guards found me curled up in a corner, my lip dripping blood on the floor just in front of my knees. I had become paralyzed with hysteria and was quickly taken to the infirmary, where a medic injected me with a light sedative. Later, the doctor stitched up the tear in my lip and after a much-needed, albeit, drug-induced sleep, I was led back to my cell. My lip was swollen and throbbing; my brain was still numbed by the sedative. I spent most of the morning curled up on my cot. I picked at my lunch soon after it arrived. The last thing on my mind was eating, but at that point, the oblivion of sedation was far more preferable. Now, I understand why some people become addicts. Sometimes, pain can be so great that the only thing that can blot it out is drugs.

After shaking off the remaining effects of the sedative, I was led outside. For thirty minutes out of each day, everyone was allowed outside into the recreation area. It was a large, fenced-in square of asphalt lined with basketball hoops and a few picnic tables. Regulations made it mandatory that all inmates spend thirty minutes outdoors. Illness was the only exception. Once outside, I felt the warmth of the sun as it floated in a clear blue sky, its harsh light exploding into my slightly hazy mind. Raising a hand, I shielded my eyes from its blinding intensity while searching for a shaded place. I would rather have been left alone in my cell, but I needed the temporary relief from its claustrophobic tension while getting some badly needed air.

Every day, I sat on the same patch of grass, letting my fingers move across its fine, green blades. I took great comfort in that sensation as it helped me to feel somewhat grounded, knowing there was something of the real world that I could reach out to, if only for thirty minutes a day. The sun beat down on my face as I gazed up into a blue, cloudless sky. Now, it suddenly occurred to me that we all see it, but we never really look at it.

Like so much else in the world, we take for granted the things that are the most deeply connected to us. We just don't think about things like the sky. It washes over us like a temperamental sea, sometimes filled with the turmoil of odd, sullen shapes. It is the air we breathe. We are one of the universe's smallest creatures, barely aware of our true standing in the broader picture that nature has painted and constantly given the opportunity to experience so much, and yet, we choose to see so little. I realized this while sitting on that patch of grass, set behind a military prison - a place that had become my home. Enlightenment can come at a very high price.

Chapter 30

The appeals process is both complicated and lengthy. One is only allowed three appeals before a final rendering of their sentence is made. In a capital case, you either win your appeal or die. My mind wandered to a disturbing topic. If I lost all three appeals, would the government allow an alternative to lethal injection? Instead of fading away under the heavy, sudden weight of drugs, I thought it might be an interesting last experience to meet my demise in a somewhat conscious state. In New York State, the condemned conclude their lives in the electric chair. The initial one thousand volts would induce neural shock, a state of painless unconsciousness achieved in mere seconds. At least, that was the idea. The voltage is then turned up until the heart stops. It seems reasonable to think that the abruptness of this method would be humane and while that may be true, there's a reason some states no longer practice it. The fact is that electrocution is ugly. No one knows how much if any, suffering is actually experienced. But, as I understand it, the body of the condemned often catches fire as the eyes are suddenly pushed out of their sockets. The restrained body shakes violently while blood exits from the eyes and ears. It is considered by some to be inhumane, based solely on the harrowing scene it produces. I guess the idea of an 'eye for an eye' can be pretty comfortable for people until they come face to face with it. The idea of a more gradual process of conscious death also occurred to me. In the past, this was accomplished by the use of the gas chamber. The condemned would, again, be strapped into a chair in a more or less, sealed chamber. Toxic pellets would then be dumped into a small container of acid, releasing hydrogen cyanide. The condemned would be conscious throughout much of the process, as instructions were given for deep breathing in order to speed the execution and minimize any suffering. A state of panic often ensued, followed by seizures and eventually death. Is it noble to want to die a living death, to meet the reaper on one's feet? I used to think so. I used to think that to stand defiantly as one faced certain death required both courage and character. Now, I think that this willingness to stare down death is likely the result of military indoctrination, the goal of which is to produce walking weapons, willing and able to kill and die on command. We create these soldiers, so politicians never have to go to war. Perhaps the world's issues could be more easily resolved if, instead, this were the case.

Chapter 31

Randall arrived for my first appeal. My parents sat behind us as he, essentially, repeated the argument he made at my sentencing trial. There was no magic bag of legal trickery, no brilliant twists of logic. The repetition of his argument did not inspire my confidence, so it was no surprise when the jury ruled in favor of upholding my sentence. My mother was inconsolable, as she saw my life slipping away in front of her very eyes. But, Randall reassured us that we had two more appeals left and that we would not go down without a fight. I don't think any of us were convinced, and the legal team assigned to me had proved to be of little use.

I debated the idea of refusing any further appeals. My parents were already going through hell and if I was going to lose the next two appeals, then why should be they forced to continue sitting by in agony? It was likely that my sentence would be carried out. I had accepted that. What I could not accept was that my parents would suffer to a much greater degree. Maybe if I just brought an end to it, my parents might not have to experience such lengthy pain. They would still grieve, but they would eventually begin to heal. At least, that's what I told myself. I did understand that they wanted to be there for me. I suppose any decent parent would do the same for their children, regardless of what they had done. I just didn't like what this process was doing to my mother. Every time I saw her, she looked ten years older. Pain and sadness had etched themselves into her face, and her eyelids had begun to droop slightly as her body started to take on a wilted appearance.

As I look back, I became quite certain that my mother's emotional collapse probably began shortly after announcing my plans to enlist. I didn't even really talk to them about it. I just told them what I was going to do. There was no discussion, and I never considered how my decision would affect them. I did what I thought was best for me. God, I felt like such an asshole. It's important to consider the direction one's life is taking, but you can't live your life at the expense of someone else's. By the time I realized it, that was exactly what I had done. The damage I had caused could never be undone, and I would likely die having left my parent's lives in ruins.

We met in a private room just before my second appeal was to get underway, two long months later. By this time, I had been prescribed a minimal dose of a sedative that I took twice a day. My mother, however, was now taking an antidepressant as well as a mild sedative. She was able to function and, yes, she did look better, but the scars that had been left as a result of my mistakes were permanent. When a child falls and bumps its knee, we like to think that a kiss will make it better. I don't know how fair it is to a child that something, so simple could dissolve such a painful experience, but it does allow for the offering of kindness and support to the child, whose mind operates on a simplistic approach to life; we fall, we cry, we get back up and receive a gentle pat on the head. Off we go, ready to stumble over our own feet, get another pat on the head, and do it all over again. But in the real world, learning to walk can be cripplingly painful and there's no one there to pat us on the head, to tell us that everything's going to be okay. In the real world, you have to dry your own tears.

Randall outlined his strategy for my appeal. Maybe it was just me, but it sounded oddly like a replay of my last appeal, and I was left wondering if Randall was just going through the motions. Maybe there was nothing more to be done, and he was just trying to buy me a little time - trying to do what he thought was right.
"What if I didn't want to do this anymore?" I asked.

The room suddenly went silent as all eyes suddenly became fixed on me. My father leaned toward me with a look of both concern and confusion.

"What do you mean, Clarence?" he asked.

I looked around at their wondering faces with hesitation.

"What if I don't want another appeal? What if I just don't want to do this anymore?"

My mother reached out and gently put a hand on my arm.

"Clarence," she began. "What are you talking about?"

I took a deep sigh as I gathered my thoughts.

"Randall," I began. "I'm sure you're doing everything you can, but it's not working. And the longer this continues, the more my parents suffer. I know you're trying to do the right thing, but maybe it's time to stop."

I wasn't being ungrateful, it's just that his plan for my appeal was the same as my last appeal and that was a near carbon copy of the argument he used during my sentencing trial. The words were different, but the argument was the same. Benjamin Franklin once described insanity as doing the same over and over again while expecting different results. I guess I wasn't the only person who was going crazy. My parents turned and looked at Randall begging, as if trying to prompt him into saying something that might regain my confidence, and thus, give me a reason to hope. Without moving a muscle, Randall brought his eyes up from my case file, hesitating long enough to find just the right words. But, it wasn't his words that spoke the loudest. It was his hesitation. It was the look in his eyes. Sometimes, silence can be the most efficient conduit for communicating something one does not wish to say out loud, and Randall's hesitation spoke volumes. He knew there was no hope of winning an appeal and was just going through the motions. I didn't care what his motives were, but I immediately developed a deep resentment of what he was putting my parents through. I know that he didn't intend that they live with such agony.

Again, I was escorted by armed guard as the fluorescent lights glinted off the polished chrome of the handcuffs holding my wrists together. Occasionally I would glimpse its reflection, briefly dancing near my feet as I walked through the corridors of the Norfolk legal building. Shortly, I found myself standing as the judge entered and took his seat behind the bench. But, there was something different this time. Up to this point, I had entered the courtroom with a strong feeling of impending doom. Maybe it was the uncertainty that seemed to be inherent in the trial process. You don't know what will be decided until it's decided. I know that's a strange way to put it, but my point is that you are forced to wait, to give up control, while your life is directed by a handful of complete strangers and not knowing what they're thinking as they make their decision is, by itself, a terrifying experience. But, something was different. There was no tension, no anticipation. I was struck by a feeling of quiet resolution and for the first time in months, I actually felt relaxed. I was confident that the entire process would finally be over.

The courtroom was called to order. The judge reviewed the documentation from my previous appeal.
"Counsel for the defense," the judge began.
"Please present your case."
Randall looked at me with obvious concern.
"Are you sure?" he whispered.
A slight nod was my only response. He stood up and straightened his suit jacket.
"Your Honor," he began. "After careful consideration, my client wishes to waive his right to appeal."
The room instantly filled with a tense stillness as the judge looked up at Randall with startled concern.
"Counselor," the judge replied. "Does your client understand the gravity of this request?"

Randall's expression continued unchanged. If he had developed any emotions regarding my decision, he was hiding them very well.

"Yes, Your Honor," he answered.

The judge shifted his eyes to me.

"Private," he said.

I stood up, prepared to explain my decision.

"Yes, sir," I responded.

"Given the nature of your case, do you realize the consequences of waiving your right to appeal?" he asked.

I paused for a split second as I realized what I was about to do.

"Yes, sir," I answered.

The judge looked at me intently.

"Private Taylor," he began. "Right now, I see no reason why I should grant your request. You are entitled, by military law, to three appeals. Now, convince me why I should grant your request."

Randall stood up next to me, ready to give an explanation on my behalf.

"Counselor," the judge continued. "Sit down. I want to hear this from him."

The judge looked back at me as I stood nervously trying to compose my thoughts.

"Your Honor," I began. "The moment I joined the Army, I fully realized that my chances of dying were pretty high. Granted, this wasn't how I imagined it, but I accepted it nonetheless. I had made a terrible mistake. I let myself be driven, not by the Army's ethics, but my own. I let myself lose control, and now two men are dead. Would I do it again, given the same circumstances? I honestly don't know. I was there to protect the innocent as well. I take full responsibility for my actions, and I'm willing to pay for my mistake. But, this isn't about me anymore. Since I arrived, my parents have been right here next to me. The crime I've committed has affected them far more than me. Do I want to die, your Honor? Of course not, but I was found guilty, sentenced to death, and lost my first appeal."

I pointed back to my mother.

"Since this began, my mother has aged dramatically. Now, she's taking an antidepressant 'and' a sedative for anxiety. And if I'm not mistaken, the appeals process can take months - sometimes years. My parents shouldn't have to go through that. It's just not fair that my parents should have to suffer more than me. I don't expect that my death will make things any easier for them, or undo what I've done. And yes, they're going to grieve, but they shouldn't have to sit here and continue watching this, knowing that I'm going to die anyway. Every time they come here, they look ten years older. My father's trying to be strong, but I see him starting to slip too. Your Honor, I'm not asking this for myself. I do want this to be over, but I want it to be over for them. Please, your Honor."

Having nothing more to say, I sat back down. Randall sat silently next to me as the judge contemplated my words.

"Counsel," the judge began. "A word in my chambers."

I felt as though I had acted out of desperation, and I guess I did. Randall and the lead prosecutor followed the judge into his chambers. I was left to wait with my parents sitting behind me. My father sat with his arm around my mother's shoulders, who leaned towards him in a near catatonic state. I turned to my right and leaned toward the large wooden rail that separated us.

"I'm sorry, Dad," I began. "I just don't see any other way."

At this point, I expected him to be angry with me. I had put them through so much. He leaned in towards me and inhaled as if he was about to speak when the judge reentered the courtroom with Randall, the lead prosecutor, following behind. After taking his seat behind the bench, the judge paused to compose his words.

"There is what is correct and there is what is right. In court, doing what is correct is a matter of procedure and legal precedent. Doing what's right? Well, that's something we've never really been good at, in spite of our desire to accomplish it. And why is that? Because we're always going to second guess ourselves - did we do the right thing? Private, your guilt has been established; your sentence has been prescribed in accordance with military law. Should you die? The rules say yes because, in the end, the rules are all we have. Is it right for you to die? Honestly, I'm not in a position to make that decision, but I can see what your parents are going through, and I hope I never find myself in their situation."

He paused to glance down at my file.

"Now," he continued. "I understand that you are currently taking medication for anxiety. Your psych exam shows you to be stable and mentally competent. So, I will ask you again. Private Taylor, do you understand the consequences of waiving your right to any further appeals?"

I stood up and made eye contact with the judge, holding my head high with clarity and determination.

"Yes, I do, your Honor," I replied.

The judge looked closely at me for any sign of doubt or hesitation. He gave a deep sigh and nodded his head, while still maintaining eye contact. Glancing down at his desk, he tried to find the words for his decision.

"Private, based on the nature of this case and the sentence that has been imposed on you, it is the opinion of this court that your request for a waiver of your right to appeal be denied. As long as there is a chance that your sentence can be overturned, you should take advantage of it. If nothing else, this will give you more time to spend with your parents."

I don't know why I was so surprised. The judge obviously chose to take the path of least resistance by following the rules. I suppose it was just easier that way. But, he was right. He could only do what was correct, not what was right. Had I followed that perspective, I would probably still be in Afghanistan. But, for just one moment, I saw the light at the end of the tunnel, only to see it snuffed out by jurisprudence and the need to maintain a clear conscience. My appeal would continue and, as I expected, Randall's argument for the overturning of my sentence was the same as my last appeal. The words were different, but it was the same argument. Same shit, different spoon.

By that time, I realized that Randall was not the expert his reputation claimed him to be. The only thing he'd done for me was to keep the court from branding me as a murderer. And, yes, I was grateful for that. But after withholding information from me during my sentencing trial, my confidence in him as an attorney had taken a sudden nosedive, and secretly, I wondered how he ever managed to pass the bar exam. I felt like a castaway, having just been plucked out of a tumultuous sea by a ship of fools. The only people who seemed to know what they were doing were the prosecution, and the judge just wanted to follow the rules.

My second appeal ended with the jury ruling against me. What a surprise. Randall was visibly uncomfortable as the judge commented on his repetitive line of defense. Without a new approach, my third and final appeal would be resigned to failure. I suppose that was okay. I had a strong feeling I was going to die anyway, but I wished the court had allowed me to waive my rights. I just wanted it all to stop and had come to see the process of the courts as nothing more than bullshit dressed in the cloak of formality. I mean, if you're going to put someone to death, or throw them in prison, just do it and move on. I had reached the opinion that Randall was just another asshole looking for a paycheck. I'm sure there are plenty of good lawyers out there. Randall, apparently, just didn't seem to be one of them. As it also turned out, the only reason he was brought on as my attorney was that he and my father were close friends in college. I guess loyalty doesn't always produce competent results.

Upon returning to the detention center, my father asked to speak to Randall privately. I had never heard my father raise his voice, and I wondered if I was hearing the same person, yelling at the top of his lungs. Apparently, I was not alone in my opinion of Randall's abilities of persuasion. To put it simply, my father was pissed, and he demanded that Randall start doing his job and threatened to have copies of the court transcripts sent to the bar association with a complaint of incompetence. Randall left without the usual post-trial meeting. I'd put all my faith in him that he would, somehow, use his legal skills to pull me out of the fire I'd started. But, I had one more chance; one last appeal. I suppose that one can hope for the best and prepare for the worst, and I was hoping that Randall might suddenly come up with some brilliant piece of persuasiveness that would turn the tide in my favor. But, I was also prepared that he wouldn't.

I spent a lot of time reading Gloria's letter. I wasn't planning to write back to her, mostly because I just didn't know what to say. How do you tell someone that you've been sentenced to die for killing two of your own? The most eloquently penned words would fall far short of even the simplest truth. I did, however, come to a point where I could direct my anger against Randall in the journal I was writing and asked him, politely, to return what I'd already written. He was good enough to do so, and I continued to forge my anger into the determination I needed to keep writing. I lost myself in it and by the time my appeal date arrived, I had written well over three hundred and fifty pages.

Chapter 32

Most of that day was little more than a blur. Randall said he'd spent a great deal of time developing a new approach for the negotiation of my sentence. My parents were highly skeptical, and I honestly refused to believe a word of it unless I saw it for myself. As usual, the prosecution was ready. They presented a thorough, yet brief, review of the events that led to my conviction, noting that nothing substantial had been produced that would cause the jury to reconsider my sentence and in not so many words, they remarked that my punishment should be held up as both an example and a deterrent. Randall stood, unfazed by the prosecutor's argument that I should be used as, more or less, the poster child of the military's wartime moral compass. He argued that the death of one soldier, under any circumstances, has never been held by the military machine as a significant consequence of war. He argued that all efforts should be made to prevent the loss of life during times of war, and this was an opportunity to start. His argument was eloquent to a fault and left me wondering why he couldn't do this before. I was truly impressed as I glanced back at my parents, who seemed both moved and hopeful. Maybe this would end well after all. What is the expression, 'third time's the charm'? Unfortunately, the jury seemed deeply entrenched in wartime patriotism and was either unable or unwilling, to see beyond the tunnel vision of indoctrination and all twelve officers voted in favor of upholding my sentence. There was nothing hypothetical about it anymore, and the reality of my fate struck me like a falling brick. Part of me was hoping to see my sentence overturned, but another part of me was glad that it was over.

After the jury's decision had been announced, the judge looked at me with a sympathetic expression. "Private Taylor," he began.
I stood up at attention, feeling my legs wobble a bit under the anxiety of knowing that my death was now a certainty.
"I am truly sorry, both for you and your parents. If it were up to me, you'd be going to prison. Unfortunately, I can't be the one to make that decision."
He paused to fumble through some papers that lay in front of him, taking a brief moment to write a few notes.
"Private, the warrant to carry out your sentence will go before the President for approval by witnessed signature. Thereafter, your sentence will

be scheduled, and you will be put to death by lethal injection, as decided by this court."

Why did I have to wait so long? I spent months locked in a cell, waiting for the gears of military law to do what I knew they would probably do all along. I'd spent a very long time believing that I would go to prison, wait out my time, and start over. Now, it was time to do some serious reflecting. I needed to find a way to resolve my life, even if I had to resort to some grand rationalization that I had somehow made a difference. But being young, I lacked life experience and, therefore, any opportunity to achieve something significant. Sure, I went to college, but a degree in Philosophy? What was I going to do with that? And instead of moving on to grad school, I ended up on a personal mission to kill terrorists by joining the military. What the fuck was I thinking? The answer to that question was simple. There are thinkers and there are fighters, and soldiering is best left to soldiers. If you put a weapon in the hands of a thinker, it will probably never be fired. If you're going to become a soldier, you must realize that following orders takes precedence over thinking. Thinking can get you killed. On the other hand, acting without thinking can also get you killed. Is there a boundary between the two? If there is, it has to be very thin.

So, what do you do? You follow orders; you do what you're told; you aim and fire; you keep your head down. But, I was not a soldier and I had no business even considering military service. What exactly did I think I was going to accomplish?

Over the next few days, I had put enough thought into my oncoming oblivion to realize one simple, but important lesson. The most terrible lie you can ever tell is the lie you tell to yourself. You can learn to read people and catch them in a lie, but catching yourself in a lie is a very different matter. It's far too easy to bring yourself to believe in your own version of the truth. It's just more convenient to believe you are innocent, despite any overwhelming facts to the contrary. In my case, my lie was that I had taken up a calling - if you will - to cure the world of its newfound ills. I actually thought I could make a difference, but as it turned out, the only world I had changed was my own. Worst of all, I had dragged my parents down with me. My lie had destroyed their world as well.

Again, I waited - always with the waiting. I tried to keep myself from rotting away by continuing my journal. Writing had become a bastion of sanity for me. As for hope, hope had predeceased me weeks ago. I guess it would be okay if no one read this. I don't think anyone would really care anyway. As I said, any remaining hope I once had was gone, and I now wrote not for the sake of writing something meaningful, but so I wouldn't have to deal with where I was going. It had turned into a compulsion, something I had to do.

I'm not really sure how much time had passed, but one morning, the officer in charge of the cell block notified me that I had a court appointment that afternoon. I didn't think that I'd have to do this again. Maybe I thought they'd just kill me and be done with it, but everything had to be formalized. All the T's had to be crossed; all the I's had to be dotted. Randall stood waiting outside the courtroom doors as I arrived in handcuffs, led by an armed guard. My parents were strangely absent.
"Randall," I began. "What's going on? Where are my parents?"
He waited as my handcuffs were removed.
"Clarence, you are receiving notification," he answered.
There was a noticeable tone of seriousness in his voice.
"Notification of what?" I asked. "And where are my parents?"
His slight hesitation only added to the seriousness of his tone.
"Clarence," he began. "The President signed your death warrant two days ago."

A long pause went by as I absorbed this painful fact. I'm not even sure I'd call it painful. I don't think there's a word that could even come close to describing my reaction. Randall also informed me that there had been no media present and the only other person there was the Attorney General. And he was only there as a witness.
"Shouldn't my parents be here for this?" I asked.
"Clarence," he replied. "You have to be formally notified by the court. It'll take five minutes. I don't think that your parents should have to fly down from Bangor for a five-minute notification, do you?"
He was right, but, it felt strange to glance back at the two empty chairs where my parents usually sat.

I stood up as the judge entered the courtroom. The prosecution's presence was no longer needed. They had done their jobs and had likely been assigned to another case. The officers of the jury were also absent and had been sent back to do whatever it was they did before receiving their summons. Only two other people were needed, a guard and the court transcriptionist. The room felt cold and sterile as I acknowledged the 'official' notification of the signing of my death warrant. I wondered what the President might have been thinking while signing the piece of paper that was, in effect, a government permission slip to end my life. Did he

hesitate? How much thought did give before signing it? I know it doesn't really matter, but if your signature is the only thing needed to terminate someone's life, how much thought would you put into it? The judge's words took only seconds to be spoken. The rest of those few minutes were taken up by courtroom formalities. There were papers to be signed and one last appointment to be made. Before leaving the courtroom I was, again, handcuffed and as I was escorted by two armed guards, Randall accompanied me back to my cell.
"You were right," I said. "My parents didn't need to be here for this."
It wasn't the trip down from Bangor I was thinking about. I just didn't think they needed to witness this particular step of my demise. At this point, the date of my execution was irrelevant. Keeping a calendar while behind bars serves absolutely no purpose, other than to make yourself crazy. And having a clock in your cell will only speed the process. At any rate, my death was now a certainty. There were no more appeals and the judge would not allow any delays. The images from that day in Afghanistan continued to run loose in my mind, and I was no longer able to justify my actions as the exercising of some grandiose personal mission. If I could distill all of it down to one word, it would be 'stupid'. The

Sergeant who walked down into the village with me that day paid for his mistake with his life. Now, I was about to follow that same path. Why didn't we wait for backup? A small patrol could have quickly and easily been put together. But, I guess there's no point in thinking about that now.

I continued to bury myself in my journal and had made remarkable progress. Sometimes, escapism can actually help to accomplish a great deal. But, when Randall and my parents arrived two days before my sentence was to be carried out, writing no longer served as an adequate escape and their arrival forced me onto a collision course with a debt that was soon coming due. There was no hiding from it anymore, and I felt my sense of control rapidly slipping away.

My mother was now walking with a cane and one side of her face drooped slightly.
"Jesus Christ," I thought. "My mom had a stroke!" We had been writing back and forth since the very beginning, but in none of my parent's recent correspondence was there anything about this. My father thought it was best not to mention it unless it was absolutely necessary, but I have to say that despite her condition, she was doing remarkably well. Although, it did force her into retirement. I credited her force of will as the primary reason for

her recovery, but from a mother's perspective, I was likely her motivation for surviving this assault on her body. We spent a great deal of time just talking, with no mention of Gloria, or why they were actually there. Randall spent most of his time in his hotel room, making phone calls in an attempt to have my sentence commuted. I still can't believe he had the balls to try to call the President. He got as far as the President's secretary only to be told, repeatedly, that the President was not available. In the end, he had done his best and I considered his job to be done.

We spent the entire next day talking about things that seemed unimportant. I think my parents wanted to keep my stress level to a minimum. But being my parents, they were able to read me like an open book and were very aware of how terrified I was. By this time, the private rooms had grown very small and my mother, in spite of the fact that she was now forced to use a cane, insisted on going for a walk.
"Oh, I don't know, mom," I replied. "I don't think they're going to let me do that."
"Why not?" she asked.
She seemed surprised to be told that, as a condemned prisoner, I would not be allowed to go outside for even a simple walk.

"A mother can't go outside for a walk with her son?"

I could see that the medication she was taking was working well, and I felt better, seeing that her willful personality was beginning to display itself again.

"Well, we'll just see about that."

She got up from her chair and started towards the door, as my father jumped up in an attempt to stop her. The ensuing commotion attracted the attention of the guard, who entered the room with his hand instinctively placed on his holstered sidearm.

"Is there a problem?" he asked sternly.

She lifted the end of the cane several inches off the floor and pounded it back down with a heavy, determined thud.

"I want to go for a walk with my son," she demanded.

The guard glanced at my father, who'd thrown up his hands in resignation, and I was speechless. Seeing there was no threat, the guard dropped his hand.

"Ma'am, we don't ordinarily allow that," he replied.

"I don't give a rat's ass what you allow!" she said, as she beat the end of her cane against the floor again.

Ten minutes later, after my father and I had picked our jaws up off the floor, we found ourselves walking on the front lawn, between the two fences that surrounded the detention center. My mother's right hand firmly gripped her cane, while her left hand held my arm. My father followed behind, while a guard trailed us by about ten feet. Together, we walked the length of the lawn several times. Sometimes we talked, other times we said nothing. All she wanted was to spend those last few hours on my arm, even if there wasn't a lot to say.

The evening crept up on us far too quickly, and the guard walked me back to my cell, while another escorted my parents to the parking lot. Just before entering the building, I glanced back at my parents. My mother's eyes pierced through me with a look of bleakness and grief. Her face had taken on an ancient, wizened expression, as though she'd witnessed a lifetime of tragedy. She looked despaired and lost. I wished I'd never seen that look. I would rather have been dismembered with a hammer than see that look on my mother's face.

I spent half the night writing down my thoughts. It was the last chance I had to put pen to paper and after bringing my journal to a close, I sat back on my cot, letting the emptiness of the night envelop me, like a blanket of cold snow, blackened by guilt and regret. Morpheus, the Greek god of sleep, passed me by that night as I was left to the whispers that echoed from the surrounding darkness. Perhaps the whispers were the voices of my conscience, taking one last jab as my psyche had finally taken flight and disappeared into the veil of the inevitable. The only hope I had left was that my life would be brought to a swift, merciful end.

My parents were waiting for me the next morning for what would be the last time we would be in each other's presence. There were no words spoken, only tears. We huddled together in one of the private rooms and for the first time in my life, I saw my father break down. I had no idea what to say. I did tell them that I loved them, but those three words would not be comfort enough, as they would soon witness my execution. I tried to be strong for them. However, the more I tried to hold the tears at bay, the faster they came to the surface and like my parents, my silent strength had become fractured by an outpouring of emotion. My mother's tears had slowly turned into a loud wailing as she let loose her deepest pain and grief. It was that sound, as well as the expression on her face, that brought me furthest into my guilt. The choice I had made back in the sands of Afghanistan had torn my mother's soul to shreds.

I don't know how much time had passed and it felt like forever, but at some point, there came a tap at the door. When it opened, I saw Randall in the hallway standing with two guards.

"Clarence," he said. "We have to go back to your cell."

The grave tone in his voice told me that the process had begun. My mother suddenly reached out as I stepped toward the door and clutched my arm as though she might hold me back. Her loud crying left her unable to speak clearly. My father gently took her by the shoulders and pulled her into his chest, where she buried her face and continued crying hysterically. I stepped into the hallway, where another guard stood holding a five-point harness. Ordinarily, they trusted me enough to just apply the handcuffs, but this was a very different situation. They removed the handcuffs I was already wearing and replaced them with a wide leather belt, tethering four heavy chains that attached to stainless steel shackles and cuffs. Once the harness was secured, I was led down the hall and back to my cell, where several more people were waiting. Once inside, only the handcuffs were removed. I sat down on my cot as the commanding officer of the detention center entered. According to military law, he was required to offer me a last meal. They could have offered me a porterhouse steak with a glass of vintage red wine from the finest vineyard in France, and I would have turned it down. Well, perhaps not the wine. But, truthfully, there was only one thing I wanted - water. I remembered that right after my sentencing trial, I'd experienced an epiphany, of sorts when I was given a glass of water. For something that's supposed to be tasteless, it seems that there is nothing better than a glass of cold, clear water - the stuff of life. So, that's what I asked for - just plain, ordinary tap water. And with at least half a dozen people standing outside my cell, I drank down a tall glass of water. It ran down over my chin and dripped onto my clothes. It was a wonderful experience.

The commanding officer left with the empty glass as I wiped my chin off with the sleeve of my shirt. At this point, there was no need for decorum. The next person was a doctor. He walked in with a sheet of paper and sat on the other end of my cot. It was required that a review of the execution process take place. Essentially, they wanted me to know how I was going to die.

I would be taken into a procedure room where I would lay on a stretcher. An IV would be placed in both my arms, with the second being used in the event the first failed. The doctor would be there to perform this task, but would not administer the drugs. I guess doctors aren't allowed to kill people, right? From there, I'd be taken into a nearby room that was referred to as 'the death chamber'. It seems a bit dramatic to use such heavy-handed words to describe a place that is nothing more than a space surrounded by walls, but I suppose that even the delivery of death can't exist without a label. I would be strapped to a surgical table and asked if I had any last words, as though there could be anything of meaning I might have to say. I'm sure that whatever I said would be documented, even if no one but my parents gave a shit.

Three drugs would then be introduced. The first would be a lethal dose of sodium thiopental. The doctor told me that its effect would be almost immediate. It would be flushed through with saline while the next drug was prepared. A high dose of Pancuronium Bromide would then be injected and flushed through with more saline. This was a paralytic and was used as the 'cosmetic' step. I was afraid to ask why he used the word 'cosmetic', but I asked anyway. The answer I got was nothing short of horrifying. It seems that, on occasion, things don't always go according to plan and sometimes, the initial drug can cause violent seizures. The paralytic is given to mask these effects and give witnesses the impression that the execution was being carried out in a humane manner. The last step is the injection of two large syringes of potassium chloride. The dose is large enough to stop the heart. The downside of this drug is that a dose this large turns on every pain receptor in the body. So, if the first drug doesn't work, you will be fully aware of your inability to breathe and feel as though your entire body is on fire. No one will know but you.

Hearing this forced me into a moment of clarity, long enough to realize that it wasn't necessarily death I should be afraid of. We all die. That's just the way the universe works, but the idea of dying in silent, burning agony was one I found truly terrifying. Now, it was official: I was scared shitless. Any more information was pointless. The review was required because someone sitting behind a desk thought I should know. But, I didn't need to know. More than that, I wished I'd never asked.

The doctor offered me five milligrams of Valium. I thought it was a bit odd to offer someone drugs who was about to die by an intentional overdose, and when I asked why, the doctor told me it was required that it be offered in order to make my execution less stressful. I actually thought he was kidding until he held out a small plastic cup containing an orange pill. I was no longer the type of person who believed it was noble to stare down death in the face of insurmountable odds. Like I said, soldiering is best left to soldiers. However, at some point, I'd made up my mind that I wanted to experience that last glimmer of lucidity. I wanted to know if there really was anything on the other side of that last heartbeat. Everyone has their own ideas of what might lie on the 'other side'. Even if you believe there's nothing, nothing is still something, right?

You've probably guessed by now that I did, in fact, refuse the Valium.
"Are you sure?" the doctor asked.
"Yeah, I'm sure," I answered.
Was I absolutely sure? No, not really, but I didn't want to die in a drug-induced haze. The first drug was going to be a sedative anyway and considering how quickly it was supposed to kick in, I thought there might be a chance to experience something of the divine. Maybe I would find out if Christianity was right - that there is a God. Not that I was planning to convey the experience to anyone. I just wanted to find out for myself.

The handcuffs were, once again, secured around my wrists. The commanding officer stepped into the doorway and told me to stand. I looked around at all the books, the notebook containing my journal, and the letter from Gloria that stuck out from between the pages of 'The Teachings of Buddha'. My mind drew a blank. There were no profound thoughts, no literary quotes, or sudden religious awareness.

"Private Taylor," he said. "It's time."

I stepped out of my cell and sat in a waiting wheelchair and, with armed guards in tow, I was taken to an isolated area of the detention center and wheeled into a small procedure room. Everything for the IV' had been set out on a small stainless steel tray. I was told to lie down on a gurney that had been placed under a ceiling-mounted surgical light, where a small amount of local anesthetic was injected under my skin, leaving a bubble of the drug a hair's breadth from the doctor's chosen vein. The insertion of both IVs was painless. The doctor had obviously done this many times. He connected it to a bag of saline and hung it on a pole that folded out from somewhere under the gurney. It was at that time I noticed a blank look on the doctor's face.

"I'm sorry you have to be a part of this," I said.

His expression went unchanged and there was no response, not even eye contact.

As the doctor began cleaning up the used supplies, the commanding officer walked in accompanied by the chaplain.

"Private Taylor," he began. "There's nothing in your record pertaining to any religious preference. Would you like to speak to the chaplain?"

I've never been a big fan of faith, especially after nine eleven. Yeah, I guess it would be nice if there was something or someone out there that could make evil obsolete. But, if that were the case, I probably wouldn't be where I am.

"Sir," I answered. "I really think my parents would get more out of that than I would."

At this point, I honestly thought that talking to a chaplain would feel more like talking to a brick wall. I think it's great that there are people around to give others that kind of comfort. I just didn't think that there was anyone out there who would listen or care.

I was helped off the gurney by one of two guards that had entered the room. Still, in chains, I was walked a short distance into an adjacent room. It was much smaller than the procedure room and contained only one piece of furniture - a surgical table. It had been bolted to the floor by a large steel cylinder, with several heavy leather straps attached to its frame. There was a small window on one side at about shoulder height, probably for whoever was charged with the grim task of injecting the drugs. I would never see that person's face. On the opposite side of the room was a large

window, covered by a black curtain. I was told to lie down. The two guards were present to ensure my cooperation. I had never given them any trouble, so I wasn't about to start now. The straps were buckled over my chest, waist, and legs. My ankles, arms, and wrists were also restrained as the chains were removed. The IV bag and tubing were fed through a small, square hole just beneath the executioner's window. Everyone left the room, leaving me to wait for the inevitable. All my emotions had suddenly been replaced by an odd feeling of calm dissociation. It was an experience that seemed to remove me from the unwavering certainty of death. The curtain was then pulled open and turning my head, I saw a roomful of onlookers, including Randall and my parents. The chaplain had seated himself next to my mother, with my father sitting at her other side. I was not able to clearly see her face, but I could hear her crying softly. A voice addressed me through a speaker mounted near the ceiling.
"Private Clarence Taylor," it began.
The voice did not sound familiar.
"You have been found guilty of the crime of involuntary manslaughter during a declared time of war and have been sentenced to die by lethal injection. Do you have any last words?"
I had spent what felt like an eternity thinking about what to say. I told my parents how sorry I was that

I had caused them so much pain. My voice quivered as I told them how much I loved them. I also asked that the families of the two marines I had killed be told how deeply sorry I was and that I, alone, was responsible for their deaths. I turned my head back and faced the ceiling.

I've heard it said that when someone dies, they see their life pass before them in one momentary flash of retrospect. So, you would think that the entirety of my short life would suddenly burst into my consciousness as my existence was about to come to a close. But, of all the things that could have entered my mind - my parents, Gloria, college, winters in Maine, basic training, the teachings of Buddha -- only one thought occurred to me, and as I lay strapped to the table, watching the whitish fluid of the sedative enter my veins, I wished that I could see the sky one last time.

End

Printed in the USA
CPSIA information can be obtained
at www.ICGtesting.com
LVHW052356021124
795330LV00012B/458